# THE TRUMPET SHALL SOUND

## A Novel

# THE TRUMPET SHALL SOUND

## A Novel

EIBHEAR WALSHE

SOMERVILLE PRESS

Somerville Press Ltd,
Dromore, Bantry,
Co. Cork, Ireland


©Eibhear Walshe 2019


First published 2019



Designed by Jane Stark
Typeset in Adobe Garamond Pro
seamistgraphics@gmail.com



ISBN: 978-1-9999970-5-2



Printed and bound in Spain
by GraphyCems, Villatuerta, Navarra

*To Donald O'Driscoll*

# ACKNOWLEDGEMENTS

The rewarding process of bringing Handel back from the dead needed a great deal of support and I was helped and encouraged by many people. I want to thank my colleagues in the School of English, UCC, Cork, Steve Enniss and all at The Harry Ransom Center, Austin, Texas, Adrian Farrell, Irish Consulate, Austin, the Handel/ Hendrix House, London, The Handel House, Halle, Germany, Jonathan Williams, Lee Jenkins, Andrew Carpenter, Claire Connolly, Padraig Dempsey and Ruth Hegarty at the Royal Irish Academy, Liz and Niall Keogh, Ottawa, Goran Stanivukovic, Nova Scotia, James H. Murphy, Boston College, Heather Bryant Corbally, Wellesley College, Boston,  Jose Francisco Sanchez Fernandez, Almeria, Ladette Randolph, Emerson College, Boston,  Charles Foran and Mary Ladky, Toronto, Edmund White, Emma Donoghue, Pilar Villar Argáiz, Granada, Teresa Caneda Cabrera, Vigo, Mary O'Donnell, Carlo Gébler, Éilís ní Dhuibhne, Dermot and Ann Keogh, Julian Walton, Gerard Dawe, Kathleen Watkins, Liz Nugent, Joseph O'Connor, Sarah Bannon, Michael Finlay, Juan Jose Delaney and Veronica Repetti, Argentina, Asier Altuna Garcia De Salazar, Bilbao and Nora Hickey M'Sichili and the staff at the Centre Cultural Irlandais, Paris.

I wish to thank the Arts Council of Ireland for the support of a Literature Bursary Award and also a Travel and Training Award and thanks also to Cork City Arts Council for an Individual Artists Bursary award. In my research, I was greatly helped by the scholarship of Handel experts like Ellen T.Harris, Jonathan Bardon and Jonathan Keates. I would also like to thank the School of English for research and publication grants, and CACSSS at UCC likewise for research and publication grants.

I want to thank my agent Christopher Sinclair-Stevenson for seeing the novel through with his kind dedication and support. Andrew and Jane Russell of Somerville Press brought my novel into being and I want to thank them for all their care and professionalism throughout, and for making it happen. On a personal level, I am very grateful to Anne Fitzgerald, Ria White, Oonagh Cooney, Ciaran Wallace, Celine Walshe, Rory O'Boyle and Saul Perez.

I dedicate this novel to Donald O'Driscoll, who encouraged it, lent his considerable knowledge of Handel to the project, read and proofed the text and was, again, the main reason I found the motivation and encouragement to write.

# HISTORICAL NOTE

Historical fictions imagine past lives where biographical facts leave us in the dark. Little is known of Handel's private life and so my novel is an attempt to imagine what he may have kept secret from his public and his patrons. All of the characters mentioned in the novel existed, except the key figures of Luca and Lorenzo. The Cardinal is also my invention, a composite of some of his real life patrons. It is entirely possible that the personal life I imagined for Handel did really happen but this is a novel and therefore not true or real or honest.

*Eibhear Walshe 2018*

# DUBLIN
## November 1741

Angry Dublin rain whips against the window as he prepares to write a birthday letter to a dead woman. He picks up the old leather folder, full with writing paper. Luca. Years ago, on an airless summer afternoon, they had wandered into a small bookshop near the Pantheon, and Luca insisted on buying the smart new leather folder for him. He protested that it was too expensive. 'Then go and fill it with operas and come back to Rome a rich man,' Luca said, and, there in the dimly-lit shop, ignoring the sour young woman watching from behind the counter, they kissed. Luca and his Caro Sassone. The two of them just twenty.

Rome. Endless sunshine, buildings gleaming like golden sand, the prospect of adventure filling his chest with a choking excitement as he prowled the streets, glances of desire like unexpected miracles. Then, his future was vague, limitless, like the blue sky over Rome. Now the future harried him nightly, the petty scrabbling after scant resources, the royal pension that kept him barely solvent, alive for more worry. Rome. Here we have no abiding city. No, indeed. He had hurried away too quickly and this frayed folder was all that remained of Rome now that the silver statue of Orpheus was gone.

Another rattle against the window. Almost nine o'clock and fully bright now, despite the rain. He shakes his head, takes up his pen, dips it in ink and writes.

*18th November, 1741*

He pauses, forgetting for a moment, and then writes beneath.

*Abbey Street,*
*Dublin,*
*Ireland.*

Before him on the desk is a small oval portrait. He looks up, touches the corner of the silver frame with his finger and then continues to write.

*Dearest Mother,*
*As always, I send you my most affectionate greetings on your birthday.*
*This address will come as a surprise to you – Dublin, the chief city*
*of His Majesty's Kingdom of Ireland. So far from my homeland, the*
*furthest I have travelled yet and the clearest sign that I have fallen from*
*fashion. London has finished with me and now, an old man, I must*
*repair my fortunes in this rain-sodden outpost. I write this week to my*
*dear niece, and, naturally, I will mention nothing of this. Indeed, with*
*some difficulty, I am sending a gold watch to her fiancé, the doctor,*
*and a diamond of the first water to her, your namesake. To do so,*
*I sold my silver statue of Orpheus, the gift of the Cardinal all those*
*years ago in Rome, my first and kindest patron. It was necessary to*
*maintain the illusion that their uncle has made a great success of his*
*life in the English Court and a fine fortune to boot. Only to you, my*
*beloved mother, dare I utter the truth, that I have wasted my time,*
*and worse than that, I have wasted over ten thousand pounds putting*
*on unwanted operas, wasted it all as surely as if I had scattered each*
*banknote into the English Channel. Only to you, my truest friend, can*
*I tell the truth, and this truth is possible between us only because you*
*are long dead and in your honourable grave.*

He stops writing, signs and then tears up the letter.

# ROME
## 1706

Rome. His first morning. Christmas Day and every church bell in the universe suddenly bursts into wild clamour, startling him awake from a heavy sleep. In his attic over the music shop, he struggles up and drags the heavy shutters open. The brightest light he has ever seen fills the dank room and the sapphire sky overhead is an unending ocean of crisp blue water. He hurries into his clothes, anxious to be out on the busy streets, his plans now come to flesh. Rome. He has two hundred crowns from his father's will, a letter of introduction to the Cardinal from the recently dead Queen of Prussia and no fixed plan beyond getting to the Cardinal and playing music for him.

Cold bright air and he bites into a fresh pie as he pushes his way along the crowded streets under St John Lateran. The Romans are all in their best for this holiday and, realising that his heavy brown coat and his hat are wrong, he vows to spend some of his precious gold on smart new clothes. His old cousin, a lifelong servant of the Prussian King, warned him, starve yourself, sleep in an attic but dress as a nobleman when you call on the Cardinal.

The wild sound of pipes draws him into a wide square and he follows the throng of holiday makers towards the fountain at the centre. A group of young men are playing bagpipes, while two girls bang cymbals and laugh with the noisy crowd. He asks a young couple next to him about

11

the musicians but the woman shrugs with incomprehension. The man, jiggling his plump baby along in time to the pipes, tells him to slow down and he repeats his question. They are pilgrims from Abruzzi, the man says, and they play here in Piazza del Popolo every Christmas Day, a tradition as old as Rome. It is a relief that he can follow most of what the man says, his year of studying Italian in Hamburg with Signor Bacchi paying off.

Then, one of the pipers strikes up a lively new tune and the girls whoop with delight, startling the plump baby into a roar of outraged crying. One of the girls grabs hold of the arm of a young nobleman and drags him into the square. She has chosen well, he thinks, the elegant young man dark and handsome, but clearly embarrassed and his discomfort amuses his friends all the more, and they shout out encouragement and laugh at his predicament. Watching the young man, he fails to notice the other girl bearing down on him and, to his horror, pushes him out into the square. He tries to resist but the crowd, cheering at the spectacle, block his escape and help push him out. The girl laughs as she delivers him to his trapped companion. The young man looks down at his brown coat with disdain and then the musicians strike up and the girls link the young men to make a circle and start the dance. It is a simple folk dance but he and his fellow victim are equally inept, stumbling as the girls push them through their paces. He starts to enjoy himself as the crowd clap along merrily and somehow they complete the set. Only when the music stops and the cheering starts and coins are flung does he realise that he is still holding the young nobleman's hand, and he smiles at him and presses it. The young noble gives him a sudden smile, his disdain revealed as simply the acute embarrassment of a shy boy, barely out of his teens like himself. Then a shout from his companions and the noble drops his hand, bows stiffly and walks away.

For his first few days, he walked the city into his very bones, spending hours on the streets and in the churches, tracking down music wherever he could, mesmerised by the buildings and by the singing and by the light. Each night, he falls into bed exhausted, his head throbbing with all he has seen and heard. He rises early to write down the music filling his head, longing for a proper organ to play on. Sometimes, he tries to sound out his compositions on the old harpsichord at the back of the shop. Although it is January and cold, each day is filled with bright dazzling light and he never tires of looking at the rich sheen of the buildings, the endless clarity of the soaring sky, the feel of crisp biting air in his lungs, pumping life and a thousand songs into his brain. Back in his father's house in Halle, the Yellow Stag House, on the corner near the church, slush and snow would just now be backing up against the dirty walls of the house, the skies shut in by unrelenting winter clouds, the sun a lost memory. He hugs himself with delight at the ease with which he has escaped that small town, the solid house, the law practice his father had chosen for him, the unending delight in local news and gossip and self-importance.

At night in the narrow cave room, he writes to his mother and his sisters, telling of his perilous journey through the imperial armies in Tuscany, and boasting of the concerts he attends and the commissions he will attract. They write back cheerful letters that belie their fears, the few coins they include under the seal to prevent his imminent demise in Papish Rome the only clue of their dread. At first he keeps his gold coins in a heavy leather wallet, hidden under his mattress but, one night he notices that the wallet has been moved in his absence, and one of the smaller coins gone. It could only have been old Giovanna, the woman who cleans the room and washes his linen and tells him what a sweet face he has. Unsettled, he takes his gold to a counting house and has it lodged in the strong room, keeping a few coins in his boot.

Every day, he eats from the cheap food stalls on the Corso, cabbage the prevailing aroma, and one day, dispatching some soup and a lump of coarse bread with gusto, he notices a tall young man standing nearby and smiling at his vigorous eating. He smiles back. The stranger is fair-haired, like himself, and so he strolls over and tries out a few words in German, only to be met with a kindly look of incomprehension. The man's smile lingers, as does his look of appreciation but he remains silent. Georg notices that he has become aware of his own breathing and of a slight thudding sensation in his chest. Finally the stranger inclines his head almost imperceptibly towards a tall building opposite and walks there, glancing back only once. Georg leaves his unfinished soup and quickly follows him into an empty courtyard and up to a half-opened door at the top of the stairs. He stands for a minute or two, uncertain as what he should do and then walks in, pushing the door closed behind him as the stranger comes forward out of the dark corridor to kiss him. His tongue darts into his mouth and then he laughs. 'Cabbage.' It is the only word he says. Georg can hear birds twittering in a cage somewhere inside the apartment in their brief few minutes standing there and, afterwards, the stranger strokes Georg's face lightly and then gently guides him back to the stairwell. Georg stares at the closing door for a minute, and then buttons up and leaves. Later in his room, he finds it difficult to concentrate on his music, the urgency of that kiss still alive on his lips.

He has himself outfitted in the latest fashion and likes the new cut of his sleek black coat and his elegant hat but the abrupt departure of too many of his father's gold crowns to the fancy tailor frightens him so he writes to the Cardinal for a third time, begging leave to pay his respects and mentioning his cousin's patrons, the King and Queen of Prussia, who had kindly furnished him with a letter of recommendation. This letter he sends via the apprentice in the shop to the Cardinal's palace but a week passes and no response comes. He continues to compose feverishly, wandering the streets but he can feel a thin sheet of glass beginning to form between himself and this most wonderful of cities. He watches as the Romans go about their lives in complete and blissful ignorance of his very existence, as if he were becoming invisible. He knows that if he does not find some musicians to work with, he will very soon become maddened with melancholy.

Every morning he speaks with his landlord about the music he has heard but, polite as he is, it is clear that he has his shop to attend to. He spends his evenings alone in shabby taverns, scribbling down music he has heard and staining the paper with the coarse food he eats. He sits writing songs, cantatas, even making plans for an opera despite the ban, all the time prolonging the return up the narrow stairs to the little attic room and the unending silence of the dark, soundless night. He wakes early, too early, in the dark mornings and lies there, fighting the thoughts and dreads that assail him, the dwindling money, and the empty days stretching ahead in this city of strangers.

One morning, in Piazza del Popolo, before he knows it, he passes his dance companion, the elegant young nobleman, in animated conversation with two companions. He watches as the three men walk down the street, unaware of all but their own debate. In sheer loneliness, he contemplates running after him, offering to buy them all a flagon of wine, just to sit in company again but he decides against it and watches as they make their way down the street.

Early next morning, he rises early, washes with care and then dresses in his new Roman clothes. He risks some of his money on a chair to the Cardinal's palace, only to find the heavy wooden doors at the gateway shut and, for a few dark moments, he stares helplessly at the huge square building frowning back at him. Eventually, he notices a pair of clerics approach the entrance and stands to one side. When one of them unlocks a small side door, he slips in behind them and, keeping his eyes down and his stride purposeful, he follows them into the deserted courtyard towards an open door on the ground floor. He is about to step into the palace when he feels a hand grasp his arm firmly.

'Your business, Signore?'

He turns. A tall, dark-haired servant in red livery stands behind him, looking stern, and he gives a reassuring smile and says in his most accented Italian.

'I wonder if you might assist me. I have a letter for the Cardinal, from Berlin?'

'Give it here,' the young man raps out, firmly but not unpleasantly, his smile clearly having some effect. Georg hands it over.

'I will see that it reaches His Grace's secretary today.'

Another letter to be ignored. The man is now pleasant but business-like. Georg feels in his pocket for a small coin and presses it into his hand.

'Will you allow me to present it in person?'

He takes the coin but keeps his hand on Georg's arm, steering him away from the open door.

'His Grace is not at home at present, he is preparing for High Mass at noon today.'

'Where?'

Something in the desperate look in his face seems to soften the young servant, and, with a glance down at the coin and another at his cloak, he offers.

'Would you care to take a look around the courtyard, Signore?'

Keeping his elbow gently within his grasp, he walks Georg around, takes great pride in pointing out His Grace's apartments, the windows of His Grace's private music room and the open doors by the side of the main entrance where a bakery is situated, paid for by His Grace and giving away free loaves of bread day and night to the poor of Rome.

'On Wednesday nights, we have concerts in the blue drawing room.'

His Grace. That's what I should call him if I ever get near enough, he thinks.

All the time, as the servant proudly boasts of His Grace's many fine possessions, Georg is aware that he is pleasantly but firmly being walked back to the front entrance. The servant puts his hand out for the letter and assures him that he will deliver it personally. As he is walked out, the servant suddenly asks.

'You are a visitor to Rome?'

He nods.

'Have you been to the Basilica of St John Lateran? It is his Holiness's own church? I would advise a visit there...today if you have some time.'

With that, he is led out the door. Another door shut in his face. He turns and hurries away, back to the basilica on its perch over the city. He makes his way into the crowded church, pushing his way into one of the last seats right in front, the canopy over the altar frilled with carved marble like a fancy four-poster bed. As he kneels, he smiles at the thought of his father's indignation, his son at a Romish mass, dressed in the finest black bought with his own hard-earned life savings.

Ahead of him, somewhere to his right, behind the main altar, the organ suddenly crashes into triumphant music and the congregation shuffle to their feet. He turns to listen to the music, the best heard yet in Rome, until the man behind him pokes him in the back, and nods reprovingly towards richly-clad priests, processing out from the side of the chapel. He watches as they walk across to the dome of rich gold, with what appears to be deer nibbling in the fresco behind the altar. He recognises the Cardinal at once, not just because of his rich robes but because of the way in which the surrounding prelates pay him covert attention. Mesmerised by the music, the lengthy ceremony means little to him. Again and again, he lifts his head to one side to hear the glorious sounds of the organ and so it come as a shock when the Cardinal kneels before the altar and then turns to process away. The congregation streams out past Georg while he sits looking at the closed door in the side chapel. Cursing his lack of foresight, he gets up and wanders slowly up to the left aisle of the deserted basilica. The place feels suddenly huge and forlorn and he wants to run out as quickly as he can. He decides instead to look at the organ, housed high up in its own balcony of highly polished twisted marble. He is staring up when a voice behind him startles him.

'Here is the young man who turned around to listen to the music instead of listening to me.'

Behind him, the Cardinal stands, in a simple dark cassock, and with a train of amused priests clustered behind him.

'Your Grace.'

He pulls off his hat and bows. His hair, grown longer than he noticed, tumbles down across his brow. He pushes it back with his hand, noticing the Cardinal staring at his hair and annoyed at himself for letting it become so unkempt. The Cardinal collects himself and asks graciously.

'By your accent, you are a visitor to Rome?'

'I am from Saxony. I had the honour of writing to you. My patrons, King Frederick and the late Queen Sophia Charlotte, wrote to recommend my music.'

The letter had clearly never got as far as the Cardinal. Another lesson. Letters are beneath the notice of the powerful.

'Ah, you are a musician. That's why you were listening to the organ and not to me?'

The priests around the Cardinal begin to pay him some attention, this young man favoured with more than a few words.

'I wish to play my music here.'

The Cardinal frowns in mockery.

'You, a heathen, in his Holiness's own church? What blasphemy, young Saxon!'

His cousin told him, never fail to laugh when they jest, and never interrupt.

He smiles broadly and the Cardinal seems a little taken aback but gestures back towards another smaller organ in a side chapel.

'Well, your wish can be granted in some degree, young heathen. Play for us here, if you would?'

Without a moment's hesitation, with the thought of his attic room in his mind, Georg takes his seat while the Cardinal and his retinue stand respectfully at a distance. He thinks of doors closing in his face. Finally, one slightly ajar. A chaplain of the church starts to move swiftly towards him but, with a nod from the Cardinal, he backs down. He strikes a note or two while he thinks, the tentative sounds he makes filling him with excitement, and then he begins. A new composition, played on the old harpsichord at his lodgings. His music, lively and playful, fills the vast space of the basilica, empty except for the men ranged behind him. For a while, he forgets about the need to impress this man and relishes the beauty of the magnificent sounds issuing throughout the church and the dramatic energy spurring on his music. When he finishes, he stands up and bows. They all look at him in silence. Finally, the Cardinal speaks.

'Your hands, they are like wings. What music do you play?'

'My own, Your Grace.'

One of the priests, a red-faced older man asks.

'Where were you trained to play like that, young man? Were you employed at the Prussian Court?'

'No, sir, I taught myself in my own attic room, on a spinet that my mother smuggled in. My father, rest his soul, chose the law for my profession and so music was forbidden.'

'And where is that home, my son? '

He realises the old priest was well-intentioned despite the sour look on his face and he answers more gently,

'Halle, in the kingdom of Prussia, Father. We have a church near our home and my father finally allowed me to learn from the local cantor. Papa then thought that I might become a cantor but I disappointed him again.'

He says this lightly but it strike him as true and a finger of remorse touches his heart, beating strongly in the excitement of this fortunate gamble and the Cardinal's attention.

The Cardinal looks bemused.

'How could he have been so foolish?'

A chaplain whispers in his ear. The Cardinal nods, his face closed off again.

'I must leave, young Herr . . .'

'Georg. Georg Handel, Your Grace.'

'Signor Giorgio. I must leave but we have music on Wednesday. Come after eight.'

The Cardinal speaks with the clarity of one who is always listened to and they all smile politely.

He stands there, watching as they leave. Soon the rustling of their robes dies away and the vast square cave of the church is deserted, yet it is not big enough to contain his sense of excitement. He wanders out to the front of the Basilica, reluctant to leave and steps outside into the sun, the doors tall and narrow with a dark staining around the handles. Just then he wishes the stranger with the fair hair was here for him to kiss.

The following Wednesday, his hair freshly cut, he dresses in his new fawn-coloured coat with the light gold trim. Old Giovanna has polished his boots and brushed his hat until they gleam and stands admiring him as he checks himself in the mirror, telling him that he is like a young god. He smiles. No more money. The small coin she helped herself to was sufficient payment.

At the Cardinal's palace, he rings the bell by the door of this solid block of stone, heavy with money. By good chance, the same servant is waiting and is a great deal more cordial.

'You are the Saxon, yes?'

He ushers him in.

'My name is Lorenzo, Signore. When you are visiting His Grace, ask for me.'

He smiles at Georg. The small coin. He produces another.

He leads Georg upstairs into a small ante-room, and taking his cloak and hat, motions him toward the open doors of a much larger music room. He hurries in to find it almost deserted. The blue and gilt chairs are arranged in a semi-circle around a harpsichord and the long room is reflected and made immense by wall-length mirrors on one side and brightly lit with heavy gold candelabra on all the tables. A few dispirited clerics stand around, watching intently as the servants lay out heavy crystal glasses and bottles filled with colourful liquors. At a far table, trays of ices in porcelain cups are being unloaded. He is hungry but unwilling to join in a sudden rush for refreshment and catches a glimpse of himself in the mirrored wall, unexpectedly sleek in his fawn velvet coat. He wanders over to the grand harpsichord and stares at it, resisting the temptation to touch its keys and instead stands and examines it intently, assuming an indifference he is far from feeling. After a while, the room starts to fill up and the clink of glasses and the sound of chatter warns him that the liquors are disappearing fast and so he goes back to a table and helps himself to a glass of some warming green concoction. As he drinks, an old monk drinking Madeira next to him picks up a rich damask napkin, dabs his face with it, and then stuffs it into his pocket. A moment later, the glass follows the napkin. When the old monk notices him watching, he smiles and gestures at another napkin.

'Help yourself, my boy, plenty for all.'

Unnoticed by Georg, the musicians have entered and are tuning their instruments and the front rows are now full and so he makes his way towards an empty row of seats at the back of the room. A rustling noise begins as the Cardinal enters from a side room, smiles at those in the front row and makes his way to a slightly larger circle of gilt chairs next to the singers. The music begins, and Georg finds it hard to listen, keeping his eyes firmly on the Cardinal.

When the music ends, they stand and the audience start drifting into another reception room, while the Cardinal stays talking to the musicians. Georg manages to get some food and a glass of wine, and, bolting it down, stands watching the Cardinal. He realises that he is not the only one straining for his attention and so he pushes his way into the group surrounding him and blurts out, as quickly as he can.

'Thank you, Your Grace, for the chance to hear such music.'

The Cardinal starts to speak but then someone takes his arm and murmurs something about the ambassador and Georg stands staring at his crimson silken back. The noise of the room seems overwhelming and he thinks about getting his cloak but a tap on his shoulder stops him. It is Lorenzo.

'His Grace would like a word in his study. Please come with me.'

He follows Lorenzo out of the room, and, at the door, a group of young men start filing in and so he stands to one side. One of them is the young nobleman from the dance and he pauses while they stare at each other. Finally Georg bows and the young man smiles back. Up close, he looks younger and less sure of himself, and his dark skin is slightly mottled with pimples, just below his soft dark beard. His eyes are dark and shine with interest. His friends call him.

'Luca. Are you coming?'

He hurries on. Luca. Georg stands at the door looking at his retreating back and then Luca turns and glances back at him. Lorenzo is standing waiting, watching the exchange of glances impassively. Somehow, Georg would have preferred Lorenzo not to have witnessed this encounter.

The Cardinal's study is a small, dark room across the corridor from the music room, with a fire blazing and a prim-looking young priest writing at a desk. Lorenzo motions towards a comfortable chair by the fire and Georg sits and watches him leave. The secretary ignores him and the scratching of his quill and the crackle of the fire are the only sounds. Georg looks around the room, surprised at its lack of decoration, in stark contrast to the lushness of the music room and notices the neatly stacked documents, the tidy pile of books and the lone note of wealth, the silver statue on the desk.

'The statue?' He ventures to ask the scribbling priest.

He looks up and frowns.

'Orpheus,' he says briefly and returns to his writing.

Orpheus. He wants to look at it but dare not. The chair is comfortable and the fire warm and despite himself Georg finds himself nodding off. He awakes with a start to find the Cardinal standing over him, watching him with a slightly sardonic smile. He struggles to stands up but is motioned to remain in his seat.

'Sit, sit, Signor Sassone. You looked as if you were enjoying your rest. Gianni, have the letters gone to the Cancelleria?'

'Not yet, Your Grace. I can take them down to the messenger now, if you wish.'

The Cardinal nods and the secretary, now all smiles and attention, bows and leaves the room.

The Cardinal pulls up a chair to join him by the fire and fixes him with a shrewd, friendly stare. Seen up close, his face is lined, pale, a few deep lines creasing his forehead. His hazel eyes are humorous but bright with a kind of unsettling intelligence that makes Georg feel the need to be thoroughly awake, something the warm fire is preventing.

'Now, young Saxon, tell me, why are you in Rome and at a time of war? Are you a spy for your royal masters?'

The Cardinal holds the letter of the dead Queen of Prussia in his left hand and taps it with his right. Georg tries not to look at the Cardinal's right hand, clearly smaller and hidden in a dark leather glove.

He considers all the possible answers and selects the truth.

'I want to perform my music, Your Grace and I want to work with good musicians.'

The Cardinal nods.

'What do you wish to compose?'

'Sacred music.'

Not quite true. Opera is what most possesses him but he cannot say this to an eminent Prince of the Church, in a city where opera is forbidden. The Cardinal is watching him closely and so he keeps his face as blank as possible, wishing he was standing up. The Cardinal's face gleams a little in the bright firelight and he looks tired.

'And is your Lutheran faith in danger here, in Rome?'

'Music is my profession, Your Grace and, if it is not too dangerous to say so, my only concern.'

'Good, good,' the Cardinal seems pleased, 'I promise not to report you to your master the King of Prussia.'

'He is not my master, Your Grace.'

Too sharp, he wondered? The answer seems to please again.

'Good. A musician should be free to work where he wishes and be above suspicion. It makes him…useful. And how have you travelled to Rome?'

His face is pleasant and his tone gentle but each question feels as if there is a larger audience outside the room weighing his words and so he keeps his answers short.

'My father's small legacy brought me here.'

'Rome can be a costly city. A small legacy will not suffice and soon, if Prince Eugene has his way, we will all be in flight from the Emperor's armies and you will need your father's gold to escape to Naples.'

Georg smiles, remembering the damask napkins disappearing into the old monk's pocket and knows that cost has no real importance for this smiling man in front of him.

'Why do you smile?'

'Forgive me, Your Grace, I was thinking of my father's wrath at his savings disappearing in Rome. I should not smile, I am aware of time running out.'

'Do you miss your city?'

'Not at all.'

Was that true? Just that morning, he had woken up dreaming of his father's house in the summertime, and of his mother ordering all the windows to be opened, to fill the old house with the sweetness of the summer air and he was surprised to find tears on his cheeks at the dream of her beloved face, her eyes closed in happiness as the scent of the lime trees drifts through the house. The Cardinal stands up and Georg hurries to his feet.

'I was born here in Rome, I can imagine life in no other city.'

The secretary has comes back into the room and the Cardinal takes Georg's hand and presses it into his. It is cold and the smaller gloved hand feels somehow unpleasant to the touch.

'More letters to answer. I will think on this further. I envy you your youth and freedom. Good night, young Saxon.'

Outside Lorenzo is waiting for him, and escorts him downstairs and out of the deserted palace. Outside the streets are dark and gloomy, Luca long vanished, and he walks slowly back to his lodgings, unwilling to face the long climb of those stairs back up to his room. Luca. That is his name. And nothing from the Cardinal except questions about his master, the King of Prussia! Youth. Freedom. Freedom to rot in this attic. He kicks at one of the dirty wooden steps as he mounts the narrow stairs to the attic.

Two days later, Giovanna knocks on his door early and thrusts a letter into his hands before he is fully awake.

'By hand!'

She stands there smirking, waiting to hear the news. He ushers her out.

It is short.

'Signor Giorgio, We cannot waste any more of your father's legacy. You may stay here for the next few months, and compose for our musicians. If this is agreeable, my man Lorenzo will call for you at noon and arrange all.'

He puts the letter down and calls the hovering Giovanna back, giving her a resounding kiss and a small coin. He packs as quickly as he can and flies down the narrow staircase on feet that feel as if they could take flight, and has settled all his affairs with his landlord by the time Lorenzo arrives at noon.

'Just these, Signore?'

Georg attempts to lift his bags onto the carriage but Lorenzo stops him. On the way, Lorenzo explains that His Grace rarely eats with his household but that Georg will dine with the chaplains and can use a household carriage when he requires to travel. Again, the gates of the palace open wide for him and Lorenzo conducts him to his room on the third floor, next to a large music room, where a fine harpsichord stands.

'His Grace's regular musicians will attend on Thursday afternoon at three to rehearse, the day after the concert.'

He looks around the comfortable, sunlit room. 'If this is agreeable.' How did this happen so quickly? A fear that it will evaporate grips him.

'May I call on the Cardinal to express my thanks, if he is at leisure?'

Lorenzo smiles.

'His Grace is rarely at leisure. He leaves today for Milan, on His Holiness's business with the Austrians. A dangerous journey. We all of us pray for his safe return.'

His Grace seems to loom large in Lorenzo's life and Georg wonders for the first time about the life behind the servant's impassive, handsome face. Without the Cardinal, this busy, richly upholstered palace would be emptied, all the Madeira and ices vanish and the priests, servants and musicians thrown out on the street.

'I will leave you to unpack. Here is a key for the little door by the courtyard.'

Georg moves out to the window and glances down on the busy inner courtyard, and then looks around at the comfortable room, the large bed, the good furniture. On the wide desk, there is a packet. He tears it open. Another short note from the Cardinal.

'Your first commission, Signor Sassone. A setting for my singers and players, to be performed on my return next month. Here is the text.'

He finds a sheet inside the note.

*Dixit Dominus*
*The LORD said unto my Lord, Sit thou at my right hand, until I make thine enemies thy footstool. The LORD shall send the rod of thy strength out of Zion: rule thou in the midst of thine enemies.*
*Thy people shall be willing in the day of thy power, in the beauties of holiness from the womb of the morning: thou hast the dew of thy youth.*

*The LORD hath sworn, and will not repent, Thou art a priest for ever*
    *after the order of Melchizedek.*
*The LORD at thy right hand shall strike through kings in the day of his*
    *wrath.*
*He shall judge among the heathen, he shall fill the places with the dead*
    *bodies; he shall wound the heads over many countries.*
*He shall drink of the brook in the way: therefore shall he lift up the head.*

Another paper has fluttered to the ground. He picks it up. It is a bank draft for fifty crowns.

He sits down later that day at the harpsichord and begins rewriting music he worked on in the little attic room, the sound now cleaner and richer in the plush music room. He is determined to use the music he played in St John Lateran but he wonders about the setting of each of the sentences. 'Thou art a priest for ever after the order of Melchizedek.' That was easy, a paean to the Cardinal himself. 'Thou hast the dew of thy youth.' Luca, flushed and smiling in the dance in Popolo.

Full of ideas, he sets out from the palace in the carriage, lodging the draft with his bankers, taking enough gold to pay for another new coat and hat and some good shirts. From there, he buys turquoise rings to send to his mother and sisters, with the letter of triumph setting out his new commission. As the carriage drives him through the gates of the palace, a sense of dread returns, and the sense of the unreality of this world.

It occurs to him that Luca may well be at the next musical evening the following Wednesday, and so he dons his new blue coat, preparing himself with care to rival the elegance of the young noble and his aristocratic friends. He keeps an eye out for them but, by the time the music begins, it is a sparsely attended affair with the Cardinal's absence in Milan, the majority of the audience hungry curates intent on filling their bellies and pockets. He watches for Luca but to no avail. He listens to the musicians, determined to pick the best for his music. The chorus are good, well-chosen and the musicians are all of a high quality but the soloists he finds unsympathetic, apart from one woman singing alto.

Then a tall, slightly ungainly young woman takes her place in front of the musicians to sing. He listens with pleasure. A soprano and a good one, despite her youth and her undistinguished features, a richness and an assurance to her voice that he is determined to use. He makes his way to the front after the music has ended and bows to her.

'Signora Durastanti.'

'Sir' she blushes and looks around. An older woman, evidently her mother, comes over to deal with this interloper.

'His Grace has asked me to compose for his return and I was hoping to include you in my recital.'

Mamma, elegantly dressed and laden with gold rings, is staring at him and so he bows and introduces himself, repeating his request.

'If His Grace wishes, then we are happy to oblige. Come, Margherita, we must have our supper before all the locusts descend on it.'

Next day, the day of the rehearsal, the palace is in a state of some excitement, and, in his music room, he can hear the bell for the porter constantly jangling but Lorenzo is uncharacteristically absent. Georg goes down himself to the porter to collect the scores for the performers and so it is well after three when he arrives back in the music salon to find all the singers and musicians waiting for him. He makes his way to the harpsichord and introduces himself over their chatter, his voice sounding harsh and strange to his own ears, while the men and women in their sober black watch this foppish youth in his blue coat with some amusement. His second mistake. He has overdressed for the occasion. When he asks if all present can read at sight, he is aware of a ripple of resentment throughout the room. He is acutely aware that he is the youngest person in the room, apart from Margherita, and so keeps his demeanour business-like as he hands around the music and tells them that he will play himself on the harpsichord and will only require the violins at first. He asks the singers, who look remarkably indolent, to stand and Margherita blushes when he asks her to sing the soprano aria.

As soon as the violins strike up, the energy of the music somehow dissipates the indolence of the singers and they respond well to the demands of the opening. He pauses and then motions Margherita forward to sing. It is better than he had hoped, her ability to read quickly and accurately evident, her voice strong, young, true, full of rich notes, and she sings happily, at ease with the slow and complicated arias he has created. Outside, through the open door, he can see Gianni, the secretary, listening and hopes that he will send back reports to his master of the hard work of the young Saxon. It takes these skilled musicians a little over thirty minutes to perform the piece and when it is ended, the atmosphere in the room is very different. Even the sun has come out to light up the music salon, and the musicians stand up, stretch and chat happily among themselves.

He asks for another rehearsal, and this time the piece sounds even clearer and more confident.

At the end of the rehearsal, he thanks those present and one of the singers asks, 'When will we perform your piece for His Grace?'

'On his return from Milan at the end of the month, I believe. We can rehearse again next week at this time?'

He asks and they all nod.

As they stream out and Georg is collecting some of the unused music sheets, Gianni makes his way towards him.

'Signor Endell, a word. You must not refer in public to His Grace's destination. It is not safe. We are in times of war.'

Georg, flushed with happiness at the music he has created, merely laughs.

'Really, Monsignore, I doubt that a group of harmless musicians like ourselves are much concerned with public matters.'

Gianni frowns.

'On the contrary, a number of the singers are known to be in the pay of the Austrians. That Madame Durastanti for example.'

'I did wonder at the vast quantity of gold rings. Maybe the Empress gave them to her?'

The man looks even more annoyed.

'His Grace will not appreciate your flippancy tonight when I inform him.'

'Tonight? But he is in Milan.'

'He returns today and wishes to hear your new composition next Wednesday.'

Some of the older musicians have lingered to listen as Gianni chatters on. So much for discretion, Georg thinks.

'Yes, he was turned away just before Milan, despite his status as papal envoy. It was a great humiliation for him.'

The atmosphere in the palace becomes more frantic that evening and the following morning, Lorenzo calls to the music room and tells him that a tray of food will be brought to his room, as the dining room must be kept free for a council meeting. Georg stays in his room and eats, while the courtyard below is filled with the noise of loud steps, carriages drawing up and a murmuring on the corridors. He looks over his music scores, marking his own sections, and wonders if he should fetch some of his gold.

Next morning, all is calm again in the palace but Georg leaves for his bankers, draws some gold and then orders a special money belt at his tailors. On his return, the palace seems emptier. The porter tells him that the Cardinal has gone away again, to confer with the Pope in Frascati. Later, he hears Gianni chattering in the loggia with another cleric, saying with some pleasure that His Holiness is displeased with His Grace and it is possible that he will be removed from all of his offices.

On the morning of the concert, Lorenzo calls into the music room to tell him that, despite the rumours of invasion, the Cardinal is returning from Frascati to attend the recital. That night, the music salon fills up quickly, despite the threat of a curfew on the streets and the rumours of an Imperial army fifty miles from Rome. Georg stands by the harpsichord in his sober black suit, assuming as much gravitas as possible. As he waits and the room becomes fuller and the air heavy with chatter and excitement, Georg can feel his chest becoming tighter and his breathing constricted as he realises what he has done. He has written this awful, childish score and the finely-tuned ears of the Roman audience will laugh it to scorn. A momentary glimpse of himself in a mirror only makes him feel more foolish, he looks like a fop, a silly lad in fancy clothes, masquerading as an adult. He turns and looks wildly at the singers, marveling at their apparent calm in the face of impending humiliation and some of them smile back at him and others look questioningly.

Margherita, who is standing near the harpsichord, moves nearer to him and murmurs, 'All will be well, Signor Giorgio, it is a fine piece of music.' He smiles his widest smile at her.

Just then, punctually at eight, the Cardinal enters the salon and makes his way directly to Georg, shaking his hand warmly and bowing his thanks to the musicians courteously, who all smile. He looks tired and a little shaken as he takes his seat. Georg wonders if, as Gianni whispered, his carriage really did come under fire outside Milan and that the Holy Father was loud in his remonstrations against him.

A hush before the music begins. Georg stands as if frozen, the airless room about to smother him. The musicians look at him in some alarm and finally he takes his seat at the harpsichord and nods to them to begin. The violins attack the opening, lively and full of fire and the singers come in, proud, assertive and Georg watches with wonder when Margherita takes up her part, swaying slightly. His music, cobbled together in a shabby attic room, takes its proud place in this blue and gilt salon, as fine as any heard here on a Wednesday night. As they play and sing, full of seriousness, his music takes on a new life, drawing in confidence from the attentive, well-dressed audience, the rich voices, the expert playing and even the gloss of the gilt chairs and the winking lights in the candelabras. Georg finds himself relaxing, enjoying the music, even admiring it, and forgetting it was ever his.

At the end of the piece, there is a silence and then the applause begins. He turns to the Cardinal, who looks happy, even flushed. It occurs to Georg, for the first time that the Cardinal is not quite as old as he thought, no more than ten years older than himself. There is some polite cheering at the back and Georg smiles and looks down the hall. Luca and his friends are on their feet, clapping, a little ironically but with good humour. He catches Luca's eye, bows in his direction and the young man bows back, a shy beautiful smile, a glimpse of white teeth in his dark beard. Tonight, Georg tells himself, I will speak to him. The Cardinal stands up and takes his hand, and, turning to the crowd, holds it up. They cheer and Georg turns and bows at the singers and the musicians.

In a low voice, the Cardinal tells him.

'For your music, it was worth braving the Austrians, Signor Sassone.'

The Cardinal presses his arm warmly and the musicians file up to shake his hand, intent on gaining some appreciation from the Cardinal. Gianni, smiling as if they were bosom friends, comes to tell him how much he admired the work.

'Beautiful setting, Signor Endell.'

The Cardinal presses his arm again as he prepares to leave and tells him that he will call to the music room and congratulate him again in the morning. Georg bows and then he scans the room, half listening to Mamma Durastanti's lavish praises. Excusing himself, he goes into the supper chamber, again to be stopped with congratulations. He mutters his excuses, fetching his cloak and key, and dashes down the staircase and out of the palace.

Outside, he hesitates, then takes a chance in the direction of the Corso, following a group of young people walking away from the palace. Hurrying to catch up, he sees Luca ahead, walking along with two young women. Georg follows, keeping them in sight as they drift along. They stroll towards the Forum and then onwards to the Arch of Constantine, where they halt to listen to a young man pointing at something near the base of the Arch. All around, intense light glaring down from a huge moon high over the Caelian hill makes the January evening seem like pale day again, the streets thronged with evening walkers, the threat of war lending an excitement to the night time city caught in this silver light. Georg stands to one side on a slight incline, watching the young people as they listen to their friend, recognising faces from the concert, some of whom glance over questioningly and nod to him. The young man finishes talking and they all laugh and, as his friends begin to wander away from the Arch of Constantine, Luca remains standing there. When he is finally alone, Georg slowly walks over and they look at each other. Georg smiles. One of the young women of his party calls for Luca from the other side of the street to hurry up, but then, a young man, glancing back too, nudges her and she turns back to her friends. Georg is not sure, but he thinks the young woman may be Margherita. The two men stand looking at each other for a few moments, all his urgent desire to meet Luca gone and Georg suddenly has no words.

Finally Luca says, in a surprisingly deep voice for one so slight.

'You are Signor Endell? '

He pronounces it as Gianni does but, this time, Georg finds it charming rather than annoying.

'Georg, I am Georg.'

Luca smiles. In the glare of the moonlight, Georg can see his face clearly, everything about him drained of colour except for the colour of his dark beard and the clear whites of his eyes. He has never, he thinks, seen such dark hair, such white teeth, and admires the sharp curve of his nose, the glint of a silver ring in his ear. This close, Georg gets a slight scent from him, a light verbena, and it makes him want to touch him, to stroke his hair. Instead he just stands there.

'Georg.'

He imitates him and then laughs.

'I don't like the way you say it. Giorgio is better.'

He puts out his hand.

'Luca.'

His hand feels warm and Georg wants to keep holding it but they let their hands fall and stand, staring at each other. He wants to say, I know your name, Luca. I've been looking for you every day for weeks now. But he says nothing. Some people pass by, and look at the two men standing staring at each other, and then Luca speaks up.

'So you come from …?'

'Saxony.'

Luca nods gravely.

'German. I heard that at the concert.'

'And you?'

'I am from Sardinia.'

'Not Rome?'

'No.'

Luca looks around. A group of clerics have stopped by the Coliseum and are chatting loudly. Something about the relentlessly bright moonlight makes Georg uncomfortable, the faces of passers-by gaunt and hollow-eyed, every detail around them nightmarishly clear.

'Come. Let's walk for a little.'

They walk on in silence, by instinct moving away from the late night strollers and instead drift in the direction of a grove of Cypress trees ahead. Luca pulls his cloak around himself more tightly.

'Cold?'

'A little.'

'Shall we get some wine?'

Luca pauses. Georg wonders if he has said too much.

'No. Everywhere will be closed now.'

He pulls out a hat from under his cloak and puts it on.

Georg tells him.

'This is summer for me. In my town, the snow has been falling for months.'

Luca makes a face of mock horror at the thought of such cold and boasts, a little.

'In my father's villa in Sardinia, by now, blossoms are already on the trees.'

They reach the trees and Luca leads the way towards a shaded pathway. Now, far away from other walkers, Georg finds himself looking more and more at Luca, who returns his stares with frank interest.

'Do you miss your home?'

'No. You?'

'No. Rome is where I want to be.'

'To play music?'

'Did you like my music tonight?'

Luca nodded and smiled at him.

'Very much. Your singers are not good enough but, yes I liked your music.'

Georg thinks, my singers are the best in Rome, which means the best in the world. He knows very little.

'Do you sing?'

'A little.'

'You must come and sing at the next concert.'

Luca shrugs.

'Perhaps. I am not so good.'

'I will teach you.'

I have my studies. It is not easy.'

'You are studying?'

Luca pulls a face of boredom.

'Law. My father insisted.'

Georg laughs.

'Law was my father's choice for me, too. And now I am a travelling musician.'

While they talk, Georg is keenly aware that they have wandered deep into the deserted glade, screened off from the noises of the late night city and the scrutiny of the moonlight. Light breaks through the trees here and there, making the trees even darker and more threatening. Luca stops and looks around.

'Is this safe, I wonder?'

Georg wonders what he means. Safe from robbery or safe from prying eyes.

There is a wooden seat under a nearby tree and Luca gestures towards it. They sit, side by side, and the silence grows. Luca shivers.

'Cold?

He asks again, but this time, Luca is silent. The seat is screened on one side by a tall hedge running away from the Cypress trees and Georg wonders at the care with which Luca found them such privacy. A slant of moonlight falls across Luca's hand, lying right next to him on the seat. They sit in silence and the whole world now just this seat, the hand so close, the waiting night and the wind brushing through the tall trees behind them. In the distance, a church bell strikes. Eleven o'clock. Georg remembers a door closing in his face in the Corso and, steeling himself, reaches over and takes the hand. He begins to rub it lightly, as if to warm it. It already feels warm and he holds it between his own two hands while Luca sits, as if made of wood like the seat. Georg turns it over and, raising it to his lips, kisses the palm lightly while Luca's breathing is now the only sound, apart from the slight rustle of the January night breeze in the trees. He lifts Luca's palm against his cheek and, then, with his other hand, he reaches over and touches his hair, heavy, soft, and presses his face against it. The scent of verbena is strong in his hair, some kind of musky pomade and he breathes it in, murmuring Luca's name while his lips search to kiss his ear, feeling the cold touch of his earring on his mouth. Suddenly Luca presses his face against Georg's. A kind of scuffle takes place and their noses clash but, somehow, their mouths find each other and their lips brush and rub together and Georg moves awkwardly forward to kiss him. He feels Luca's tongue dart through his teeth and into his mouth and that slight movement travels deep down into his body, setting his blood racing. He learns quickly to breathe deeply through his nose while their tongues slide against each other and their kissing becomes stronger and more confident. As they kiss with increasing abandon, Luca makes a deep sound in his throat, a kind of murmuring groan, and puts his hand behind Georg's neck to push him closer, their kissing becoming more urgent, almost violent. He puts his hand on Luca's slender leg, surprised at how strong it feels and moves upwards. Luca pushes it away.

'I hear a noise. We should go.'

Georg hears nothing but he stands up to stamp his feet awake. He also wants to hide from Luca the consequences of their kissing, embarrassed by his excitement. Luca stands up with him and looks around him.

'Your friends, they are long gone.'

Luca shrugs.

'They will not care. Walk with me to my cousin's house.'

Georg follows him out of the dark glade with reluctance and they make their way back to the bright streets. As they walk, Luca tells him of his cousins here in Rome, the house where he lodges, near to St John Lateran.

'My uncle is strict. He is always checking on my studies, threatening to tell my father.'

They reach the house and Georg laughs when he realises Luca lives on in the same street as the print maker.

'You could have seen my terrible hovel of an attic…and my narrow little bed.'

Luca ignores this, looking up at the darkened house anxiously. Georg checks around him first and then moves to kiss him goodbye. Luca pushes him away.

'No, my uncle may be watching for me.'

So Georg wonders. Is this all? Will he vanish like the fair-haired merchant? Is this even his house?

'You will meet me tomorrow?'

'Yes. Noon.'

'Where?' Georg asks.

'Popolo. I will be finished with my classes then.'

He runs into the house, leaving Georg on the deserted street. He stands and watches him go in, even though Luca turns to wave him away from the house. As he lets himself quietly in by the side door to the palace, Lorenzo emerges from the courtyard.

'His Grace was asking for you.'

Georg apologises, tells him that he needed some fresh air after the concert and that he will be in the rehearsal room after breakfast. Without replying, Lorenzo hands him a packet.

He runs to his room and opens it. Another draft, this time for one hundred crowns. He drops it on the floor of his room and throws himself on his bed, his head buzzing with thoughts of Luca, of his lips, the scent of verbena on his hair. That night he sleeps fitfully, and wonders if, by any miracle, he could have Luca beside him in this comfortable bed.

He is at the harpsichord early next morning, playing a new melody that seems to sing of Luca's beautiful mouth and of their kissing, but it is nearly eleven when the Cardinal finally comes into the music room. He goes to stand up but the Cardinal waves at him to stay sitting, closing the door softly behind him and walking over to stand at his shoulder.

'Please, keep playing. A very sweet air.'

Georg keeps playing, aware of the Cardinal standing behind him, and the music, formerly a delight, seems to betray him, to tell all his secrets. He ends slowly and turns to find the Cardinal beaming down at him.

'Next week, can we hope to hear your music again? I expect a visitor from Hanover and he will appreciate your work.'

Georg nods.

'We would be delighted, Your Grace. Will I prepare something new?'

The Cardinal shakes his head.

'No, Elector Georg must hear your wonderful composition of last night. His visit is something of a secret. He comes from the Emperor and we value his intervention. He is a great lover of music and so I know you will entertain him.'

Georg smiles his thanks. All of this could have been relayed by Lorenzo. He waits.

The Cardinal stands and looks out of the window. He turns.

'Have you met him, the Elector, Giorgio?'

Georg is puzzled. He shakes his head.

'No, Your Grace, I have never been to Hanover.'

'But he is the brother of your late Queen of Prussia.'

Georg is about to admit the truth, that his cousin got him that letter of recommendation, that he only met the Queen once, years ago, at a crowded reception, but the Cardinal presses on.

'Never mind. He is an important ally for us, and will be even more so, when he is King of England.'

'I know little of politics, Your Grace.'

'Now you must learn before you meet him. We are caught between the King of France and the Emperor and the Imperial army is, at present, nearest to Rome. That Madame Durastanti can teach you. She is in the pay of the Emperor.'

Georg feels a little uncertain and remains silent. The Cardinal looks down at Georg kindly. The Cardinal, a smaller man than he, always puts him at a disadvantage by making him sit. He hears a bell toll outside. Past eleven thirty already.

'I mention this only because you and her daughter are working together.'

He pauses and looks inquiringly.

'Perhaps she is your favourite…?'

The Cardinal looks at him, genuinely curious. Georg hesitates. He wonders if he should pretend an interest but then he remembers Margherita's kind empathy last night in his moment of terror and replies, 'No, Your Grace' and almost before he can stop himself, he adds, 'I have no interest in women, in that way.'

A sudden vivid recollection of the sensation of Luca's soft, vigorous tongue pushing into his mouth makes him flush but his answer seems to please the Cardinal and after a moment, he answers, softly, almost irrelevantly.

'In that, we are alike.' And he looks away.

This interchange seems to relax the Cardinal, but, instead it has the effect of making Georg more uncomfortable. The Cardinal walks over to the window and takes a seat, facing him directly.

'Forgive me for prying. I hope we are becoming friends.'

He rubs his face with his hands and Georg mutters some suitable noise of agreement, but sounds unconvincing even to himself. He wonders when he will leave and contemplates standing up but stops himself. The Cardinal notices nothing.

'England supports the Emperor and, if Elector Georg is to be King of England, we need his friendship and goodwill.'

'Will the Imperial troops invade Rome, Your Grace?'

The Cardinal looks at him warily before answering, darkly.

'The Emperor has promised to protect Rome, but…he has already taken Piacenza from us.'

Georg nods, assuming an air of interest, already aware of time slipping by. It will take him at least twenty minutes to get to Popolo and he should be leaving now, but he makes himself stay sitting, apparently at ease, while the Cardinal explains the dangers of war to him. Finally, he stands and Georg hurries to his feet.

'I'm glad we have spoken again. I welcome our conversations. I have few moments like this.'

'Your Grace has been very kind to me.'

He bows and then waits and then, a few moments later, dashes to get his cloak. As bad luck would have it, there is no carriage in the courtyard and so he begins to run up the Corso, hearing the bells for noon everywhere. It is long past midday when he gets to Popolo and he stands in the centre, scanning the groups of students walking past in the unexpectedly warm day, but no Luca. He hears the bell ring for twelve thirty and suddenly feels the need to sit down, the physical disappointment is like a blow to his stomach. He slumps on the church steps where he first saw him, overwhelmed by his run, and to his horror, he finds himself in tears. As he buries his face in his hands, he hears his name, a great shout. Luca runs up.

'Giorgio, forgive me, I was delayed by my professor. I though you would be gone.'

He grabs Georg in relief, his face flushed and happy with his running, his white shirt stuck to his chest with sweat. Georg laughs with relief.

'And I was delayed by the Cardinal.'

He puts his hand up to his face, anxious to hide his foolish tears, but Luca notices nothing.

'Where can we go?'

Luca looks at him with open desire.

'Not the palace. Your house?'

Luca shakes his head.

'My uncle's bankers from Florence are there today. Come, let us walk. We will find somewhere. We must!'

They set off in the noontime sun and as they jostle through the crowds, Luca contrives to press against him for time to time, and soon the need to kiss him, to touch him, becomes unbearable. A juggler is keeping the crowds entertained and Luca motions to him and they slip into the crowd jammed right up against a church. In the crush, Luca slips his hand into his and squeezes it and they smile at each other.

'I want to kiss you again,' Georg whispers in his ear.

Luca nods and then puts his hand on Georg's back and slips his hand up under his shirt to stroke his back. His white shirt is open at the neck and Georg longs to run his hand over his chest but the juggler has finished and a shift in the crowd means that they need to move on.

Luca motions in the direction of Flaminio, away from Popolo, towards some open fields and they walk silently away from the city, Romans out enjoying the mild January air and the fresh breezes. Away from the streets, families sit around in the open green spaces, some eating and others playing with their children, and there seems little chance of privacy until Luca points ahead to an embankment, leading down to an open-air amphitheatre. At the corner of the amphitheatre is an overgrown clump of trees and they climb down as quickly as they can towards the trees. Luca gets there first, laughing and then leads the way into the dark green gloom at the corner of the old stone building, where they find themselves soon screened on both sides by some jutting branches. As soon as he can, Georg pushes Luca firmly up against the wall and, taking his head in his hands, attacks him with kisses. Luca squirms up against him, their bodies responding immediately, and Luca grabs two handfuls of his hair and pushes his head about as they kiss. Just then, above them, they can hear the chatter of a family as they approach the edge of the embankment, and, a moment later, a mother calling her child back from the edge. A child's head appears through the branches above and she points down.

'Kissing,' she cries, before running off.

They spring apart and Luca curses.

'This is intolerable.'

They climb back up the slope and stand together for a few moments, scanning the wide, busy fields around them. At the far side of the parkland is a fenced off enclosure, a row of vegetable gardens and Luca suggests they make their way over there. As they get nearer, Luca nods towards a dense hedge running behind the gardens, and then runs forward and, without a moment's hesitation, pushes his way through into the depths of the hedge. Georg plunges after him, tearing through the prickly branches at some cost to his coat, at a loss in the dank green undergrowth, the poking branches and the slimy mud underneath. The bright sun has vanished and all sense of direction gone but, just then, Luca whistles softly somewhere from deep within the bushes. He wrestles with the tangle to follow the sounds of the whistle and almost falls into a small clearing right in the heart of the bushes. Luca stands in the centre of the tiny muddy clearing, with a shaft of light falling down on him, his coat hanging on a branch, his shirt nearly off and he throws the shirt deftly on another branch. Standing there, bare-chested, Georg watches him as he pushes down his breeches and then stands carefully at the edge of the shallow mud pool, beckoning him. Seeing him naked for the first time, he stares at Luca's slender muscular body, his legs and stomach, dark with fine hair, and his eyes intense with lust.

'Now you.'

Georg pulls off his clothes in a rush, while Luca, naked and brazen, stands near him in this little clearing, his hand resting on his hip, watching, proud of his body. Georg moves unsteadily towards him through the muddy undergrowth, almost stumbling into the water and reaches out to put his arms around him. There is the shock of intimacy, skin against skin startling, the warmth and softness, the firm muscles and fine dark hair, and Georg finding himself making a noise, a whimper of delight. This closeness, Luca gathered into his larger, taller frame, makes him so excited that he is afraid he will bite him, and so he slides his arms down his back to draw him in closer. As they squirm and kiss, Georg imagines he is somehow passing through Luca, that they are becoming one and he calls out his name as if hurt or in pain. They both use all their strength to press into each other, no gap possible between them and almost as soon as they kiss and feel the excited shock of each other's naked bodies close together, Georg shudders and groans and presses Luca even tighter against him, his fingers digging into his buttocks. It is all over.

'Sorry, sorry,' he mutters.

However, Luca is now pressing against him and moaning himself and so Georg holds his head against his shoulder while he groans and shudders too and pushes into his stomach and calls his name. All too soon, it is over and they both stand there clinging to each other and panting for a minute or two, shocked by the sudden intensity of their pleasure. Luca takes his face in his hands and stares at him, smiling, and Georg finds himself blushing, wishing somehow to escape the intense scrutiny of Luca's eyes on him. They cling together and, all in a moment, Georg is unpleasantly aware of how cramped it is in this little cave of branches. In this muddy dell, he has become somehow self-conscious again and so he stands back, looking down at their glistening bellies. He reaches over to his coat and draws out his linen neck cloth and begins to clean them both off, the action of wiping somehow comfortingly maternal, but also a chance to look away from the gaze from Luca's eyes. His patting and wiping over, he goes to throw the linen away but Luca grabs it.

'For me. To sleep with, tonight,' and he kisses the damp cloth and then stuffs it into his breeches.

As their bodies cool off, the cold of the undergrowth begins to chill them, despite their caresses and the slight shiver of winter forces them back into their clothes. With some difficulty and very little grace, they pick them down off the trees, and then push their way out into the parkland, with some vigorous horseplay on the way, and when they do find their way back out, they laugh at the disapproval of an old farmer's wife, frowning at these two well-dressed young men tumbling out of the undergrowth.

Back in the fields, they sit in the sun lying against a fallen bough and watch the world stroll past and Luca falls asleep against the tree. Georg watches him sleep, his face relaxed and gentle, his features fine, as if carved and reaches over to take a twig from his hair. He mutters something, wakes up and looks at Georg crossly until he realises who he is.

'Giorgio, you must be careful.'

The afternoon is rapidly cooling and the chill of early evening drives them back down into the city. Luca suggest some wine but Georg finds himself exhausted and longing for the peace of his own room. Before they part, Georg promises to find a way of getting him into the palace someday and slipping him into his room.

Luca tells him that he must study for the rest of that week but he promises to write to him at the palace to arrange a meeting when his exams will be at an end. The days seem endless and when no letter comes, Georg takes to wandering past the university buildings near Popolo but to no avail. At night, he dreams of Luca in the narrow little thicket, with a sense of nightmare or menace and awakes, despairing, wondering if his clumsy lovemaking has driven him away. A week passes and then early one morning, Lorenzo brings his letters from home and amongst them a note from Luca, with no address, suggesting a meeting at three o'clock that day at the front steps of Santa Maria Maggiore. Suddenly, the air is filled with a kind of lifting excitement. He floats down the stairs to the rehearsal room. Georg hurries through a rehearsal with Margherita, her mother sitting by her side beaming at Georg. She sings her aria with her usual skill and grace and, during a pause, when Gianni calls in to gossip with Mamma, Georg cannot resist asking Margherita quietly about Luca. She smiles, with a glance at her mother.

'Oh yes. He studies with my cousin, Marco. I always give them my tickets for the concerts.'

She looks around again and drops her voice. 'You are lucky to find such a friend…I envy you. He is very handsome.'

Georg blushes at her frankness but is pleased and nods in agreement. 'Of course, I envy him too,' she adds, before her mother bustles over, wondering what they are whispering about.

'The Empress, of course,' Georg tells her. 'She has just sent me this silver ring,' and he waves it in her disapproving face, laughing, before resolving that he will buy Luca a ring. Margherita tells him not to be so rude to her Mamma and he smiles at her.

Luca is standing waiting outside the crowded porch of Santa Maria Maggiore and Georg watches him for a moment, unseen, confident, holding a large artist's portfolio against his hip, by the far the most beautiful on that crowded porch. Luca sees him, flashes his best smile and they embrace, like good friends and he risks a kiss to his cheek. Georg looks down at the folder.

'Do you paint?'

'A little.'

He is smiling in the chilly January light, his coat a cobalt blue, with yellow trim around the buttons and collar. Georg wants to tell him that someone should paint him in this clear Roman light, his dark hair, his blue eyes, the red of his lips, the blue coat, all his bright colours but they stand smiling at each other in the busy crowd, saying nothing.

'Come,' Luca finally says, 'I want to paint and you can watch.'

They walk away from the basilica, crossing the road and Luca leads him down a narrow lane, towards a terracotta-coloured building, with an old church in front. It seems deserted but Luca knocks at the closed door, it swings open and a little old priest peers out. He recognises Luca, smiles broadly and opens the door fully for them.

'Ah, my little artist friend, I knew it was you. The light is perfect just now. Come in, come in.'

Luca motions Georg into the dark, deserted church, and he sniffs the faint smell of stale air, incense and of damp while Luca walks ahead to the altar with the old man.

'You wish to paint today, my boy?'

The priest asks him, anxious to please.

'Will I light some candles for you?'

'Yes, Father.'

Luca follows him across the gloom of the main aisle and stands by the altar while the old man begins lighting some candles. Georg lingers, a little sulky, wondering why they were wasting the precious time together in this dull little church when Luca calls him over and points upwards to the roof above the altar.

'Look.'

High overhead, the cave-like dome above the altar is startlingly beautiful, the shaft of sunlight from the side windows lighting up thousands of tiny gold and blue tiles, that are beginning to also catch some of the reflection of the newly-lit candles. Framed by two broad arcs of beaten, shining gold, a grave figure of the Christ stands confident and benign, with great white figures of the saints around him, edged in gold and arched by red and gold mosaics. Further out, clusters of saints stare out calmly from underneath palm trees, and in the panel under the feet of the Christ, a flock of pristine, docile-looking sheep line up to worship him. With all the candles now alight, the whole gloomy little church shimmers in the afternoon light with these figures above them, facing them down and blessing the dark.

'What do you think?'

Georg walks back down the main aisle, the better to see the whole pageant, and smiles back at him. He nods.

'Wonderful, Luca. Wonderful.'

'Come.'

They sit in the front row of the church where Luca opens up his sheaf of drawings and paintings and spreads them out on their laps. Each drawing or painting shows a detail from the mosaic above, sometimes a saint or one of the animals. Georg picks up one small painting, a detailed portrait of a little bird, perched high on a palm tree right over the Christ figure. The bird has a halo of its own and looks down happily, full of scrawny self-importance.

'This is good, really good.'

'It is yours now.'

'You should be a painter.'

'My father will not allow it.'

'Neither did mine,' thinks Georg, 'but here I am, playing my music for the Cardinal', but he says nothing because Luca, as if by accident, has placed his hand on Georg's knee, hidden from view under the paintings. The old man shuffles over towards them, his candle duty done, and stoops down to admire the painting, his hand resting on Luca's shoulder. Luca moves his hand higher on Georg's leg, the movement only partly hidden under the painting and the old man nods approvingly at the paintings.

'You have a talent, my boy. You, my friend, are you also an artist?'

Georg nods, not trusting himself to speak, as Luca's hand moves again. As if nothing is happening, Luca tells the old man that Georg is a musician of great renown and that his masses will be sung for the Pope in St John Lateran. While Luca tells him this, the old priest has casually moved his hand upwards to stroke Luca's hair gently and while he does so, he tells Georg that he will pray for his success with his music. There is a silence for a moment or two, while Georg glances upwards again at the watching saints above them and then the old priest gently pushes Luca's head towards him and Georg begins kissing him.

He has the small painting of the little bird on the gilded branch framed and places it by his desk in the music room and Lorenzo admires it on the morning of the recital the following week.

'The Elector will dine with the Cardinal after the performance tonight. His Grace asks you to join him.'

So much the better, thinks Georg.

'You like the painting?'

'Very much,' Lorenzo replies, after a pause.

That night, Georg slips into the small music room a little before the concert where Luca finds him. They risk a brief kiss.

'Here is the key to my room, next door. When supper is being served, come back upstairs, but be sure to lock the door. I will knock four times. Open the door only for me.'

'I will be naked in your bed,' Luca tells him.

The thought almost makes him want to abandon the concert but he ushers Luca out and waits there, for a discreet interval.

When he enters the concert room a little later, he can see Luca at the back of the crowded hall, but they are careful not to acknowledge each other and Georg takes his place by the harpsichord and then precisely at eight, the Cardinal ushers in a low-sized middle-aged man, who glances over at the musicians and then points out a seat at the front to the tall pretty young woman at his side. Everyone in the packed hall knows who he is, the Elector of Hanover, the friend of the Emperor, the man who will be King of England when the present Queen dies. For once, all eyes in the room are on this man and not on the Cardinal, the man that Gianni had told him was travelling with his mistress, a woman with the picturesque name of Melusine because he has locked away his wife in some remote castle for taking a lover. This woman is now by his side, this Melusine, sweet-faced and charming despite her weighty exotic name, with eyes that crease with pleasure when she smiles back at the Elector, Gianni had whispered that this mistress is also his half-sister, an illegitimate daughter of his late father. Where does Gianni hear all this, he wonders, as they take their places.

At a nod from the Cardinal, Georg bows and then motions to the singers and the players to begin. During the performance, he keeps a surreptitious eye on the Elector and, despite a somewhat sleepy demeanour, Georg is pleased to notice that he is clearly following the music, paying particular attention during Margherita's solo arias. During the prolonged applause, Georg carefully avoids catching Luc's eye while the Cardinal comes forward to make a gracious speech welcoming the Elector. After all, this is the man who could usefully interpose himself between the palace and the rampaging Imperial troops. The Cardinal makes a graceful gesture, and the Elector processes out, with Georg in tow behind the Cardinal. They are brought to a room across the loggia, a richly furnished room Georg has never entered, where Lorenzo awaits with an elegant table set for supper. Without a word, the Elector seats himself heavily at the head of the small table and Georg and the Cardinal stand while the willowy Melusine settles by his side, Georg pausing to sit last.

Looking a little bored, the Elector ignores the general pleasantries of the Cardinal and stares at the exquisite food with a slight air of contempt but, when he picks up his fork, he manages to work his way through a great quantity. In contrast, his mistress sister takes a drink of her wine, nods approvingly, looks around at the elegant room and then points at a painting over the fireplace, smiling at her host.

'Veronese, perhaps, Your Grace?' she asks, in French.

He beams. 'Yes indeed, Madame, my prize possession, from my late uncle.'

The Elector, who is engrossed in spearing some beans on his fork, suddenly shoots a glance at the painting and throws a question out to the table in German, cutting across the Cardinal in mid-sentence.

'Veronese…the Venetian?'

The Cardinal smiles with incomprehension while both his mistress and Georg nod. The Elector points his knife at the painting.

'My brother has one in his house in Venice.'

He turns towards Georg, continuing to speak in German, while Melusine accepts more wine from Lorenzo.

'So, Herr Handel, you wish to compose?'

'Yes, Your Highness.'

The first time in months that someone has pronounced his name correctly. He hopes Highness is the right form. He had checked with Madame Durastanti. An Elector is the same as a prince, she opined.

'Sacred music? Opera?'

Georg glances at the Cardinal. The Elector waves his hand dismissively. His fine, slightly bulging blue eyes have a keen glance. Georg has seen this look before, in the Cardinal's eyes and also in the eyes of the King of Prussia. It is the gleam of power, of unquestioned authority.

'Oh yes, I know, this Pope has banned opera. Old fool.'

He gobbles down some food, chews for a few moments, apparently without pleasure and then barks out.

'There are opera houses in Venice. I will write to my brother about you.'

The Elector used few words and Georg knew that these words were not used as conversation. He puts down the chicken bone he is attacking and continues.

'He is a Bishop, my brother.'

He smiles at this, a curving, not entirely unpleasant smile.

'But that never stops him sampling more' . . . he pauses . . . 'exotic pleasures of Venice.'

He glances at the Cardinal as he says this, at this moment, complimenting Melusine and then turns a keen glance back, sweeping over Georg.

'I prefer simpler pleasures myself, young man.'

He raises his glass to Melusine and she smiles back, her eyes creasing with pleasure at his attention.

A sudden chill of fear makes Georg's chest tighten, this rich table, the kind glances of the Cardinal, the friendly interest of Elector Georg and upstairs, Luca waiting for him in his bed. What kind of stupid risk has he taken? Something tells him to be careful with this plain-spoken man. Madame Durastanti says he is stepping over the heads of fifty-two other Catholic cousins including her patroness, the Empress, to push his way onto the British throne. Taking those kind of steps requires a definite measure of ruthlessness.

The meal is coming to an end and, despite the Cardinal's best efforts, the Elector makes it clear that he now wishes to leave.

Melusine tells him first he must send a purse to the young woman, Margherita and Georg likes her for this.

'My agent will write to you,' he tells Georg, curtly, in German. 'I liked your music.'

The Cardinal escorts the pair downstairs to their carriage and, as they leave, Georg asks Lorenzo if he should wait for his master to return.

'No, the Pope is expecting a report tonight, His Grace's carriage is ready to take him there now.'

Even better. Georg races to his room and pauses for a moment, making sure the corridor is empty before doing something as strange as knocking on his own bedroom door. He knocks gently, four times. Silence. Then he waits and knocks again and, after a moment, the door opens a little.

Luca peeks out. He is wrapped in Georg's cloak. He looks relieved.

'Someone was knocking a few minutes ago. I dared not open it.'

Georg hurries inside and then pushes the desk against the door. The fire is almost out. He throws some logs to revive it, while Luca tears at his clothes, anxious to have him naked as soon as he can.

Just after dawn, Georg wakes up, Luca now deep in sleep, lying unconscious in his arms. They had forgotten to draw the heavy curtains and the early morning sun has come slanting into the room, making the most of its unaccustomed freedom to flood the room with brilliant light, stinging his tired eyes. Luca's mouth looks unbearably soft and beautiful, his expression trusting, as he concentrates on his slumber, and Georg is careful not to disturb him, despite his increasingly sore arms, the room gradually filling with a blinding light, his body warm and heavy, his breathing loud, all cares smoothed away from his brow. From this coming together, to this closeness, they can never be separate again, Georg thinks, as he watches Luca sleep.

Noise from the corridor, the awakening servants, makes Georg anxious and he kisses him awake, whispering that he will slip out and get them some food and hot water. He throws on his clothes, runs downstairs and orders some food to be brought to his music room and then smuggles it back to his room. They breakfast together hurriedly, and then Georg slips him into the music room, a little before Margherita's arrival, with Mamma in tow.

They begin rehearsal, the leap from bed to music room unsettling when Georg pauses to think about it. Lorenzo brings in the new sheet music, a little surprised to see Luca there but says nothing and Mamma Durastanti is all fawning interest in Luca, the friend of her nephew Marco, the son of a wealthy Sardinian, and Luca is his usual sullen self, which seems to charm her even more.

Georg hands Margherita a sheet of the new song he has been working on, watching her as she reads it and hums to herself, uncertain as to where it belongs yet and when it should be performed. It is clearly not sacred music. Luca helps himself to a copy, in an effort to ward off Mamma and Georg is heartened to see him follow the notes, obviously able to read the music on sight, his chest filling with pride. He had composed this air in the days waiting for Luca's summons, trying to work off his sense of fear and desolation, using words from the *Dixit Dominus*. When she is ready, Margherita stands next to the harpsichord and bows her head for him to begin playing the slow opening chords.

It is better than he could have imagined. Her sorrowful voice fills the room, silencing Luca and her Mamma and even chattering Gianni, who has dropped in for his habitual gossip with Mamma, all listening intently as her rich voice draws out the stately notes with confident intent. Georg is unsure about the words, borrowed from the text the Cardinal gave him, the music is right, but he wonders about the text.

'Thy people shall be willing in the day of thy power, in the beauties of holiness from the womb of the morning: thou hast the dew of thy youth.'

Luca smiles up at him when she sings this phrase and he nods, yes, this is for you and he remembers their glistening bodies in the glade beyond Popolo and wonders if Luca does.

Midway through the song, to Georg's dismay, the Cardinal appears in the open doorway. He places his fingers on his lips, nodding to Margherita to continue and, as she finishes, they all applaud softly.

'Signor Sassone, Mademoiselle Durastanti, another gem. The Elector was very pleased with your music last night and I thank you.'

They both bow their thanks and the Cardinal's eyes fall on Luca, a smile of inquiry on his lips.

Georg hurries to explain.

'Your Grace, I am seeking to expand the choir, may I present…'

His second name…what is his second name.

Margherita comes to his rescue.

'The good friend of my cousin, Signor Luca Bartolome.'

'You are welcome indeed, Signor Bartolome, I know you as a regular at our musical evenings but we have never had the pleasure of meeting. Will you sing for us today?'

The Cardinal smiles and Georg is struck with horror. All this talk about singing lessons and he has no idea if Luca can even sing.

'It will be an honour, Your Grace', Luca bows and takes his place by the harpsichord.

Georg thinks quickly, and moves the opening notes down a scale, to bring it to Luca's possible range. Is he a tenor? Luca begins to sing, a competent tenor, although the song is a little high for him, perhaps more naturally a baritone but the youthful sweetness and strength of his voice carries him and he accounts himself well. He can clearly read by sight and something of himself escapes in his singing, a tenderness that Georg has not seen, even in bed.

They all applaud again, with relief but for once, there is something less gracious in the Cardinal's manner, and he turns to Georg, just in time to avoid seeing Luca's look of slight anger and contempt.

'I have another commission for you. A few lines I have scribbled myself. Perhaps you might find some music to make them fly.'

He hands Georg a paper and Georg tells him it would be an honour and the Cardinal smiles around him, somehow avoiding looking at Luca again, and leaves the room, begging them all to continue. They play for another hour or so and then Mamma Durastanti invites Luca to accompany them back to her lodging to dine, which Luca accepts and Georg demurs, pleading work. Georg is gathering his music when Lorenzo returns to the room, filling him with a sense of foreboding.

'His Grace has asked me to deliver this.'

Another bank draft. More than Georg has ever had, nearly three times his legacy from his father, but somehow it makes him more uneasy. Then, just as he is leaving the room, Lorenzo asks, casually, 'Will Signor Bartolome be joining the singers on a regular basis?'

'No,' Georg rushes to tell him almost before he has time to think again. 'I have sufficient tenors for the time being.'

He opens the paper from the Cardinal.

'A graceful youth, awakens sweet delight,

With enticing tones,

His hand has wings

Or rather he makes with his hand music more than mortal.'

He knows never to show this to Luca, who would simply snigger.

Nothing prepares him for the sense of desolation waking up alone in his bed the following night. It is as if the cold night air has reached inside his chest, with the absence of that warm body lying into his, the scent of verbena on his hair, his breath moving next to him. Finding it impossible to stay in the deserted bed, he gets up in the dark of the night to put on his cloak and pour himself a glass of wine. The room has grown cold and he puts more wood on the dying fire and resolves to use some of his gold to hire them a small room, somewhere, anywhere, rather than continue this nightly sense of mortal desolation. He looks out onto the deserted streets below, lit up by another powerful moon, and an image of Luca sitting on the same wooden bench near the Arch of Constantine, but this time with the old priest from Santa Prassede and he groans and clutches his head at his tormented thoughts and his longing for Luca.

As he makes his way back towards his bed, he stumbles, feeling a little dizzy, as the floor seems to shake under him and he blames his tiredness. Sitting down on the bed, he hears a shout on the street and then notices that a log has fallen from his fire. He stands up to replaces it when the room shakes again, this time more intensely. A noise like a distant roar of thunder fills the palace and there is more shouting from the street. The Imperial Armies, Georg thinks, and he thrusts his feet into his boots and runs for the door when another shudder in the floor knocks the wine glass from his desk. An artillery attack. He grabs a candle, drags open his door and runs out into the dark corridor where he is thrown against the wall by another shaking of the palace. Unhurt, he hears shouts below in the courtyard and sees a glimmer of candlelight at the far side of the corridor by the Cardinal's study and runs towards the light. Lorenzo is standing looking out from an open doorway, holding a candle, blood on his forehead, dressed only in a long white nightshirt with a cloak thrown over his shoulders. As Georg gets nearer, the Cardinal's face peers out from behind Lorenzo's shoulder

'Your Grace, are you safe?'

'Who is it? Ah Georg. What is happening?'

He comes out into the corridor looking ashen, and Lorenzo quickly steps to one side, next to Georg and faces the Cardinal.

'It seems to be an attack of some kind. Perhaps the Imperial armies?'

The Cardinal shakes his head,

'Impossible, they are still at Parma. It seems more like an earthquake.'

Georg whistles. 'Of course.'

By now the corridor is filled with voices and Gianni has arrived, full of excitement.

'Your Grace, the streets are thronged with people. They are saying this is a judgment from God.'

They all follow the Cardinal to look out of the windows and, indeed, the streets are now full of people, crying, praying, some carrying crosses and icons. He turns and starts issuing orders.

'Have wine given out at the palace gates and open the kitchens and the bakery. Dress, everyone!'

He steps back into his room to dress and Georg sets out to do the same. On the balcony outside his room, he finds Lorenzo leaning against a wall.

'You have cut your head, come with me,' he orders, despite Lorenzo's murmur of protest and he puts an arm under his shoulder to help Lorenzo into his room nearby. The palace is now full of noise and some shrieking can be heard outside the palace. He looks again at the blood trickling down Lorenzo's face.

'We need to clean that wound. Come here, sit over here on the bed.'

Georg guides him and then fetches a cloth and some wine to clean his forehead. He dabs gently at the wound, while Lorenzo speaks, saying more than he has ever heard him say before.

'When I heard the noise, I ran from my bedroom up to His Grace's room, to see if he was safe. I was afraid of an assassin. I must have fallen against the door as I knocked, just as you arrived.'

As Georg cleans around the already healing cut with his kerchief, he thinks, but you came out of the room. He says nothing, however, intent on preventing any pain, and, despite himself, remembering another time when he cleaned a man with a linen kerchief.

'Yes,' Georg says as he cleans away the blood, 'I think I saw you fall, I heard a cry ahead of me as I ran up the corridor. It was a great relief to see His Grace was safe.'

Lorenzo smiles, a wide smile of gratitude and, not allowing himself any time to think, Georg brings his face close into Lorenzo's and kisses him on the mouth. Lorenzo receives his kiss for a moment or two and then shifts away from him slightly on the bed, touching his face apologetically.

'I'm sorry but His Grace ...'

Outside they can hear the clear sounds of hymns being sung on the street, the voices, shrill with fear.

'Yes', Georg answers, 'of course...the Cardinal.'

Warm May air draws out great tangles of hedge roses and honeysuckle along the country lanes where he and Luca walk in the drowsy afternoons. The day's rehearsal finished, Georg meets him in Popolo to walk out of the city where they lie together in the overgrown meadows and woodlands beyond Rome, the screams of the darting swifts overhead following them home in the golden evenings back through Piazza del Popolo and on to the Corso. With the Cardinal away in Naples negotiating with the Spanish, Georg sometimes smuggles Luca into his room, using Lorenzo's key for a little side door. They spend the long May evenings on Georg's bed, the bright light stealing gradually across the ceiling above them, the clatter of the Corso outside the window, the hum of prelates about their business in the loggia below. He holds Luca for hours, his slender body becoming as familiar to him as his own – the darkness of his eyebrows, and the sheen of white in his eyes, the curves of his shoulders, his thin arms and powerful thighs, the dark hair on his body. Sometimes he wonders at the long thin scar on the side of his left arm, but asks nothing, unwilling to break the spell, the lively sweat of their bodies as sweet to Georg as the clean, delicate scent of honeysuckle in the Roman countryside. In the bright mornings, Georg often wakes first, Luca asleep in his arms, breathing heavily, the clean lines of his face almost unbearably innocent. Very early one sunlit morning, he lies in his bed and watches Luca dress himself in a clean white shirt and new suit, hurrying out to his morning exam. At the moment of parting, his lover comes back to the bed and kisses him and Georg wonders out loud at the luck of such a moment.

One weekend, they decide to walk far out of the city, to a village at the foot of the hills where an old cousin of Lorenzo's keeps an inn and, tired from the walk, they stay for the night. In the morning, they wake up, tangled together on one of the beds in the little room under the eaves, to find that a tray with bread and cheese and cold milk has been left quietly for them. A little worried, Georg offers the old woman an extra coin as they leave, money she vehemently refuses, telling them to return again, to brighten her home with their beautiful faces, like young angels, and they delay their walk home, stopping to swim and to sleep in the meadows below the farm house.

In the Cardinal's absence, Georg continues to write music for an oratorio on the Resurrection, to be presented in celebration if this war ever ends. Georg fills the score with trumpets, loud acclamations of triumph, especially the lively opening aria written for Margherita. When she hears the oratorio, her mother shakes her head gloomily.

'When this war ends, the Pope loses more territory. More trouble for the Cardinal?'

Georg is a little bored by her political chatter but nods politely.

'His Holiness is no friend to our dear patron, you know,' she tells Georg. 'He resents the fortune his uncle, the late Pope, left him but he needs the Cardinal in this time of danger. Any loss to the papacy – then the Cardinal will be blamed.'

Georg wonders what it must be like to have all that worldly, bleak knowledge always at one's command, as Madame Durastanti has, and yet to always look so sleek and self-satisfied.

As the days go by and no word comes from the Cardinal in Naples, the musicians take to wondering out loud if this triumph will ever be performed. Then, all in one morning, two letters arrive for Georg.

The first is from the Cardinal, written from Naples in his own neat hand.

*Caro Sassone,*
*Despite all our hard work in creating a new kingdom here, I have amused*
*myself in my spare time with a little writing. Perhaps you could set this*
*to music, with our Margherita in mind, to be performed on my return.*

There was a second sheet, enclosing a draft for one hundred crowns, with a poem written on it.

*When I said goodbye and left that memorable place where my love was born,*
*In a fit of madness, I thought I could turn my heart's heat to frost*
*Alas! I'm seized at all times, by all parts of love.*
*And all light and day and at all hours in my mind's eye,*
*My beloved is ever present.*

He puts down the second poem, unwilling to read it again, and takes up the other letter, which, to his great puzzlement, comes from Madame von der Schulenburg in Hanover. Who on earth is she, he wonders as he reads? Suddenly he realises. The Elector's mistress, Melusine of the smiling eyes.

*My Dear Herr Handel,*
*I am writing at the request of the Elector, who was entranced with*
*your music, and is sending you a token of his regard.*

He stops reading and opens the wrapped box that comes with the letter, to find himself staring at a miniature of Elector Georg, edged with small diamonds, and looking like a disgruntled bloodhound.

He picks up the letter again. Her handwriting is as seductive as her smile.

*We will be returning to Italy soon and the Elector wants you to come to*
*Venice next Easter, to compose for His Highness's musicians. He asked*
*particularly if you have plans to compose an opera. I will be writing to*
*dear Mademoiselle Durastanti to extend my own invitation and hope*
*that she may be prevailed on to sing in your composition.*

He locks the letters and the miniature into his desk, but leaves the 'Orpheus Ode' and the love poem out on his table to begin work. That night, Luca finds the ode on his desk, snatches it up and reads it aloud as he lies on the bed.

'I am seized at all times by all parts of love.'

He laughs and rolls over in the bed, gripping himself between his legs for emphasis. Georg remains silent, standing there, watching him.

'Who is the Cardinal pining for, Giorgio? Do you know?'

Georg laughs, wishing he had hidden the cursed poems. He waits for his chance and then snatches them back up and bundles them into a drawer.

'Yes, isn't it obvious? Madame Durastanti.' Georg tells him.

Luca turns towards him, his face becoming dark as Georg locks the poems away.

'Or, maybe, it is you?'

'Nonsense.' Georg snaps back, a little too quickly.

'But who else. Do you know who it is?'

Georg nods at Luca down on his bed.

'Perhaps.'

'Who? Tell me!'

Georg waits a moment. Then speaks,

'Lorenzo.'

Luca whistles.

'The servant. Who can blame the Cardinal! He is very handsome… but a servant?'

Something like jealousy mingled with a kind of desire brings him back on the bed, catching hold of Luca and drawing him roughly towards him. He grabs his arm, and, to distract him, draws a finger delicately along the thin scar.

'How did you get that?'

'An old story. I was caught in a fight between two brothers, my friends from home, a boring old tale.'

Luca grabs his head, kisses him, and murmurs.

'His hands have wings indeed.'

Luca laughs again and he kisses him to stop the laughter.

Next day, after rehearsal, when they are alone, he gestures towards a new opal brooch pinned to Margherita's cloak.

'Melusine?'

She nods.

'So? Venice next year?' he ventures.

She smiles, looks around and then nods again.

'Don't tell Mamma! But…yes. You?'

He nods too.

'Tell no one.'

'Will you write an opera?'

'Perhaps. If I do, can I show it to you?'

She smiles and gathers her music to leave and he returns to his room and takes out the miniature and stares at it again. The Elector's face seems to have been formed entirely from discontent and a kind of knowing contempt for the world. His sour-faced stare is a direct challenge to him. 'Will you do this, young man? Do you dare?' He takes a sheet of paper and writes quickly, presenting his humble services to Melusine and to the Elector, promising that he will be in Venice next Easter.

Sealing the letter, he feels uneasy and sets out from the palace, carrying the framed miniature of the Elector to his jewellers. The man there tells him that the diamonds are valuable and agrees to buy them, and to replace the setting with inferior but impressive-looking gems. Georg uses some of the money from the diamonds to order a fine ring and chain. For Luca's birthday, his twenty-second, just one year younger than Georg.

On his return to the palace, Lorenzo is by the gate, standing in the warm sun, a rare smile lighting up his face and he greets him with a wave.

'The news from Naples is good. The treaty is signed and His Grace will return next week.'

'Excellent,' Georg tells him. 'We can perform the new oratorio in his honour. Can you ask him if this will be acceptable?'

Lorenzo smiles back, a kind of light in his eyes. It strikes Georg for the first time that Lorenzo has not smiled like that since the night of the earthquake and he feels happier about the second ode to the beloved.

The following week, a special celebration to honour the Cardinal's return is announced, in the outdoor amphitheatre high above on the Janiculum. Invitations are sent out all over Rome, Gianni tells him, summoning ambassadors and envoys, and all at the Papal Court. A lavish display of fireworks is planned, to celebrate the peace proposals, and all the musicians are ordered to wear their best finery. Lorenzo tells him that the new composition, the *Resurrection,* is requested as the centrepiece of the evening and there is a rumour that the Holy Father himself may grace the evening. Georg orders a new white satin coat with silver embroidery, and rehearses the *Resurrection* oratorio with the musicians until it is polished and smooth. Then, at the last minute, he gives them the 'Orpheus Ode' and asks Margherita to sing, noting a smirk on the face of Gianni as he listens.

The night of the performance, Georg dresses carefully in his new clothes, and has the carriage bring him to the amphitheatre. The sun has long set and the dark parkland around the decorated stage is lit with painted lanterns, the rich scent of the shrubs heightened by the perfume from braziers filled with lavender and incense, the many candles catching the faces of the singers, dressed in white, behind the harpsichord. He looks for Luca, and sees him standing in the crowd in front of the stage, near tables laden with food and wine. Georg is surprised to see Margherita and her mother standing next to Luca. She should be on stage by now, Georg thinks. He walks over to her, bows politely and offers his arm to escort her there. She shakes her head, a glint of a tear in her eye.

'No women to sing tonight,' her mother snaps, her face stern with anger. At that moment, Georg loves her for that anger. 'By orders of His Grace. No female to defile the sacred music in the presence of His Holiness.'

'One moment. We shall see.'

Seeing the Cardinal alight from his carriage moments later, he stalks over towards him and bows as low as he can.

'Welcome. We are all delighted at your safe return.'

The Cardinal beams with pleasure.

'Caro Sassone, a welcome sight indeed.'

Georg cuts him off.

'We are honoured to perform. With your kind permission, Mademoiselle Durastanti will sing your own 'Orpheus Ode' tonight, to express our thanks?'

The Cardinal looks at him with some sadness.

'Giorgio, you are looking well indeed,' glancing down at the snowy white coat, the gilt buttons.

Georg feels like a painted fop. He persists.

'And Mademoiselle?'

'Not tonight, I'm afraid. By order of His Holiness. Her place will be taken by the sopranist, Signor Videtti.'

Something in his face, his eagerness to placate Georg, to will him into acquiescence, disgusts Georg and he bows again, his face a mask and makes his way back to the musicians, where Videtti is waiting. They shake hands and Georg thanks him for taking on the role in so short a time and asks if he needs some time to rehearse. Videtti, a tall, elegant man, shakes his head. He has had an hour or so to study the score. An hour or so and no one had the manners to tell him, Georg thinks, as he takes his place by the harpsichord.

In a few moments, it is clear from the fuss and the murmurs that His Holiness has arrived and all bow, and the signal is given for the music to begin. Georg has heard Videtti sing before and admires his skills, and the quickness with which he has learned the demanding aria. His powerful frame gives a depth to his rich, high, ornamented singing. Georg glances into the crowd from time to time but Margherita seems to have gone, as has Luca. Georg wonders if he should have also left. As soon as the music ends, Georg gets up from the harpsichord, bows his thanks to the musicians and singers and makes his way quickly back to the Cardinal, who smiles in welcome.

'Ah, Giorgio, wonderful music. My thanks to you. And here is His Holiness's Chancellor, Cardinal Ottoboni now. Come and I will introduce you and you may even receive the blessing of the Holy Father.'

He makes to usher him over to a nearby group, standing around the old pontiff, seated in a splendid crimson bower of silk, but Georg remains standing where he is, as if rooted to the ground.

'Please forgive me, Your Grace. I am tired and wish to find my friends, who have all gone.'

The Cardinal looks a little hurt.

'You have friends here too.'

But, without replying, Georg bows again, turns abruptly and walks away. At the edge of the park, he finds Luca sitting on a bench, waiting for him, with some bottles of wine taken from the festivities. Luca tells him that Margherita and her mother have taken their carriage home and so they make their way back to the field beyond the Arch of Constantine where they first met and spend the night lying under some trees, arms wrapped around each other as they drink the wine, waking up in the cold dawn on the ground, their cloaks beneath then, their heads aching.

Much the worse for wine, his new satin coat grass-stained and ruined, Georg creeps back into the palace and falls into his bed. Later, he tries to ignore the discreet raps on his door but is forced to get up when Lorenzo murmurs.

'His Grace wishes to see you. This afternoon. At four.'

Georg groans and answers.

'I will be ready. Send me some food and some water to wash at three.'

When he wakes up again, he dresses, tries some food, without success, and makes a note of the money with his banker. Nearly seven hundred crowns. More than enough to get the two of them to Venice and to keep them while he writes his opera and waits for the Elector to arrive next spring.

At four, he is at the study. Gianni opens the door, doom written all over his face. He ignores him and makes his bow to the Cardinal, who is standing quietly, looking out the window. Gianni withdraws and the Cardinal comes over and takes his hand.

'You were missed last night, Giorgio. His Holiness's Chancellor wished to meet you. He left this as a token of his delight in the wonderful music.'

He points to a heavy purse on the desk. Good. More money to get him away from this embarrassing failure and the dismal fall from favour. He murmurs his thanks and remains silent. Georg wishes he would let his hand go and waits for the dismissal to come.

'I have arranged for you to play in St John Lateran next week. Remember, when we first met, you said that this was your ambition.'

His grip on his hand tightens and then he lets its drop. Georg is silent, his head aching from the wine and the night with Luca under a tree.

'But surely His Holiness will not allow a heathen German…?'

'His Holiness is anxious to please me, especially since our success in Naples.'

So he is not to be dismissed for his disappearance last night. He feels unwell and is aware of the Cardinal watching him, waiting for him to speak.

'Are you not pleased?' The Cardinal asks in a tentative voice.

Something of his rudeness crosses his mind and he begins to realise that the more disgruntled he appears, the more the Cardinal wishes to appease him. It is a power that Georg does not relish and so he begins to apologise.

'I fear I was a little ... abrupt ... .'

'We will not talk about that. You showed loyalty to your friend. I too was disappointed not to hear her sing. But I have a plan.'

He walks across the room and opens a drawer. A manuscript, tied in leather. This is not at all what Georg was expecting.

'An idea of mine. Something that kept me amused in the long carriage journey back from Naples.'

Georg takes the manuscript from his hands and opens it, his head reeling, and the effort of trying to read it makes him feel a little faint. He staggers and the Cardinal, alarmed by his sudden change of pallor, reaches over and takes hold of his upper arms. Georg curses his weakness and wishes the Cardinal was not holding him again. A drumming begins in his ears.

'Forgive me, Your Grace. Too little sleep.'

With this, he finds his knees start to trembling, and, to his horror, he begins to slip towards the floor. The Cardinal grapples with all his strength to keep him on his feet, holding him under his arms, and slowly guides him towards a chair, allowing him to collapse into it.

'Keep your eyes closed and your head down.'

He feels the Cardinal's thin arms hold him, his breath on his neck, as his head spins and his stomach churns. Minutes seem like years as they stay there, Georg slumped on the chair, leaning into the Cardinal who crouches over him. Georg curses the wine he drank and prays that the Cardinal's lips, so close to his ears, will not move any closer or that Gianni or Lorenzo will knock on the door. Something of this communicates itself, as the Cardinal gradually disengages himself, carefully pushing Georg back into a sitting position. Fetching him some water, all the time telling him to keep his eyes closed and his head downward, he helps him to drink. At last, feeling somewhat better, Georg risks opening his eyes. He mutters his apology and stands up very slowly, thanking him again and avoiding his eyes, while the Cardinal speaks soothingly, telling him that he will send his doctor. Georg begs him not to do so, making his way slowly out into the corridor, thankfully meeting no one on the way back to his room. There he drinks more water and falls into a troubled sleep, filled with dreams of the Cardinal and himself, intertwined in the Roman meadows or asleep together in the fields beyond the Arch of Constantine.

The next day, nearly recovered, Georg stays in bed and reads the Cardinal's manuscript, a tale of ancient Rome that seems immensely complicated but with many dramatic moments about renunciation, love and fidelity. The central character Agrippina, wife of the Emperor Claudius and mother of the monstrous Nero, is full of cunning and subterfuge and Georg smiles at the idea of his gentle, good-humoured friend Margherita as this imperial schemer. The other parts, Nero, the tyrant Claudius, the heroic general Otto and the beloved Poppaea, Georg can fill from the singers he knows in Rome, perhaps Signor Videlli for Nero. Lorenzo calls into his room to bring him some food and the Cardinal's compliments, and asks if he wishes to have the doctor called. Georg reassures him that he is recovered, allowing the sheet to fall from his body and smiling at Lorenzo in such a way that the servant hurries from the room. That evening, Georg makes his way to the Cardinal's study, carrying the manuscript, but is stopped at the door by Gianni.

'His Grace is not free. Come back in the morning.'

Gianni's sharp eyes look at the bundle of papers under his arm.

'Is that his opera there? He allowed me to read it. It is all a political metaphor. His Holiness is the deceitful Agrippina and His Grace is the noble warrior Otto.'

'The music interests me, the politics not at all.'

'Well, you should think of the politics, Herr Endell. It won't be performed here in Rome because the Pope will never allow it.'

Georg thinks the same but the temptation to compose is too strong. Over the next few days, with the Cardinal back in the palace and Luca taking his exams, he spends his evenings alone in the rehearsal room, writing music for the somewhat convoluted and tedious plot, thinking of ways to display Margherita's voice. It takes him nearly four weeks to complete, working late into each night with increasing enjoyment but, when it is ready, he hesitates. He sends it out to be copied but takes care that Lorenzo brings it back to him directly. For a day or two he wonders what he will do. He supposed he should show it to the Cardinal but he waits. Luca's birthday approaches and the ring and chain have arrived but his performance at St John Lateran will take place on the same day, and he has seen little of his lover, caught up with his studies. With some shock, he realises that it has been a few days since they were together, the excitement of the composition filling his life, and he longs to make love to him again.

At last, he decides to write a note to Margherita and ask if he can call to her mother's lodgings on the next evening. A letter comes back, bidding him for supper, and he makes his way there, the manuscript of the opera in his hands. He is ushered into their apartment which turns out to be a surprisingly large set of rooms on the first floor of their gloomy old house, near the Pantheon. He had always assumed that they were not rich but a servant girl brings him into the very comfortable dining room, where Margherita and her mother are waiting. Sitting with them on a sofa, eating quietly from a plate of fruit, is a young girl, very beautiful, around sixteen or so, clearly Margherita's sister by the resemblance between the two but with delicate features and darker hair. Georg is surprised as they never mentioned her, but speak often of Papa, a busy merchant with business interests in the silk trade in France. Madame greets him warmly and Margherita smiles but the girl stares at Georg wildly, and makes a kind of noise, like a bird in distress. Georg bows to them all. Margherita takes the girl's hand and strokes it and says to him,

'This is our Anna, Georg, our little darling.' The girl smiles at Margherita and goes back to her plate of fruit, at peace and ignoring them all. Madame takes his hand and it is made clear, somehow, by the way they avoid direct eye contact, that Georg is not obliged to engage with the beautiful girl, and so he follows Mamma when she tells him, 'Come over to the table, Herr Handel. It is time to eat.'

Madame extracts all the gossip from the palace from him while he enjoys the fine food and Margherita stays and watches her sister eat, the girl making odd random noises and pausing once to embrace her sister roughly. The girl begins to get restless, jumping up from her seat and attempting to draw the curtain, even though the evening is still bright. Before Georg finishes eating, Madame turns to the girl.

'Come, my darling, it is time for your bed.'

Madame takes the young girl by the hand and leads her willingly from the room, Margherita's eyes following her every step with anxious love. When she is gone, Margherita thanks him.

'Our little darling enjoys company, she gets out so little. Assunta takes good care of her while we are at work and while Papa is away travelling in France for his business but she is happiest when Mamma and I are at home.'

Georg takes out the manuscript.

'I have finished it.'

She claps her hands.

'The opera! So quickly. What does the Cardinal say?'

'Forget about the Cardinal.' Georg tells her. 'I want you to look at it.'

She takes it up and for the next half-hour she reads, while Georg sips his wine and looks around the room. The table is littered with papers, colouring pencils, small toys, and he amuses himself by perusing the books on the shelves, anything to keep himself from looking at Margherita as she reads the score with a slight frown on her face. From the other room, he can hear the murmurs of Madame and of the servant, and, once in a while, the discordant sounds made by Margherita's sister. He regrets the haste with which he composed, the tunes he had flung into being, all now exposed to Margherita's kind but expert eye. He wonders at the life of the beautiful girl here, her loving sister and mother and regrets all of his silly jokes at the expense of Madame, who never expresses a hint of complaint about her unending care for her lovely, alien child.

Suddenly, Margherita looks up, her eyes shining, and his chest lurches. She puts down the manuscript.

'Perfect.'

He smiles, almost tearful at her glowing eyes.

'Perfect. I long to sing this.'

She jumps up and runs to the harpsichord.

'Here...Play.'

She finds Agrippina's first aria and places it on the music stand. He sits and begins to play while she reads faultlessly from over his shoulder. Her powerful voice sweeps the room and Georg admires again the ease with which she found her place within the song. As she sings, the door quietly opens and her sister comes in and stands silently in the middle of the room, listening to her and swaying slightly. Madame follows her in and, seeing the girl standing quietly watching the music, withdraws.

They finish the song and the girl applauds. Margherita turns to kiss her and tells Georg over her head. 'She loves music. You know, that's one of the reasons I started singing.'

He smiles.

'The Elector has asked for you.'

'But the Cardinal...?'

'He cannot help.'

'So? What is your plan?'

'Venice next year. Will you come?'

Without hesitation she nods vigorously, rocking her sister in her arms.

'Oh yes, Mamma will make it happen. When Mamma sets her mind to a thing, it always happens, even if we have to walk the whole way... and swim the last few miles.'

He slips out before Madame can return. The next day, he arranges for a copy of the opera to be sent to Hanover, to Melusine.

The Cardinal is delighted to tell him, the following week, that His Holiness will attend the mass in St John Lateran on the eighteenth of June. Georg asks that he might be allowed to present his respects, aware that he must make up for the rudeness of the night in the Janiculum. On the night itself, the great and good are assembled for the mass, Gianni attending His Grace at the front door as he awaits His Holiness's arrival,

and Margherita and her mother and her cousin Marco in the front row
with Luca. Georg waits by the high altar, Luca's birthday ring in his
pocket and when the congregation rise for the entrance of His Holiness,
he quickly ascends the small staircase into the balcony and seats himself
at the great organ. Lorenzo, perched on the balcony, is keeping a watchful
eye on the proceedings and when the Cardinal reaches the high altar,
he touches Georg on the shoulder as a signal to begin. As he plays, the
music proudly filling the largest space he has ever played in, his fingers
moving over the keys, he remembers six months previously staring up at
this impossible height. The choir sing with great beauty and when it is all
over and he descends from the organ loft, the Cardinal bustles over to tell
him that His Holiness wishes to thank him.

Seated at the high altar, dressed in white and surrounded by his
admiring entourage, the Pontiff is a surprisingly robust, even florid man
for his advanced years. As Georg kneels and kisses his hand, he looks up
to see the face, more like that of a successful butcher than a pontiff, with
a downward turn to his mouth. His manner is gracious as he blesses him
but he takes a firm hold of Georg's hand and begins to question him,
each question apparently met with less and less satisfactory answers.

'You are . . . Saxon, my son?'

'Indeed, Your Holiness.'

This seems mildly to unsettle him.

'We pray for all our dear brethren of the German lands.'

The implication being even the heathens, and Georg mutters thanks
for his kindness in doing so.

'You played with great skill.' He looks around him and something
is put into his large butcher's hand, the free one, and he finally releases
Georg and hands him a small, pleasantly heavy object.

'With our blessings, my dear Signor Endell.'

Georg bows his head in thanks and then backs away. The Cardinal is
waiting.

'You did very well tonight, Giorgio, His Holiness is usually sparing in
his words. This will spread the fame of your music even further.'

Margherita and her mother join them, as soon as the Cardinal bustles off to catch up with His Holiness's departing entourage. Georg looks down at the object in his hand, wrapped in soft crimson velvet. He opens it.

'What is it?' Mamma Durastanti demands.

Georg laughs.

It is a statue of the Virgin Mary, slim, elegant and with small blue stones studding the chastened cloak.

'He hopes the Holy Mother will convert me to the Romish faith.'

He hands the statue to Madame Durastanti.

'For you, Madame, with my respects.'

In an instant Madame takes it, despite Margherita's shocked exclamation.

'Mamma! You cannot take it. It is valuable and Georg has few resources.'

Already Georg is beginning to regret his impulse but Madame seems unwilling to hand it back and he decides to show a good grace.

'Please, Madame, allow me this one favour?'

He turns to look for Luca.

'He is gone,' Margherita tells him quietly, her mother busy with appraising the statue. 'Some news from home. He asked that you meet him in Popolo in an hour.'

He sees the two women to their carriage and sets off for Popolo, the streets filled with the night time bustle of the summer evening, a few stars already appearing in the sapphire, a welcome breeze blowing from the river onto the Corso as he makes his way to meet Luca. He sees his familiar figure hunched into the porch of the church in Popolo and runs over to greet him, the time almost midnight, his birthday approaching.

Luca turns towards him, his face tear stained.

Georg takes hold of him, careless of the crowd around and looks into his face.

'What is it?'

'My professors. They have failed me. I must leave the university. My father wrote today. He orders me back to Sardinia.'

Georg takes him in his arms.

'No. Stay. I have money for us both.'

Luca shakes his head.

'It is all settled. My uncle was very angry with me. All the money wasted. I am to return home.'

Standing together for so long, they are aware of those around them staring, two young men embracing and holding each other, and Georg breaks away.

'Come, we can walk.'

Luca shakes his head.

'I must return home now and pack. My uncle is bringing me to Ostia in the morning, to take the ship home.'

Georg remembers the ring and slips his hand into his pocket.

'This is for you. For your birthday.'

Luca opens it and his eye light up. He puts it on.

'Wear it and swear you will stay with me. I will not bear to lose you.'

Luca looks at him and shakes his head as the bell begins to ring for midnight in Popolo.

Easter. His last day in Rome. Tonight he leaves for Venice and he stands at the church in Piazza del Popolo, waiting to meet Luca. They have a few hours and then he must begin his journey north. He has been vague with Luca, avoiding him as much as he could for the past few weeks, ever since he heard that his opera will open in Venice at the San Giovanni Grisostomo theatre. Margherita and her family have already set out north and now his bags are packed and his travel plans set. Georg had called to see the Cardinal that morning to say his farewells. Much to his relief, Gianni came back to say that His Grace was away from the palace that day but had arranged for Lorenzo to accompany him northwards, insisting that his servant must travel as well, to carry private letters from the Pope to the Elector in Venice. Now, standing waiting by the church in Piazza del Popolo, he curses softly, wishes himself already in Venice.

When Luca finally comes up to him, unsmiling, with the bells ringing for noon, Georg hugs him. For a moment, Luca stands unresponsive but then he hugs him back, taking hold of one of Georg's pockets. They stand for a while and then Georg, growing uncomfortable, breaks away and suggests that they take a walk along the Corso. As they ramble about the city, Luca is quiet, answering Georg's comments with a curt word from time to time. They pause to stand for a few minutes by the Arch of Constantine, while Georg draws his attention to a large flock of birds circling high about the Caelian hill, like a giant net flailing about in the wind, desperate to get Luca to talk or even to look at him.

Last summer when Luca had gone home, at first his absence was a living ghost that pursued Georg, glimpsed here and there, all about the Roman streets, and so he began to avoid Popolo, the Arch of Constantine, all the places they had been, his nerves strained with physical longing for his body next to him, the sound of his voice, the taste of his mouth.

At the end of the summer, when an invitation came to compose a wedding mass for the daughter of the new Viceroy in Naples, Georg accepted gratefully. Naples proved successful, a city of feverish pleasure and excitement after the years of war. The longing to take the boat to Sardinia and find Luca was soon overcome by the commissions he received for church music. Despite several notes from the Cardinal, Georg prolonged his stay in Naples for a few more months, returning with great reluctance at Christmas. Letters from Sardinia had been few and unhappy in content but, in the New Year, Margherita gave him the good news that Luca was returning to Rome in March, his father finally allowing him to move out from his uncle's house, take a studio of his own and begin his studies in art.

They met in Luca's new studio near the Pantheon, across from Margherita's house and, from the start, Georg was uneasy. At Luca's suggestion, they walked out again to the small inn in the cold spring countryside, the old woman overjoyed to see them. After dinner, when Luca went to bed, Georg lingered over his wine, gossiping with the innkeeper about her house and her family, slipping quietly into his own bed without disturbing Luca in the other bed. Very early in the morning, Luca took Georg in his arms and began to kiss him, and Georg closed his eyes, forced to imagine that it was Lorenzo there with him instead.

The following week, a letter arrived from the Elector. He had arranged for the San Giovanni Grisostomo theatre in Venice to stage *Agrippina* just after Easter and Margherita had agreed to sing the title role. They both had a month to travel to Venice and begin the performances. Georg tells Luca something of this good news without mentioning the dates.

As they walk about the city, Georg finds himself talking, for the first time, about his home in Halle, the house of the Yellow Stag, about his old father, and of his medical stories, babbling away about anything that would keep Luca from asking about his return. They pass a small altar on the road up to the Caelian hill and Georg stops and looks.

'This must be Pope Joan,' Georg tells an uninterested-looking Luca, who stands kicking the pavement.

'Who?'

Georg keeps talking and slowly Luca moves back to his side to stare at the altar.

'Gianni told me all about her. The woman who got elected Pope, dressed up as a man.'

'Is this a joke,?' Luca, asked, bad-temperedly, unwilling to be distracted.

'No, a legend. She was on her way up to St John Lateran, to be made Pope, when she went into labour and gave birth right here on the street. Really bad luck.'

Luca shudders.

'What an unpleasant story. Only Gianni would enjoy that. What happened to her?'

'The mob killed her just here. Gianni says whenever they elect a new Pope, now someone gets the task of confirming that he is indeed a man, by touching him from under a chair.'

'Sounds exactly like the task Gianni would like to do himself,' Luca laughs briefly.

They go indoors to a crowded inn to eat. They sit, drinking wine, the food largely untouched, and, after a while, hunched over his wine, Luca suddenly erupts into talk.

'When I was in my father's house,' he begin abruptly, his eyes bright and angry, 'my dearest friend in Sardinia came to visit. He is married now and just had a son.'

Luca's voice drops a little. Georg smiles, uneasy, wondering where this story is going.

'He is my godson. He called him Luca. For me.'

Silence.

'You must be pleased,' Georg ventures.

Luca shrugs. He clearly has more to say.

'My friend. He was also my lover when we were young . . . My first.'

Georg grows uneasy at this confession, aware of those around them. Luca is speaking carelessly, loudly.

'The scar on my arm, the one you asked me about?'

'Luca,' Georg starts . . . but Luca cuts across him.

'Remember. I told you. A fight between my friend and his older cousin.'

Georg considers getting up and leaving but he knows that he must listen to this story, right to the end.

'His older cousin came to my house one summer afternoon. I was alone and we drank some of my father's wine and, before I knew it, his cousin was kissing me, although he is married too. I brought him to my bedroom. When my friend discovered us there, he got a knife and swore he would kill his cousin. I tried to get between them and he cut my arm. He cried when he saw what he had done and brought me to the doctor.'

Luca puts down his glass, his eyes shining with triumph, his mouth tight.

Despite himself, Georg can't help asking. 'And did you and your friend . . . this time?'

'No. He is married. Besides I told him all about you.'

Georg, hearing a nearby church bell ring for five o clock, stands up to go. Luca gathers his cloak about himself, preparing to leave with him.

'Will I come with you tonight? Do you still have the key?'

Georg stares at him.

'What? Tonight? But I must leave tonight at six. I am late already. I told you I was travelling to Venice today.'

Luca stands up, his face pale, his eyes stricken, and, in a moment, Georg knows that this is his chance to leave.

'I will write.'

Kissing him hurriedly, he throws down money, turns and walks straight out of the inn and down the hill towards the Corso, not daring to look back. Each step gets lighter as he moves nearer to the palace and to the waiting coach.

He sleeps for most of that night, Lorenzo by his side in the coach, and when they arrive at their first stop, a day later, the inn gives them a room with two beds. Georg says nothing as they both unpack and Lorenzo sends out for supper but, while undressing, Georg finds Luca's silver ring in a pocket of his coat. Luca must have slipped it into his pocket on the church porch in Popolo. Georg looks at it for a moment and then, in a spasm of anger, throws it towards the fireplace. It falls harmlessly onto the ground but just then Lorenzo enters with a tray of supper and some wine. Later, the candles quenched, and Lorenzo settled into the other bed, Georg rises again, to find the ring. It has fallen on the floor and, picking it up, Georg places it carefully in his coat pocket. He stands for a moment or two in front of the fire and then turns towards the other bed. Raising the covers, he slides in beside Lorenzo. The narrow bed can barely fit them both, and, for a moment, Lorenzo stays facing away from him. Then, with a swift movement, he turns and draws Georg towards him in his powerful arms.

They journey slowly northwards, sleeping together at night now as a matter of course. Two days later, a courier catches up with them, with a letter and a parcel from the Cardinal. It is the silver statue of Orpheus. Georg sends Lorenzo out for his own supper and reads by the firelight.

*My dear Georg,*
*This statue is a token of good fortune for Venice. Keep it, in remembrance of a day in St John Lateran and of a young man with hair falling over his forehead like gold spilling from the heavens. Keep it but not this letter, Pietro*

Georg sits by the fire, holding the statue in his hand, the solid feeling of silver, the figure of Orpheus and then, in a sudden movement, as Lorenzo returns to the room and crosses over to the fireplace to start kissing his neck, he flings the letter into the fire.

# VENICE

Each day is occupied with rehearsals at the San Giovanni Grisostomo Theatre and so, when his sister writes from Halle and asks him about the glories of Venice, the canals, the palaces and the churches, he realises that he has lived between three or four streets, seeing nothing but the opera house. He runs to a print shop and buys views of the Grand Canal and San Marco to send her and then hurries back to another rehearsal. The theatre is freshly painted, reopening after many months and attempting to re-establish its finances with this unknown musician paid for by the Elector. On his first day, he stands on the stage to meet the artists who will build and paint the set and stares out at the vast dark empty cave before him, wondering if anyone at all will pay a few crowns to come to hear the music of an unknown German youth in this wealthy, sophisticated city. The manager explains that the subscriptions for *Agrippina* are already promising and that his servant must take control of the money and the ledgers. Georg has written to the Cardinal, asking for Lorenzo to stay on, to handle the money and help with the printing and copying, and the Cardinal sends his permission in a gracious letter, expressing his regret that he cannot attend the opening night.

Georg works hard in rehearsal, cheered by the excellence of the musicians, trimming and shaping his music around the strengths of the soloists singing the parts of Claudius, Nero, Otto and Poppaea. Agrippina's arias are left untouched. He falls into bed exhausted but happy and sometimes, at dawn, he wakes up and imagines Luca's body lying next to his. He vows that the next day he will write, as he promised, but he never does.

Melusine insists that he take English conversation lessons in the afternoons, paying an English clergyman, Mr Delaney, for the task. This is a drain on his precious time but, despite her smiling eyes, Georg has learned that Melusine brooks no refusal. She has a way of darting sideways looks at those around her when she thinks she is unobserved that makes Georg wary of her. He has sometimes noticed the same in the Elector and wonders about Gianni's gossip that they are also half-brother and sister. He knows that they are a formidable combination and he recalls the gentle manner of the Cardinal with some regret. His teacher, Mr Delaney, a pleasant-looking young man of few words, dry, good-humoured and careful, is patient and soon Georg is speaking simple sentences in English, much to his own satisfaction. Mr Delaney is accompanying a wealthy young English nobleman, Lord Burlington, on the Grand Tour, but, at the moment, his Lordship has taken himself off to Padua to view some statues and so Mr Delaney is at liberty. Each afternoon, Georg meets Mr Delaney at the Elector's palazzo on the Grand Canal, at Melusine's insistence. She often calls in to speak English with Georg, teasing them that she wants to see that her money is being well spent. Melusine herself surprises him with her fluency in the language and he works hard to learn, amused by the refusal of the Elector himself to attempt the language.

Melusine scolds her lover, when he calls into the study to speak with Georg. The Elector grunts well-humouredly at her teasing and she turns to Georg.

'My dear, they are offering you three kingdoms. Learn the names of each country at least?'

'What are they called, Herr Handel?'

'Inga-lande, Scote-lande and Era-lande.'

Georg manages and she laughs, her deep, rather throaty laugh that disarms all in the room, and Mr Delaney nods approval.

The Elector waves a hand of dismissal at their frivolity and snaps at Georg in German. He lays a document down on the table.

'About the money, Herr Handel. I have paid 1000 crowns down to the theatre. If the opera runs for a week, then you will be entitled to a clear 800 crowns when I am repaid.'

Georg bows.

'You have been very generous, Your Highness.'

He has indeed and the subscriptions are flowing in, all curious to hear this new musician but Georg worries that the opera will not meet his expectations and spends as much time as possible at the theatre.

Georg has been given rooms at a palazzo near the theatre. It is a lavish apartment belonging to the Elector's brother, the Bishop of Osnabrück, a man with an eye for the male form, judging by the distinct themes of the fine Roman statues and paintings decorating the high walls throughout the sumptuous apartments. Georg is currently the sole occupant of the grand palazzo and the Bishop's Venetian servants treat him with great respect. His rooms look out over the Grand Canal, and from his wide balcony high above the city, he spends his early mornings watching the busy traffic below and the sun that slants over the water, throwing up unexpected light against the windows of the palaces and churches. Although it is nearly May, cold winds sometimes blow down from the Alps and blinding fogs drift in from the Lagoon and, at times, he can barely see the dim lights from the Elector's palace across the Canal. Late at night Lorenzo brings him his supper and the accounts from the theatre that day and sometimes joins him in the vast curtained bed. Lying on Lorenzo's broad chest, and feeling the swell of his breathing, Georg tries not to think of Luca.

Margherita and her family are also living near the theatre, in comfortable lodgings paid for by Melusine, who is also buying her stage dresses and wigs. Margherita comes faithfully to rehearsal each day, despite her mother's falling into some sort of low fever. When Georg offers to pay for additional nursing for her mother, Margherita refuses, with her customary gentleness.

'Assunta is taking excellent care of Mamma, and, besides, our darling Anna loves to sit by her each day and paint her paintings and stroke poor Mamma's brow.'

She looks tired and worried but puts her hand on Georg's arm.

'If you wish to please me, write to our dear Luca.'

In the evenings, he sits up late, revising the score and, sometimes he takes out a sheet of paper to begin a letter to Luca, but the sight of Lorenzo, moving about the room, preparing his supper, prevents him, or so he tells himself. He has grown to love the feel of Lorenzo's body next to his, his broad shoulders, and the wide, shapely proportions of his face but sometime when he catches a glimpse of his strong neck, almost bull-like, a slight fear crossed his mind, a fear he hurries to dismiss.

Finally Georg brings Mr Delaney to the Teatro San Giovanni Grisostomo one afternoon to see the first dress rehearsal of the opera. Lorenzo is already there, sitting in the front row, taking note of the monies received from the theatre manager and entering them into his ledger. A few moments later, Melusine arrives, taking her seat in the front row, and even the ailing Madame Durastanti slowly limps in on a stick as the musicians take their seats. Georg is shocked to see the change in Mamma Durastanti, her customary sleek look gone, her face now thin and haggard as she sits down slowly and carefully in the front row, to perch by Melusine's ear.

Without telling the performers, Georg has arranged for one of the musicians to take his place at the harpsichord. Right before the music begins, he walks to the back of the theatre and stands, a little shaky, leaning against a pillar surveying the scene before him. He can see the stage and the handful of spectators in the front row, barely visible in the gloom, and he watches as Melusine works away on her correspondence with her secretary while Madame Durastanti tries to engage her in conversation from time to time. The theatre seems unnaturally quiet that day, and there is something threatening in the vast dark spaces, a thousand ghosts waiting to laugh his Roman folly off the stage.

Just then, as the overture plays, tiny lamps begin to light up, one by one, to reveal the newly-completed stage set, high and stark, painted with rich tones of white and cream with fretwork, glittering with long thin silver and white banners, floating from white Roman columns. The music echoes a little uneasily though the vast theatre, Georg thinks, like the hollow sounds of a child running in a cave. Slowly, as the lamps are lowered, gradually filling the stage with light, the banners slip to the ground, revealing figures like Roman statues, draped in white robes, with white faces and powdered wigs. As the lights increase, these figures, Nero, Otto, Poppaea and Claudius, begin to move, all turning to look anxiously at the steps at the centre of the stage where a great white curtain ripples and shifts.

Suddenly, the curtain falls to the ground with the clash of cymbals and Agrippina is revealed standing at the top of the stairs, to the rehearsed gasps of the other performers. Georg hardly recognises Margherita in her long white Roman mantle, a dramatic red cloak caught up by vast silver clasps at her broad shoulders. She glides down the steps with all the patient ease of a serpent, her elaborate blonde wig threaded high with huge crimson roses, her eyes darkened with kohl and flashing with anger, her mouth a dramatic slash of scarlet, the only colours on the whitened stage. As if inspired by her new robes and her warrior queen paint, Margherita's voice is at its richest as she begins to sing and Georg notices Melusine putting down her letters and turning her face towards the stage. Georg listens to the others, the high clear voice of Nero, the rich tones of Pallas, Poppaea's pretty ways and sweet voice, and they all do well but, throughout the performance, he notices that the theatre manager stops looking around and stays quiet whenever Agrippina sings, either alone or with the others. Lorenzo puts down his ledger and sinks back into his seat and listens, and Mamma Durastanti stops her chatter during the solos and the duets. The other singers acquit themselves very well but he knows that, if this opera is to succeed at all, it will be due to Margherita. And it will succeed, he thinks, as she sings one of her martial arias, from under a full dark veil, her eyes flashing beneath the veil.

When they have finished, Margherita, in full costume, comes down to speak with Georg, who tells her how wonderful she sounds and her Mamma struggles up to congratulate her. They wait for Georg to speak.

He presses both their hands.

'Perfect.'

'I knew in Rome that it would be magnificent. Look at this wonderful set.'

As Mr Delaney hovers, Georg introduces him to Margherita, her rich headdress swaying comically as she bows, a shy look on her face as he tells her of his admiration for her singing. Mr Delaney is a little flushed as he speaks and Georg notices for the first time how handsome he can look.

In the middle of their conversation, Georg notices that Mamma Durastanti has begun to sway a little on her feet.

'Mamma, we must get you home, immediately,' Margherita exclaims, but her mother protests.

'No, here is Madame von der Schulenburg to speak to you. I will sit here.'

Mr Delaney makes a quick move towards her.

'Madame, allow me to escort you home. It would be my pleasure.'

Mr Delaney takes her arm firmly and begins to walk her up the aisle of the theatre while Margherita prepares to take the stage again.

The following day, when he is practising his English with Mr Delaney, the Elector comes into the study, alone. Georg and the Englishman make to rise but the Elector waves them down. He prowls around and motions that they can continue their class.

Self-consciously, they continue, sounding stilted.

'Good afternoon, Mr Handel, and how is your opera progressing this week?'

'It is progressing very well, Mr Delaney. Soon the vide vorld will say, Mr Handel, he has the genius.'

They laugh.

'They will say he is a genius.' Mr Delaney corrects him.

'You have the truth there, learned Mr Delaney,' Georg tells him.

The Elector suddenly asks him, in German.

'So you meet with Lord Burlington when he returns next week?'

'Yes, Highness.'

The Elector shifts in his chair, an annoyed look coming to his face.

'I hear from Rome that the Cardinal will appoint you to his church in Santa Maria del Popolo.'

This is news to Georg, and unwelcome news, but he keeps his face blank.

'When the opera is finished, you will come to Hanover as my Kapellmeister.'

Georg hesitates. This is even more unwelcome. He had not left Halle to become a court servant in another small German town.

As the Elector stares at him, waiting for his answer, he remembers the grotto on the Janiculum in Rome, a flunkey of the Cardinal in his white suit, while Margherita was snubbed by the Pope. He bows low to the Elector but says nothing. The Elector's sour face is not improved by the increasing annoyance on his face. He stares at Georg while Mr Delaney shifts uncomfortably in his seat. Finally, Georg manages.

'I am greatly honoured, Your Highness. May I consider your kind offer?'

The Elector stands up and looks as if he is going to kick something. Georg thinks of his comfortable rooms in the palazzo, the thousand crowns paid to the theatre, but the memory of that evening in Rome keeps him silent as the Elector turns and leaves the room.

After a moment's silence, they resume their English class but, within ten minutes, Melusine knocks on the door and comes in, apologising for interrupting the lesson. There is something about the fixed smile on her face that makes Mr Delaney get up, bow her into his chair, which she refuses and then leave, without another glance from her. As soon as the door closes, she begins, speaking in German.

'Tell me, Herr Handel. What do you want?'

He hesitates. He gives her the same answer he gave the Cardinal.

'To write music, to create operas,' he pauses . . . 'and to be free to do so.'

He saw from her face at the dress rehearsal that she liked the opera. How much can he gamble on this? Her pleasing eyes, the gloss of her dark hair, the attractive throaty laugh she sometimes lets escape, all of these charms seem to evaporate as she looks at him. She is taller than Georg and makes use of this as she stands over him.

'I had hoped.'

She stops.

'I had hoped that you would be so kind as to take a little care of our interests. That is, of course, if it is not to disadvantage your own.'

She is gentle in tone but her words sting him.

'His Highness has been very kind....'

She cuts him off. A hard look comes on to her pretty face.

'Kindness is not a luxury he can afford. Let me tell you something. I was eighteen when my daughter was born. His Highness was ordered not to acknowledge her. He had just been made heir to the English throne and no scandal could attach to the House of Hanover. My father had just died, and my child was without a name and she and I were exposed to the ridicule and the malice of the world, although he loved our girl dearly from the moment she was born.'

She pauses, then changes her tone.

'I would not be eighteen again and as frightened as I was then for all the treasures in Venice but His Highness behaved correctly. Not kindly but well. Soon my daughter will be the child of the English King.'

She looks at him directly.

'Why do you think I have paid for English lessons?'

'I have been wondering about this myself.'

Georg was aware of his risk but he held in mind the sight of Margherita descending that stairs and those heads all turned towards her in the deserted theatre.

'We need friends, in London.'

'London?'

'Yes. London is a wealthy city with a great thirst for opera.'

Watching his face as he thinks about her words, something relaxes her and she moves towards the door.

'You would like to visit London?'

He smiles, 'Of course…someday.'

'I will tell him that. You will find him to be a fair man. I have lived at Courts since I was a very young girl. Such men are rare.'

'I know another,' Georg thinks, 'in Rome', but he is silent and opens the door for Melusine, who kisses her fingers to him as she leaves. Let her think that she has extracted a promise from him, he thinks, but he is not going to Hanover.

That day he writes to Luca at his uncle's house in Rome, a short note, telling him about the opera and the great success he is hoping for. He is careful not to include his address. He encloses a miniature of the Grand Canal and a playbill for the opera. He wonders how to sign it but simply scrawls his name and places it out for Lorenzo to send to Rome. He wonders what Lorenzo makes of the name on the envelope, but the servant says nothing, his uncharacteristic passion in bed that night the only sign of any disturbance.

The following week, on opening night in late December, Georg is putting on his new coat in his bedroom, an elegant dark velvet, when Lorenzo enters carrying a small box.

'From the Signorina.'

Georg opens it to find a note from Margherita.

'To my dear friend, with my warmest thanks for your beautiful opera.'

It is a silken rose, deep crimson, just like one of the roses she wears in her head dress.

Lorenzo returns with a pin.

'Allow me, Signore.'

He places the silken rose on Georg's lapel and carefully pins it there, its rich colour even more startling against the plush velvet. Unusually for him, in daylight, Lorenzo kisses him.

'It will be a great success, Signore, never fear.'

Is his fear so obvious, he wonders? He decides the day is fine enough to walk to the theatre, needing some of the cold air from the Alps to clear his head.

He stands by the harpsichord, the silken rose rustling on his chest. The theatre has filled up, which gratifies him, yet he is frightened by the noise of the Venetians as they chatter and eat and wave at each other, all of this noise replenishing the coffers of the theatre and repaying his debt to the Elector. Mr Delaney comes up to wish him well and to whisper in his ear that the Elector is arriving.

'Madame Durastanti?' Georg asks.

Mr Delaney shakes his head.

'Too weak. The doctors say it is now a matter of months, as you know.'

Georg did not know. Margherita had said nothing to him.

The music begins and, as Georg had guessed, with a full house, the opera sparks into life, Margherita dominating the stage, the musicians playing their best, the other soloists rising to the occasion. The Venetian nobles, proud of their discovery of this new talent, stand at the end of the performance to cheer and the rest of the audience joins them to roar their approval. As he is called to lead the singers out to bow to the cheering crowds, he knows that his fortune is made. The cheering audience call him to the stage again and again, shouting for the Caro Sassone and flowers are thrown at his feet as he bows. The Elector looks uncharacteristically benign as he sits there. Melusine, by his side, beams at Georg and throws her own floral tribute down to him. He catches a glimpse of Lorenzo, cheering him in the front row, his face more animated than he has ever seen, glowing with pride.

At Melusine's salon afterwards, a throng of distinguished guests gather to shake his hand and to chatter endlessly to him about ideas for new operas and invitations to dinner, to fêtes, to country houses. Towards the end of the evening, he manages a few words alone with Margherita.

'May I call on you tomorrow, to pay my respects to your mother?'

Margherita, flushed and excited from the performance and from all the adulation, turns her kind face towards him.

'That is very good of you, Georg, but Mamma is so tired these days, too tired to see even dear friends like you.'

'Perhaps you would like to return to Rome, now that the opera has begun.'

'Why?'

'To consult your doctors there?'

Margherita looks unusually irritated at his questions but keeps smiling.

'Perhaps. Mamma has the best medical advice here and Madame von der Schulenburg has kindly sent the Elector's own private physician.'

'And what is his advice?'

'Rest. When we finish the opera, Papa will come and take Mamma to the mountains.'

She pauses.

'Only if she is well enough.'

The theatre manager comes up, shaking his hand.

'The subscriptions are beyond our wildest dreams, we will play for another two weeks at least. Mr Endell, you will be a rich man. The Elector's money has been repaid. From now on, all the rest is yours.'

At the end of the evening, the Elector beckons Georg over to say his farewells. He has a young man in his train, a slight, dark-haired youth, under twenty. The Elector introduces him in surprisingly fluent French.

'Here is Lord Burlington, Herr Handel.'

The young man, thin, with alert dark blue eyes, takes his hand, his covert look of admiration not lost on Georg.

'I hope to have the honour of welcoming the new hero of Venice to London this year. Come and perform for us. You have a home in London, at my house in Piccadilly. It is yours for the asking.'

Melusine calls young Lord Burlington over to her side and the Elector watches as the young man walks away, his eyes narrowing and the thin smile fading from his face.

The Elector, turns, frowning and points a finger at Burlington, switching to German.

'This young Lord tells me how he longs for me to visit London, to be recognised as Queen Anne's successor. I am the hope for England's future, or so he would have me believe.'

He looks angry.

'I am told that my dear friend, Lord Burlington is also in correspondence with the Stuart Pretender in France. I can trust no one in this London, I find. They court me and flatter me while, at the same time, they send their love letters to Saint Germain.'

He glares at Georg.

'That's why I need you in London. You can stay with this young fop in his London palace and keep Melusine informed of all that is happening there. Put your letters in with your new compositions, the English authorities will not bother with the post bag of my Kapellmeister.'

He puts down his glass, preparing to leave. Georg bows while the Elector takes him by the elbow and holds him in an unpleasantly strong grip.

'Be sure that you follow me to Hanover, by the end of summer at the very latest. I have work for you there and then more work for you in London.'

He glares at Georg, as if willing him to defy his command.

Georg bows but stays silent. He has already proposed a new opera to the manager of the theatre, to run in the summer. The manager, sworn to secrecy, has accepted it and is taking some of the profits from *Agrippina* as a deposit. Georg has no intention of being the Elector's spy in London, or writing little musical offerings for his dingy court players to enliven a dull winter in Hanover. Venice has shown him its appreciation and he will reap its full rewards. He escapes from the celebration as soon as he can and makes his way back to the Bishop's palazzo.

The extended run of *Agrippina* to the end of January brings Georg nearly two thousand crowns. In addition, richly appointed parcels and small inlaid cases start unexpectedly arriving at the palazzo in his absence, to Lorenzo's amused puzzlement. When he opens them, he finds that they are tokens of esteem accompanied by invitations from wealthy Venetian nobles. Letters come in seeking the company of the new maestro at their dinner table or begging him to play some of his own music at one of their evenings. Georg, busy with his new work, ignores the letters but the unopened gifts begin to pile up in the hallway. Finally, impatient at the increasing clutter that greets him when he arrives every evening, Georg has Lorenzo gather them up and bring them up to his bedroom. There, they unwrap them to decide what can be done with them all. A fine watch and chain and some elegant buttons fall out of one parcel. Lorenzo unwraps more parcels and places the contents on the bed, an ornate enamelled snuff box, the bolt of Chinese silk, a thin chain with a pearl pendant, some exotic animals worked in silver, and a pair of pewter candlesticks. A large inlaid box is found to contain an elaborate service of ruby red Murano goblets. Lorenzo is unpacking the final parcel, a heavy platter with a swan's head while Georg looks at all of these objects with disbelief, scattered all over the rich coverlet on his bed.

'Repulsive,' Georg shudders. 'What will I do with all of this? What am I supposed to do with wine glasses and bolts of silk? This is ridiculous. This room is getting too cluttered.'

Lorenzo stands there politely while Georg starts to poke through everything and finally makes rapid decisions.

'Well, this silk can go over to Margherita's house today, she can use it for a costume. You can gather up the silver ornaments, and make a parcel for them all. I can send them on to my mother in Germany. I'll keep the chain for Madame von der Schulenburg, she has an eye for jewels.'

'Here,' he picks up the snuff box and throws it over to Lorenzo, 'you might develop a taste for snuff.'

Lorenzo catches it deftly and puts it away carefully in his pocket, smiling his thanks.

'And the glasses, Signore? And this meat dish?'

Lorenzo lifts up the heavy inlaid box.

'I suppose we can't sell them?'

Lorenzo shakes his head decisively and Georg agrees.

'No, you are right. My kind patrons would be offended if they saw their gifts for sale again in the merchants' windows.'

He signs in exasperation.

'Oh Lord, what do I want with rubbish like this? Look, put the box and the platter under my bed and I can decide later. In future, all gifts to be refused at the door. Instruct the servants.'

Rising early each morning, Georg begins work on his new opera, determined to have the score to the theatre manager before the end of the month. He exchanges the pewter candlesticks for a silver case and places an expensively bound copy of the *Agrippina* score into the case, sending it off with a letter of thanks to the Cardinal. The Cardinal responds with a gracious letter, offering him a position within his own household as soon as *Agrippina* has completed its run and requesting that Lorenzo return to his service in Rome within the month. The previous night, in bed, Lorenzo agreed to stay on in Venice with him for the summer, to take care of the business side for the next opera and to manage his affairs. Georg sends him out to make discreet enquiries about new lodgings in Venice, for the day when the inevitable clash comes with the Elector and they are evicted from the Bishop's palazzo.

'We might have somewhere of our own, to use those wine glasses and that hideous platter.'

After the final performance, he calls to Margherita's dressing room, where she is packing away her costumes and invites her to supper to discuss the next opera. She declines and ask him.

'Where will you perform the new opera? Hanover?'

'No,' he replies, carefully. 'Here, in this theatre.'

'But we have promised them *Agrippina* in Hanover at the end of the summer.'

She turns away, a little tearful.

'Besides, Papa arrived today, to bring us back to Rome. Mamma needs to return home and I can make no plans for the next few weeks.'

'I will stay here in Venice.' Georg tells her, 'I am not inclined to become an Elector's pet monkey yet. But tell no one.'

He promises to write to her in Rome and, walking her back to her apartment, they say their farewell and part, both a little out of sorts with each other. Restless, Georg stops at an inn across from the theatre and orders a flagon of wine. As he sits there, wondering about his letter of refusal to the Elector, a fog begins slowly to descend on the dark street, filling the square with a thick white cloud. Gradually canal water spills over the raised bank and into the shallow courtyard in front of the theatre, the dark waters creeping slowly towards him as he drinks his wine. The innkeeper comes out to push the light wooden benches and chairs out of the path of the water, and he warns Georg to drink up, as the shallow canal water will soon fill the small square. Georg nods, pulls out a coin to give to him and stands up to go. As he does, the figure of a man walks suddenly out of the fog, coming straight towards him. It is Luca. For a moment, Georg wonders if he is an apparition, conjured up out of fog by his own imagination or his own fear. Georg thinks about asking the innkeeper if he sees him too, but the man has gone back into his shop. As he stands there, full of uncertainty, Luca strides quickly towards him and stands in front of him, his chin stuck out, his dark eyes glowing and intense. No apparition. It is Luca, improbably, right here in front of him. He speaks, almost spitting out the words.

'I have found you. Cara Sassone. The toast of Venice.'

Luca's face looks thunderous in this fog-muffled light and Georg is unsure of what he can say. As the silence in the deserted square grows, Georg forces himself to ask, his voice sounding limp and uncertain to himself.

'When did you arrive?'

'This afternoon. I went to the theatre, to see this new sensation of an opera but there were no tickets to be had. They were turning people away all afternoon. All those gold coins. You must be delighted, to be so rich now.'

Luca glances down at the fine watch on his coat, at the silver buttons. By his tone, he is attempting a tone of amused contempt for all of Georg's success but the urgent pleading look of desire in his glances towards Georg belies his assumed tone. The fog is beginning to make Georg feel more and more uneasy, cutting him off from escape.

'If you had written and,'...he nearly says *warned me* but recovers to say instead...,'told me you were coming to Venice today, there would have been tickets for you. I would love you to see the opera. I know Margherita would too.'

Luca bows his head in mock thanks.

'You are very gracious, Cara Sassone, to your old Roman friends but, to be honest, I was unsure of my welcome. Besides, I thought I might surprise you. You like giving surprises. I thought it was your turn to experience one. You don't seem to be enjoying it very much.'

Luca stares at him with what seems like a kind of fascinated loathing. In this thick blanket of fog in the deserted square, Georg realises that soon, one of them will kiss the other. He needs to prevent that at all costs and to get Luca away. Georg looks around the deserted square, where the water is now beginning to recede somewhat.

'Come, we should walk. It is late and this can be a very dangerous area at night.'

Georg has no idea at all if it is dangerous here or not, but it seems to work as, reluctantly Luca allows himself to be led out of the foggy square, Georg fully determined to get him to Margherita's lodgings and away from the Bishop's palazzo. All of the anger seems to have receded from Luca's face as they walk down a narrow pathway and over a small bridge, without a word spoken. He even allows himself a tentative smile at Georg, who smiles back and uses the opening to ask him the important question.

'Where are you staying?'

Luca shrugs.

'With you, of course? I left my bag at an inn near the theatre. I have little money for lodgings and now you are the wealthy toast of Venice, you have a grand apartment for us, no doubt.'

He thinks I am bringing home to bed, Georg realises. That is why he is silent, and that is why he has given me a smile. Outside a small church facing the Grand Canal, Georg decides to come to a stop and he turns to face Luca.

'No. You must understand this. I cannot bring you to my rooms. I stay in the Bishop's palazzo. It belongs to the Elector's brother and I am there at His Highness's invitation. The Elector pays for the theatre and for the singers and his servants are instructed to watch me. Do you want to bring my time here to an end? Do you want me to lose my patron?'

As he speaks, Georg realises that much of this is true and wonders what the Elector has been told about Lorenzo by the palace servants but servants are loyal to each other and can be bought. A conspicuous young man like Luca would be quite another matter. Georg knows Luca well enough to know that he is incapable of endearing himself with servants, his own lack of confidence often translated into petty anger at perceived slights.

Luca looks abashed and more than a little cowed by this long speech, more than he has ever heard Georg say before. He looks as if he will speak but Georg talks over him, determined to make his point.

'It is late but we can go to Margherita's now. Her friend Mr Delaney has lodgings nearby and you can stay with him.'

Without waiting for Luca to reply, Georg walks on and gets them quickly towards the section of the city where Margherita's apartment is situated, in a handsome building on a quiet square near the theatre but far from the Bishop's palazzo. They stop outside and peer up to the first floor, where lights are clearly visible in one of the windows of the lodgings despite the late hour. Georg goes to knock at the door but, before he does in the narrow porch outside the house, without warning, Luca suddenly lunges towards him. He catches hold of Georg, gripping his collar and then takes him in his arms to kiss him roughly on the mouth. As he kisses him back, he is no phantom conjured up out of his deepest fears from the gloomy fog but a ghost from the Roman spring, the man he first loved, the familiar scent of verbena on his hair, his mouth as beautiful as he remembered. It is Luca who stops, almost as abruptly, and pushes him away.

'Call here, tomorrow. At noon.'

With that, Georg raps on the door and they both stand there, waiting for the sound of the servant shuffling down the stairs, demanding to know who is there, disturbing the peace so late at night and threatening to send for help.

After a sleepless night, and a feeble attempt at breakfast, Georg sends Lorenzo to Margherita's apartment with a letter to tell Luca that he is detained at the theatre that day and must dine with the manager to settle his accounts. In the hastily scribbled letter, he promises that he will call to see Luca at Delaney's lodging that evening after the performance. Instead, when his work is done for the evening, Georg leaves the theatre as quickly as he can and walks by himself through the dark streets late into the night, dining alone in a quiet inn far from the theatre. He takes his time returning to his apartment and it is nearly midnight when he slips back into the palazzo, to find Lorenzo already gone to bed and another servant waiting to let him in and give him a candle.

He creeps upstairs and into his room where he finds a low nightlight burning on the desk beside his bed and a figure curled up under the sheets. He calls softly. 'Lorenzo.' The figure stirs and turns towards him. Luca. After all he has said to him. He goes over to the bed to order him out, and as Luca wakes up, the sheets fall away from his naked body. Wordlessly Luca reaches over to draws him towards the bed, his fingers tugging at Georg's clothes, his mouth following downwards.

The next morning, early, Georg wakes up to find the bed empty beside him. Turning towards the open window, he sees Luca standing on the balcony, looking out. Through half-closed eyes, he watches as Luca turns, shivering in the chilly morning air, to lean back against the edge of the balcony. Georg keeps his eyes half-shut, feigning sleep, but observes closely as Luca begins to rock himself slowly, backwards and forwards, his cloak wrapped loosely around his hunched shoulders. This rocking back and forward seems to last an eternity but Georg wills himself to stay in bed, to feign sleep. Finally, Luca stops rocking and turns back towards the balcony to stare out over the city. He makes a movement, as if to climb up on to the balcony. A sudden fear makes Georg finally sit up, pretend to stretch and yawn and call softly to Luca, asking him to come back to bed. At this, Luca turns around to face the room and, after a moment's hesitation, makes his way back into bed, his cloak dropping on the floor, his beautiful body a shock of chilled skin and muscle from the early morning air, their kisses all the more urgent, almost violent as Luca throws himself down on the bed.

Later in the morning, Georg wakes up again, to find Luca sleeping soundly beside him, the sockets of his eyes hollow and dark from exhaustion. Lying there watching him, he recalls Luca's story last night in bed after they had made love, the rows with his uncle in Rome and with his art academy, the breach with his family in Sardinia and the withdrawal of his allowance by his father, the sudden decision to come to Venice, and the search for Georg through the dark city. As they kissed, Luca had told him of his decision to stay here in Venice and continue his painting while Georg would write his music and of the apartment Georg must find for them and Georg had listened to all of these plans without comment.

Georg quietly slips out of the bed, dresses quickly, all the time watching Luca, who is sleeping soundly again. He makes his way downstairs to find Lorenzo waiting for him in the dining room. Over a very hasty breakfast, Georg tells him,

'I must go to the theatre to finish some business.'

Lorenzo nods, his face closed and expressionless. He motions his head upwards.

'And . . . the Signore?'

Georg would have preferred if Lorenzo had known nothing about Luca's presence in his bed but he sighs. Of course he knew. The whole palazzo knew.

'He should not have come here. Who let him in?'

Lorenzo bristles at this, his face reddening.

'He told me that you were expecting him. The servants here…well, they were gossiping this morning and I told them to mind their own business.'

Georg hits his hand off the table. Worse and worse.

'Well, he must leave now. I don't want the Elector….' He stops and starts again.

'When the Signore wakes up, tell him to go back to his lodgings. I will call for him tonight at Madame Durastanti's, sometime after eight.'

Lorenzo nods, something unsettling in his expression that makes Georg pause but the thought of all he must do today makes him anxious to go.

Georg leaves the palazzo, his head swimming with tiredness, and walks around the streets, quiet at this early hour, taking his time, thinking furiously. The morning light is pure and a strong chill breeze cools his heated face as he finally turns towards the theatre.

Luckily the theatre manager has not yet arrived, and making his way into the small office under the stage, Georg sits down, and writes a letter to the Elector,

*Your Highness,*

*As you requested, I have now completing my business here and I plan to quit Venice this week and promise to be in attendance in Hanover by the end of the summer. With Your Highness's kind grace, I must first visit my aged mother in Halle for a few months as she has been unwell. I wish to then proceed to Your Highness's Court by the beginning of September at the latest.*

*Your gracious servant,*

*G.F. Handel.*

He then scribbles another note to his mother, announcing his imminent arrival in Halle, smiling at his description of his hearty, vigorous mother, still in her forties, as aged and unwell.

A more difficult note is the one he must draft to the theatre manager, explaining that pressing family business has called him back to Germany and that his next opera must wait for performance at a later date, requesting that his deposit money to be settled and paid back to him today. He rushes to finish his letter but, as he had dreaded, the theatre manager arrives and is none too pleased with the news when Georg tells him of his change in plans.

'Young man, you have a fortune waiting here for you, and yet you scurry off to be a lackey in some dull Court, spending your day listening to His Highness's children picking out your tunes on the spinet. Are you without any sense?'

Georg has no heart to respond, or to argue. His need to leave, to escape, is growing more and more urgent by the hour. He listens to all the arguments that the manager makes and hangs his head, eventually agreeing to forfeit his deposit. At this point, Georg is prepared to make any compromise that will allow him to quit the theatre today and escape this city prison. At this, the manager relents and, taking pity on the agitated young man, gets out his money box and counts out Georg's share of the takings, returning him a portion of the lost deposit. As Georg prepares to leave, full of thanks, the manager shakes his hands mournfully.

'We could have made a fortune here, young Saxon.'

He hurries back to the palace where he summons Lorenzo to his room and begins to gather up his papers and his money while the man stands silently watching him.

'Lorenzo, my plans have changed. I must travel to Germany late tonight to visit my mother. Can you have everything ready here for me today? I will sort my papers. Can you pack everything else? I am sorry for all of this fuss but it is unavoidable.'

Lorenzo looks a little shocked but nods.

'Of course, sir, I will fetch your case and your travelling bags at once.'

'I must go out to my banker now but I will be back within the hour. I will leave money to pay the Bishop's servants.'

There is something about Lorenzo's face that unsettles him and he speeds out of the room and down the stairs to conclude his business. As quickly as he can, he arranges travel for Lorenzo and himself that evening. All of his other business is soon arranged, his gold safe at the bankers, some coin ready for the expenses of his journey and to tip the servants at the palace. On his return in the afternoon, he turns the corner just in time to see Luca walking away from the front door and a sweat breaks out on his brow. He waits in a doorway, watching Luca's retreating figure and wonders about abandoning everything in the palace and asking Lorenzo to follow him. More than a little angry, he stands there for a few moments and then makes his way into the palace and up to his room. Lorenzo has been busy with his travelling cases and Georg's fancy new clothes all laid out on the bed to be packed. Lorenzo looks up from the large trunk to ask,

'Will the gentleman from Rome be travelling with you? He called here this afternoon and is expecting you at Madame Durastanti's tonight at eight?'

Georg looks puzzled.

'No, we will travel alone. I have booked our passage for this evening at eight and so we must hurry. We will stay at my mother's house in Halle at first and then onwards to Hanover in September. I will write to the Cardinal and tell him that you will remain working for me. It is sudden, I know, but exciting? No?'

Lorenzo stops packing and turns to face him, saying nothing, a struggle evident on his face. Georg watches him closely.

'Will you have enough time?'

'No, Signore. That is not . . . All is nearly ready.'

He looks directly at Georg.

'If you please, I will return to Rome, to the service of the Cardinal. I do not want to travel tonight to Germany.'

Georg feels a lurch in his chest and his face grows hot.

'But . . . you agreed to stay with me. How can I . . . ?'

Lorenzo looks at him for a few moments with something like disbelief and then repeats firmly.

'It is better this way. I will return to Rome later this week. I have spoken with Signorina Durastanti this morning. They will need assistance in getting Madame back home and so I will move there this evening and take up service. I have already packed my bag. Let me finish this packing for you, Signore and then I will go.'

He looks back down at the cases.

'And I will deliver your apologies to Madame tonight.'

Georg says nothing. Lorenzo repeats.

'Before I go, I will finish packing for you.'

'But . . . your money?'

'If you like, I can engage another servant for you. There is a young man here at the palace who is willing to travel for a week or so, until you reach Germany.'

Georg walks over to him and touches his face. He runs his finger across the strong line of his cheek. Lorenzo stands motionless and then, after a moment, takes Georg's hand gently away from his face and steps back, his eyes never leaving Georg's.

'Enough,' Georg thinks, 'I need to be quit of everything in this place.'

He turns and fetches some money from his case and places a pile of gold coins on the table. He speaks without turning around, keeping his face turned towards the wall.

'Go. I can finish this. Here is the rest of your money. Go, if I am detaining you.'

Without a word, Lorenzo bows and walks out of the room. Georg cannot trust himself to look at him as he passes by but only turns around when he hears the door close. The pile of money still sits on the table.

For a few moments, Georg stands there, hoping that the door will open again but when it is clear that it will not, he lets out a breath. He looks around at the cluttered room and realises that he has accumulated more than he had realised. In a temper, he starts bundling the rest of his clothes into the large trunk left open on the bed. The small gifts he packs in his small travelling valise, along with the statue of Orpheus and the silken rose, but it takes him much longer than he realised to get everything ready and when a church bell rings for seven, he curses, as there is still more to pack.

He goes out to the stairs and calls down to the palazzo servants to fetch down his cases and find him a carriage. He is nearly finished and his bags tied up when he stumbles across the large lacquered box full of glasses under his bed. He kicks the box, clinking the precious glasses and then goes over to the balcony and tears open the windows. Lifting up the heavy box, he pushes it out onto the balustrade and, opening the lid, tips the contents out into the Grand Canal below him, the protest of the tinkling glass as it hits the water the only pleasure this day has given him.

# HALLE
## 1708

Georg is sitting in his mother's garden, an unopened letter from Margherita on the old wooden table beside him. Across from him, his mother is plucking the stems from cherries in preparation for jam-making, her beloved lime trees in full bloom in the early summer evening, the scent at its strongest at this hour while they sit in the shade. His six-year-old nephew sits on the ground before them, his wooden blocks all around him as he fights the Emperor and the King of Spain and, every so often, he looks up at his grandmother, who gives him a piece of fruit. The boy is grey-eyed and serious, his grandmother's constant companion, often watching his uncle with open curiosity. From the attic, his old spinet is resurrected and Georg teaches him some tunes, and sometimes the boy launches into a volley of questions about Rome and the palace that he lived in, Georg enjoying the patient, careful logic of his questioning.

Margherita's letter arrived early that morning but Georg has left it unopened, unwilling to read it, to break the spell of this tranquil time in his mother's house. He spends the early mornings composing his new opera, the afternoons in the garden telling her of his triumphs and his plans, and usually finishes the evenings drinking wine with his brother-in-law in the inn by the river. When Georg first arrived here in Halle in February, dreams of Luca pursuing him here to his mother's house disturbed his sleep. In the mornings, working at his desk in the attic, he sometimes dreaded to hear a step on the staircase outside, fearing an unwelcome visitor or a letter bearing news from Italy. As the days passed and it became clearer that he was safe here, he relaxed and began to enjoy the respite from his haunted dreams. He wrote to the Elector asking to prolong his visit to Halle and Melusine had written back, informing him of his formal appointment as Kapellmeister to the Court of Hanover and granting his request for more time at his mother's house. In the same letter, she told him of Madame Durastanti's death, which had taken place a week after he had fled from Venice. Melusine had suggested that, in the circumstance, the performance of *Agrippina* planned for Hanover would best be postponed until the end of September. Georg had immediately written to Margherita in Rome, telling her of his heartfelt sorrow at the death of her courageous mother. Now, months later, her reply has finally arrived and the possible contents unnerve him.

His mother glances over at him and at the unopened letter and, taking up her basin of cherries, rises and touches the boy lightly on the head.

'Come, Johann, your mother will be looking for you, let me bring you home, my little man.'

The boy is reluctant to leave, still full of questions about Rome.

'And, Uncle Georg, will you be here tomorrow or do you have to go back to live in the palace?'

'I will still be here tomorrow. Now, do as your grandmother wants.'

His sister is expecting another child, sometime later in this month and Georg has promised to stay and become the child's godfather. He has already purchased a heavy silver cup to present to the child, to be called Frederick if it is a boy or Frederica if a girl.

The evening light in the garden grows even more vivid as the sun slides gradually behind the trees and finally Georg braces himself to open the letter, under the welcome shade of the lime trees. It is addressed from her apartment in Rome.

*My dear Friend. Thank you for your kind words, they bring us much solace in this very painful time, we are heartbroken for our beloved one. I know how much Mamma valued you and what great pleasure your success afforded her. Little did I know that those would be her last days in Venice and now I am glad to know that your music made it a very joyful time for her? The Empress wrote a very kind letter and sent us a jet brooch, to remember Mamma, and at the end she spoke of you with love and asked me to keep that lovely statue, and I will return it to you in Hanover at the end of the summer, along with a small jewel she had reserved for you, a keepsake. We will travel north in time for the performance of* Agrippina *and I look forward to seeing you then.*

*In the meantime we live very quietly and our precious Anna is learning to survive without Mamma, a little day by day. She has surprised me with her strength and her wisdom. How lucky you are to be with your family. They must be so proud of your success and you deserve all the adulation and the respite and so do please give them my kind respects. By now you will have heard of the sad accident in Venice, on the evening before Mamma's final illness, just after you travelled to Germany. The good news is the doctors are hopeful that Luca will walk again, which is a miracle indeed, after such a fall, two storeys high. Yesterday I heard that his uncle is travelling to bring him back to Sardinia. We were fortunate to be able to do what we could but Mamma's illness became acute and we were so grateful when dear Mr Delaney took charge of Luca and engaged your servant Lorenzo to move him from our apartment and then bring him back to Rome when he was finally able for the journey. They are both good and true men and I believe Lorenzo has now returned to the service of the Cardinal, as Luca no longer requires his assistance. He has also recovered some of his spirits and is recovering also from the despair that gripped him in the first days of his illness.*

*I have more news for you, news of great changes in my life but, I beg, just for your ears. Papa has decided to give up his business to take care of Anna and myself, and so we will be leaving the apartment here and travelling to Hanover at the end of September to meet you. Mr Delaney will travel to join us at Christmas and I can tell you, just you that he has asked Papa for my hand in marriage and Papa has consented, with the stipulation that we wait a year, to honour dear Mamma and our mourning. I know you like him and also that Mamma respected him and I am myself very conscious of my good fortune and will strive to make him a good wife.*

He puts down the letter, unfinished, and looks around the garden and then sees his mother standing at the window. He waves but she cannot see him, her failing sight more and more apparent. He stands up and walks towards her, a smile breaking slowly across her still youthful, beautiful face as he gets near to the house. Before entering the house, he crumples the letter into his pocket.

# HANOVER
## 1708

As soon as he arrives in Hanover that autumn, Melusine summons him to her apartments. The pale, gleaming September sunshine fills her elegant salon, a pale silvery light giving an added sheen to the china ornaments that fill the cabinets in her drawing room and catching the lustres on the elaborate glass candlesticks. Her suite of rooms is spacious, with large ticking clocks, gilded chairs and an elaborately painted ceiling in the main salon where they sit. Above them, plump cherubs fly upwards in an impossibly beautiful swirl of cloud towards a gilded sunburst. As he kisses her hand, the strength of her confidence and self-possession, greater here in her lover's domain than it had ever been in Italy, fills the large room. He was told, as soon as he arrived, that Elector Georg had locked up his wife in a remote castle years before, a savage punishment for her adultery and there she languishes. As a result, these rooms, on the first floor and overlooking the elegant gardens in front of the Schloss, are purloined from the banished first lady of the Electoral Court. Here Melusine clearly reigns.

She is in high spirits and pleased to see him. Of all the bright objects in that drawing room, none is brighter than Melusine herself, in a rich gown of deep red brocade, cuffs of ermine at the wrists and the neck giving a deliberate hint of a regal air to her appearance. Her dark hair is simply dressed and she stands to greet him, her tall elegant figure setting off the gown to perfection. He has the foresight to bring her a gift, a thin, beautifully-wrought chain with a small pearl pendant at the base, one of his Venetian gifts, and she accepts it graciously, passing the chain through her fingers as she waves him to sit. She looks well, relaxed and in command of all around her and pours him some coffee herself, waving her servants away as they scurry forward to help her.

'Welcome, Georg. I trust your time at home was productive. We were waiting impatiently for you here. His Highness wishes for a performance of *Agrippina* in the palace and you are the vital presence, the only begetter.'

He acknowledges her compliments.

'Thank you. All is ready. I have met with the court musicians this morning. They are prepared and we can begin rehearsals today. Margherita will arrive later this week. What else must I do? I am still unclear as to my duties here?'

Melusine looks at the servants standing to attention and, smiling, commands them to bring her niece here to meet Georg as soon as possible.

As soon as the door is closed, she turns again and looks at Georg, her voice low and confidential.

'Your duties will be in London. As soon as His Highness is returned from his visit to Berlin, and your opera is performed for the Court, you will travel onwards to London.'

Georg is surprised and relieved to hear of his imminent departure to London. He was not yet prepared to resign himself to the life of the court musician here in Hanover. This is a dull place, already reminding him too much of his own home town in the short time he has been here.

'You will travel to England before Christmas and take up residence with Lord Burlington. He was here last month and has kindly offered to be your host and I have accepted, with your thanks.'

Georg begins to object but something about Melusine's implacably smiling face stops him. He would have much preferred to make his own arrangements for accommodation in London.

'He has already arranged for you to be presented at Court, to present His Highness's compliments and play some of your music for Queen

Anne. Her Majesty is something of an invalid and shy of company but she does permit music on occasion.'

Georg nods, somewhat bored by this talk of an elderly woman in London, whose health is a matter of indifference to him. Melusine's quick eyes pick up his disinterest.

'Forgive me for raising the matter of Her English Majesty's health, which might seem tedious to you but this is a topic in which you must cultivate an interest.'

He looks at her questioningly.

'We are not permitted to visit London or even to inquire directly about Her Majesty's health. However, Lord Burlington is close friends with Doctor Arbuthnot, the physician who is attending her. You will be in the position to cultivate his friendship on our behalf.'

She pauses and touches her thin coffee cup with a delicate finger, as if to hush it. It strikes him that he has never seen Melusine's ears, always hidden behind her pretty curls and her lace caps but he sometimes imagines that she can hear everything that happens in Europe, from the English Channel right over to the Baltic. No whisper of intrigue escapes her from that wide land mass, in her determination to see her lover on the English throne.

'The Stuarts watch from France, and so we must also be vigilant and you can keep us informed of the precise state of Her Majesty's health. Doctor Arbuthnot is a lover of music and will be glad to meet you. When he visits his Lordship at Burlington House, you will be able to gather any hints of his attendance at St James's Palace.'

A harassed elderly woman in London is ill, worn out, as he has heard, by many disastrous and unsuccessful pregnancies. Her husband is dead and the rest of her family watch from Hanover and from Paris with eagle eyes, wishing to ascertain the likely moment of her death. He shudders slightly at his part in all of this.

'And cannot Lord Burlington, the dear friend of His Highness…?'

'Lord Burlington, like all wise Englishmen, is friend both to His Highness and also to the Stuart interloper in Paris. We need a reliable friend in London and one whose musical compositions for my dear niece will not be read with any interest by the English authorities.'

He is uneasy and Melusine, looking at him, asks him, with a touch of annoyance.

'You seem less than pleased? This is your chance to go to London, where you can make your fortune in the theatre. This will guarantee your entry into the Court.'

'But, will Her Majesty receive the Kapellmeister of Hanover at Court if His Highness himself is not welcome?'

She looks puzzled.

'Why?'

'They will be suspicious as to my absence from the Court here? I hear that servants of His Highness are not popular in London.'

Melusine nods and clasps the ermine at the neck a little more closely to herself, the large sapphire on her finger glinting deep blue.

'I have welcomed the chance to observe you at work in Rome and in Venice and I think that you are admirably suited to the task.'

She pauses and smiles. He waits, knowing that he will not welcome her praise.

'For two reasons. Firstly, your music is such that the powerful ones of the earth desire to have it written in their honour. Queen Anne has some inclination towards music and when she hears you play, she will want you to write music for her.'

He bows his head at her compliment, knowing her next words are the crucial ones. She speaks a little more carefully.

'Secondly, you are a man of infinite . . . how shall I put it, adaptability? You are handsome, for a start, and that goes very far with most people, and then you know how to remain silent when you need to be silent and listen when great men and women want you to listen. You will make yourself agreeable to the English as you made yourself beloved to the Romans and the Venetians. Remember how they shouted, Viva il Caro Sassone.'

She smiles at him.

'Do not forget. I was there. I heard them shout out your name in Venice. I remember it all.'

Her tone is unclear, veiled, not quite complimentary, as she means it to be. She was there, as she is reminding him. What did she see or hear in Venice of Luca?

They are interrupted by the quiet opening of the polished doors and he stands up as a young girl, tall like her mother, with the same dark hair and pale skin, glides quietly into the room, her face serene and confident. Dressed, like Melusine in dark red brocade, the girl, who is no more than fifteen, comes forward to present her curtsy to him. He stands and bows back at her. Standing there in the September sunlight, waiting for her mother to speak, she is sweet-faced, dark haired, smiling, in most ways an exact replica of her tall, graceful mother, except for her blue eyes, prominent and slightly bulging like those of the Elector.

'Ma tante.'

She bows elegantly to Melusine, who smiles in a way that Georg has never seen before, as if robbed of her cool, elegant composure. Instead her face is full of anxious loving vulnerability. Melusine's eyes shine brighter than the September sun and brighter than any crystal lustres at the sight of this child of hers standing before her.

'Georg, here is my niece, Sophia. Well, Anna Sophia Melusine von der Schulenburg to be precise.'

The girl giggles at her full name.

'Yes, she is Anne for the dear queen of England, Sophia for the Elector's late mother who was her kind and loving godmother and Melusine, the poor child, was inflicted on her for the sake of her old aunt.'

The girl laughs.

'Ma chère tante, la plus belle. Sir, I am glad to meet you, please, I am Nannerl to my friends,' and she takes his hand and shakes it.

'Chérie, here is Herr Handel. I told you about his wonderful opera. We will hear it next week and he will be sending you music from London, when he travels there later in the year.'

The young girl turns to him and the light in her eyes at the mention of London makes them even more prominent.

'Thank you so much, Monsieur, you are very kind.'

She paused and looks again at her mother, with complete trustfulness. 'London, ma tante. I long to visit. Don't you?'

'One day, Nannerl, we will both visit, with His Highness. We may even go and live there, with the help of dear friends like Herr Handel.'

Melusine takes the girl's hand and presses it and Georg watches her, her face helpless with love.

'And now, my darling, play something for Herr Handel, our dear friend. He will be sending you some of his music and he must know what your tastes are.'

The girl walks over to the elegant harpsichord at the far side of the room and seats herself. After a few moments, she begins to play, a competent musician with a good ear for the music she is playing. Clearly, Georg thinks, she has inherited more than his blue eyes from her father. He will be happy to write for this girl. Like her father she appreciates music. He sits back and watches Melusine, beaming with pride at the playing of her child, her niece to the world, who will become a King's daughter or Melusine will tear the world apart with those long elegant fingers if anyone attempts to prevent it.

# LONDON
## 1709

When Georg crosses over from Holland and arrives in London early one morning in the following year, he finds this vast city alive with rumour and intrigue. As soon as he is rested, he walks out on that first day into the bustling streets around his Lordship's house and is exhilarated and a little frightened by the noise and the liveliness of this crowded city. Everywhere on the apparently unending streets, new buildings are going up, churches are being built and confident wealth displays itself in the shops off the Strand crammed with gold and silver and the well-dressed throngs in the fashionable parks and promenades. For a few hours, he walks around, excited by this new place and by the sense of vitality, unwilling to sleep after tedious hours in the boat. After a while, tired from his long journey from Hanover, he begins to be disturbed by the noise of the crowds on the streets and the sounds of loud chatter and shouts of laughter from the busy coffee houses. An unpleasant sensation creeps up on him, as if everything and everybody on the London streets are somehow all part of some great bonfire waiting to explode into flame, and he retreats back to his room to try and sleep.

From the first day in London at his Lordship's insistence, he is lodged comfortably in Burlington House, despite a slight unease with the admiring looks of the young Lord, and he refuses an invitation to dine that night, pleading a headache from travel. He is given a large, richly-furnished room overlooking an elegant Italian garden and a laden tray of food and wine appears at his door. Late that afternoon, looking out of his high windows to the grounds beyond the garden, he sees a pleasant green meadow, and he has to remind himself that this house is right at the centre of the city, very near to the royal palace. To call it a house seems a misnomer, as Burlington House is itself more like a palace. Each day, as he walks out through the great front doors, a vast horde of workmen are engaged in extending the imposing façade, erecting a magnificent set of pillars to embellish the grand entrance to the house even further. His Lordship is obsessed with rebuilding and promises to introduce Georg to his architect, Thomas Collins, his companion on his Italian travels.

As with the Cardinal's house in Rome, the hidden wellsprings of endless wealth smooth the running of daily life in every part of this vast palace, with its magnificent music room and library and countless servants and attendants, yet Georg misses the tact and the graciousness of his first patron. From the first, he sets up his desk in the music room to begin work in the mornings, his new opera almost complete, another beginning and some short pieces for the harpsichord ready to send to Melusine. In the afternoons, he walks far out into the city, anxious to explore it and excited by the feeling of wealth, of power around the royal palace and the green parks. He makes his way to the Bank of England and deposits his Italian gold. As he hands over the money, he thinks of how easily it would obtain him some quiet rooms of his own and his own servant, and he remembers Lorenzo with longing.

From the start, his Lordship treats him with great favour, requesting some music for his regular evenings and inviting him to use his box at the opera. As he did in Rome, Georg goes to hear music when he can in the churches and at St Paul's and is a constant attender at the opera in Her Majesty's Theatre. With all of that, his days are sometimes over-lengthy, as if his life has been suspended, and his bed at night haunted by the absence of Lorenzo. In darker moods, he wonders how long his supply of gold will last him, as his instructions are to stay here indefinitely and make himself part of Her Majesty's Court. Melusine had arranged for the payment of his first year's salary as Kapellmeister just as he was leaving for London. She made it clear that she requires regular correspondence from him and as much information as he can glean as to the Queen's possible demise.

On his second night in London, he is bidden to dine with Lord Burlington and he is somewhat relieved to find that the purpose of the dinner is to introduce him to some of his Lordship's closest political friends. It is a small gathering in the elegant main salon, and as Georg shakes hands with them all, it seems as if each man has a grand title of some kind or other, all of the company clearly well known to each other. There is talk of wives by some of the men but no women join them at table when they finally make their way into the magnificent dining room. Seating themselves at Burlington's immense table, they drink the health of Her Majesty in finest vintage.

The meal begins and, as a compliment to Georg, Lord Burlington raises a glass to the Elector but Georg catches one or two ironic smiles down the table. The men are all much older than his Lordship, and all connected to the Court, and they talk of Georg of Hanover with easy familiarity. It seems as if all prudent Englishmen of note have made it their business to visit the Elector's Court in the past year, as Her Majesty's health continues to decline. Raising his glass, Burlington tells him of a friendly letter just in from Melusine that very morning, asking warmly after her dear friend, Herr Handel. With the wine, tongues are loosened. Georg is told confidentially over the beef that her Majesty is expected to die within the week, being currently in the grip of a violent attack of gout that has assailed her and rendered her unconscious.

With coffee comes a late arrival to the company. Doctor Arbuthnot himself walks into the room, muttering his apologies as he comes directly from St James's Palace where he was attending Her Majesty. The Doctor is presented to Georg with great flourish by the host and sits by his side, helping himself to some wine and devouring some nuts and olives with the concentration of someone who has not eaten in hours. The Doctor is some years older than Lord Burlington and seems to Georg to be a good-natured genial sort of man, anxious to talk to the newcomer and to make himself pleasant. Georg's English is much improved but at times he has difficulty in following the man's strong accent and is not surprised when he tells him that he is from Scotland. He tells Georg that he has heard much talk of his music and is anxious to hear it for himself. Georg promises to play for him as soon as the company rises.

The rest of the company ply Arbuthnot with questions about the state of affairs at the palace and Georg listens carefully, taking care to seem to be concentrating on putting sugar in his coffee. He notices that the good Doctor manages to evade any direct comment on Her Majesty's health. Instead he diverts them by relaying the report that rumours are circulating that the Stuart Pretender has already landed secretly in Scotland at the head of a French army, poised to take London as soon as the death of the Queen is announced. When the coffee is finished, Lord Burlington rises and invites them into the music room. Georg plays for the company for an hour or more, to the pleasure of very few there, most being bored by music. Doctor Arbuthnot listens intently, his eyes shaded by his hand and his face peaceful. As he leaves, he bows to Georg, promising to have him play for the Queen.

'We must hear some of your operas here in London, Herr Handel. I've heard of your Venetian success and I will have Her Majesty's musician play some of your airs for her when she is resting. It is just the physic she requires.'

Georg duly writes to Melusine that evening to report that Dr Arbuthnot was delayed at Her Majesty's bedside that day, and to pass on the general report that she is overwhelmed with her illness. He omits the compliment about his music being a physic for the Queen's recovery into good health as this is not what his masters in Hanover are paying him to assist. He slips the letter within the leaves of a new score, a present for Nannerl.

Lord Burlington gets permission for Georg to play the next day in St Paul's Cathedral and on his way home, he stops into a coffee shop near St James's Palace to practise his English by scanning the newspapers. As he does so, he overhears two men recounting the latest news and it becomes clear that they are talking loudly for the general attention of those around them. According to one man, word has just come in from the captain of a boat out of Hamburg, tidings of the bloody assassination of the Elector at the hands of a demented Jesuit in Berlin, who cut his throat as he left the royal palace on his way back to Hanover. Georg finishes his coffee quickly.

He makes his way quickly back to Burlington House to find his Lordship in conference with Doctor Arbuthnot. The Doctor, a sensible man, listens to Georg's fears and laughs at the preposterous tale from Hamburg. Instead Arbuthnot tells him that he is in daily communication with the Queen's attendants, and reassures him that all these rumours are false, that the Elector is alive and well and the Pretender is still biding his time in Paris. The good Doctor asks to hear Georg play and brings the good tidings that Her Majesty will be well enough to receive Georg the following week at Court and wishes to hear some of his music. Georg wonders how Arbuthnot has the latest news from Paris, but this seems to be common throughout London, a close knowledge of all that is happening in Europe. He wonders if all the great people of London are not plagued with severe eye strain, occupied as they are with keeping a watchful eye on Hanover and another eye equally trained on Paris. Doctor Arbuthnot asks Lord Burlington to bring Georg to Court the following week, to attend Her Majesty at one of her rare Drawing Rooms at St James's.

On the appointed day, Georg fetches out one of his good Roman coats and joins his Lordship in walking the short distance to the palace. When they arrive, they are ushered directly into the Royal Apartments where, in a cramped, rather gloomy chamber, less opulent than any room in Burlington House, a small group of thirty or so are assembled, to wait on Her Majesty before she progresses onwards to dinner that evening. As they arrive, Doctor Arbuthnot makes his way quickly towards them and calls Georg aside.

'Her Majesty is much improved and anxious to have her Electoral cousin's servant presented to her. Can you come with me now, she is expected at any moment?'

Georg nods and they approach a dais at the head of the room where most of those assembled are gathered. There is a low murmur of talk in the room. Doctor Arbuthnot whispers in his ear.

'You should know that she is not much given to chatter, Herr Handel. She will have little to say, be prepared for this, and remember that it is not a snub.'

At that, there is something of a stir when a set of doors is thrown open and two ladies-in-waiting enter while the room falls silent. Her Majesty enters, her eyes downcast, a short middle-aged woman dressed in dowdy black, and a row of immense pearls around her neck the only sign of her regal status apart from her demeanour. She pauses at the door and murmurs something to an attendant lady, who gestures towards the dais where there is a raised platform with a seat. Her Majesty moves slowly in that direction, those around her bowing as she limps painfully towards her seat. Her ladies gather around to assist her in seating herself while all assembled watch in a respectful silence. Some chatter resumes around the room as she takes her seat and looks downwards, apparently unconcerned with those gathered around her, but all eyes in the room are intent on watching her. Under cover of a conversation between the Doctor and his Lordship, Georg watches her with curiosity, her still-youthful face plump and unlined, and an unhealthy pallor about her cheeks. There is a wary expression in her tired eyes as she settles herself into the chair, and darts a few covert looks around the room, with a fan held up to her mouth. There is very little talk while she sits there, every so often saying a few words to one of her ladies near her. A large damask stool is placed in front of her where she props up one foot and Georg notices, peeping out from under her skirts, a damp poultice, grey and unpleasant, tied around her ankle.

Nothing much seems to be happening and Her Majesty speaks to very few people but, at Doctor Arbuthnot's prodding, Georg is brought forward and bows to her. Her weary eyes are lifted up to his face as she listens to him present compliments and good wishes from the Elector, his English for once halting in the beam of her strong, slightly unsettling gaze. She looks up at him for what seems an eternity, taking in with some scepticism, or so it seems to him, his fancy velvet coat, the buttons from Venice, the watch chain. After a few moments, in a soft, careful voice, she thanks him in French and tells him that she looks forward to hearing his music. He replies in English and she compliments him on his command of the language. 'You are a quick learner, Herr Handel,' she tells him, making it not quite a compliment as she glances down at his well-cut coat.

With evident relief at her task completed, she turns to ask Doctor Arbuthnot something about her medicines, the rich pearls on her neck swinging and shifting with the sudden movement. Georg can see from the change in her expression that she trusts him, a gentler, more open look coming into her face as she listens to his words of reassurance. Suddenly he realises who the Doctor reminds him of. It is his own father and the Queen looks at him in the way that local women in Halle looked at his father and trusted him with their ailments and their worries. She is right to trust him, Georg thinks, remembering how skilful Doctor Arbuthnot was at evading all questions about her health at Burlington House, protecting her privacy from all of those important men.

'So, Doctor, I am wearing the poultice you had them make for me, as you can see,' and she points down to her leg.

'Yes, I am pleased to see that, Your Majesty, and I hope that it has brought you the relief you required?'

'Oh yes, it has indeed. I am much improved today and the darting pain in my foot has all but gone.'

There is something childlike in her eagerness to seek his reassurance, and something in Doctor Arbuthnot's manner, kind, respectful, confident, strikes Georg, and a memory from years of observing his father's manner with his patients. It seems to Georg, having seen his father doing much the same with the dying, that the Doctor knows that she will not recover. Her pallor, unnaturally white and blanched, confirms this for Georg yet Arbuthnot seeks to cheer her up with his good-natured reassurances. She can trust very few people, this tired, watchful woman, her children all dead, her husband gone and her younger brother now her mortal enemy in France and longing for news of her death to take to the seas at the head of an army. Is it worth all that betrayal and death, he wonders, to be the royal sun, the source of all majestic light, someone under constant surveillance ? He thinks of Melusine's face looking at her child, dreaming of the English crown, and wonders if he would dare warn her.

The Queen turns towards her attendant, who whispers that dinner is now ready and Georg bows over her outstretched hand, catching the distinct aroma of brandy from her breath as he makes his obedience to her. As he retreats, Georg remembers a few lines of poetry quoted last week at dinner in Lord Burlington's after Arbuthnot had left. It was from a new poem written by one of their friends and they all sniggered. 'Here Thou, Great Anna! Whom three realms obey, Dost sometimes council take, and sometimes tea.' Well, today, it is not tea, Georg thinks as he retreats. He is glad that she has some comfort while Europe watches impatiently to see if she lives or dies, and he feels slightly ashamed of his own part in that surveillance.

For the next few months, Georg settles into his life in London, his time spent writing music for Lord Burlington's musical evenings and working on his new opera, and walking in St James's Park. Despite all of his attempts to keep as busy as possible, he is fighting against the dispiriting sensation that his life is caught in a kind of limbo. He soon realises that many others in London are also living in such a state of unreality, none more than his noble patron. Lord Burlington takes a short trip to Paris, ostensibly to visit the French Court but, it is whispered, to pay court to the Stuart. There is little or nothing happening in London for him to report to Melusine, apart from the comings and goings of the Doctor to the palace, but he dutifully sends on all the information he can gather. After a week, Burlington returns looking a little bothered from his French journey and is mercifully off on his travels again, this time on a visit to his Irish estates with his architect Thomas Collins, full of plans for more beautifying of his many houses and estates. The London house grows quiet without his Lordship and the musical evenings are suspended for the time being and so Georg grows more and more restless. Once or twice in the coffee houses or wine shops off the Strand, he gets a smile, a welcoming look, the promise of more, his tall figure and fair hair attracting attention whereever he goes, but, since his flight from Luca, he finds that he has little desire to return these looks and he hurries on his way.

He is jolted out of his feeling of restlessness when an unexpected invitation arrives for him to write some music for the Court. In a letter from the Doctor comes the news that Her Majesty, as a token of respect for her cousin in Hanover, has asked Georg to set some verses to music as a Birthday Ode. This ode will be performed by Her Majesty's musicians and singers in a special service in St Paul's Cathedral and will, as Arbuthnot writes, also be performed to mark another moment of national importance. Arbuthnot adds that he is not permitted to tell him of this yet, as it is a state secret and known only to those at Court. In his letter, the good Doctor includes a copy of the verse that Her Majesty requires to be used in the musical offering for her birthday service.

He is looking over the verses when Lord Burlington makes his way into the music room. Georg shows him the letter and the verse and he reads it out with a slight note of derision.

> *The day that gave great Anna birth,*
> *Who fix'd a lasting peace on Earth.*
> *Eternal source of light divine*
> *With double warmth thy beams display*
> *And with distinguish'd glory shine*
> *To add a lustre to this day.*

Burlington hands Georg back the letter and smiles, a little ironically.
'I'm not sure His Highness in Hanover will welcome this, Georg.'
'Why not, my Lord?'
'Well, Her Majesty's government will soon be announcing a peace with France. A separate peace, leaving the Emperor stranded in his battle against Louis. This is the vital state secret that Arbuthnot is not telling you. This "Lasting Peace" deserts Hanover.'

Georg colours and feels a quagmire open under his feet.

'What has my music to do with this, my Lord? I am simply writing to please Her Majesty?'

Burlington smiles, as if to explain something rudimentary to a child, and Georg feels again the shackles of his duties as guest in this vast palace.

'The Elector is an ally of the Emperor. He will be none too pleased when he finds out that his own Kapellmeister is writing odes of joy to celebrate England's betrayal of the Imperial cause.'

With that, Burlington withdraws, leaving Georg uneasy. Later that day, he writes to Melusine, asking her advice as to the birthday music. He begins work on the music, waiting impatiently for her response, but nothing arrives from Hanover and the weeks pass without any direction at all. Finally a parcel arrives, with some musical scores and a letter from Nannerl. He throws it aside with some impatience, but later in the day, when he sits down to read it, he notices that the writing changes after the childish handwriting of the first page. He realises that Melusine has written into the middle section of the letter and so re-reads it very carefully.

*I cannot risk a direct letter to you, as we now know that your letters are being read but you must proceed with the Birthday Ode for Her Majesty and any other commissions, as we need you there in London. Be prepared for bad news from us, it may be that the Elector may have to show his displeasure and even dismiss you from his service for a time. Keep sending your music pieces to my darling Nannerl, she enjoys them so much and include any letters to me with them. I promise that your interests will be taken care of, whatever action we take in public, and your income will not suffer.*

He tears up the letter, unhappy at the dilemma he finds himself in but knows Melusine well enough to know that if her interests are served, then she will take care of him. He starts writing the music that day, making his way to St Paul's that afternoon to make himself known to the Dean and arrange rehearsals.

In the following month, the Birthday Ode is performed with great acclaim, although Her Majesty is too ill to attend the service herself, sending her ministers in her stead. She writes Georg a gracious letter, telling him that such is the reported success of his music that she wishes him to write a *Te Deum* for the declaration of peace with France. Usually this is the task of the Queen's own court musician but, as she makes clear, she requires it specifically from the young man from Hanover and he writes back to thank and to oblige.

As he expected, in the week after his *Te Deum* celebrating peace, a formal letter arrives from Hanover, written by His Highness's first minister. In unequivocal language, he is reprimanding Georg for his endorsing of the peace and announcing that His Highness will be suspending his position and his salary as Kapellmeister. It is an uncomfortable moment for Georg and he wonders how much he can trust Melusine but, when the news of his dismissal spreads around the Court, by which means Georg is not quite clear, there is a representation to Her Majesty by his new-found friends, and the following month, Arbuthnot brings the good news that the Queen has granted him a royal pension of two hundred pounds for life. At dinner that night to celebrate, Lord Burlington congratulates him on his good fortune and, when Georg mentions his plans to seek lodgings elsewhere, protests loudly that he must stay on and write an ode for him, as he has some good tidings of his own to announce,

Summer comes to London, his first in England. The sweet air in the fields around the house entrance him and, as each day dawns brighter and clearer than the last, Georg rises early to write his music, the quicker to be off into the parks around the city and beyond, each day a day of precious freedom, of wandering around this exciting, youthful place. Unwilling to sleep in these bright, unending evenings of June sunlight, Georg spends all of his evenings in the gardens around the city, drinking wine late in inns by the river with the musicians he has befriended and walking home through St James's Park as late as possible to see the beginnings of dawn and the light touching the tops of the lush greenery of the tall trees.

In late June, Lord Burlington comes into the music room to tell him of a planned festivity that evening, a late night supper party outside, to celebrate the beauty of these white June nights. His Lordship tells him to dress in his finest summer white shirt and be outside at midnight, for a special announcement. But his lordship is coy, and will not be drawn as to that good news. Her Majesty's health has worsened and Doctor Arbuthnot has not been seen for days, his attendance at the palace almost constant. He wonders if this is the long-awaited news from St James's Palace and feels unhappy at the idea of celebrating such news on a beautiful summer's night like this.

When Georg makes his way into the Italian garden at midnight and walks down the wide avenue at the centre towards the fountain, he finds that a long table has been set up in the garden. It is covered in white linen, laden with gold plate and decorated with heavy candelabras and wreaths of summer flowers. A tall circle of broad torches has been placed in the lawns around the table, bringing a new daylight back into this June evening. All around, the scents of the shrubs mingle with the overpowering scent of the lavender strewn on the low bronze braziers set around the flowerbeds. Already, some of his Lordship's friends are standing around the table, a low murmur of conversation as they await his arrival. The servants are finishing their preparations, bringing great platters of food and trays with wine glasses into a small tented pavilion set up next to the dining table. On the ground in-between the flowerbeds, are large crystal urns full of ice and replete with wine bottles and Georg stoops to help himself to a glass of wine, feeling a little uneasy and in need of a drink to sustain him. Around the table, some of Lord Burlington's friends make to sit and one or two nod to Georg and smile a welcome to him, but, he notices, there is no sign of Doctor Arbuthnot.

Lord Burlington appears, with two young men at his side and his Lordship welcomes everyone to supper and asks them to take their seats wherever they wish. The servants are now dismissed, and it is announced by his Lordship that all men must serve themselves, as this will be an informal evening where no one will be permitted to leave until they greet the dawn. There is a little cheer of appreciation and Georg fetches himself some food from the pavilion, deciding to sit down at one end of the table, away from his Lordship and within sight of the windows of the house. He eats and chats a little with his companions, while watching his Lordship and his companions and wonders who they are. The older, dark-haired man seems a great favourite with his Lordship, and speaks with authority and deliberation. In a whisper, one of Georg's dining companion tells him that this is the celebrated architect, Thomas Collins, who is redesigning Burlington's Irish castle at Lismore in the style of Chambord. Georg listens and watches but is more interested in looking at his companion, a tall young man, with large dark eyes and unruly soft brown hair, who shifts uneasily at the side of his friend and says little as his Lordship talks and then Mr Collins interrupts and they both laugh and debate. It is clear to Georg that the young man with the dark eyes is somewhat outside the company, but he hides his discomfort well.

As the evening continues, the light grows a little dimmer and the candles sparkle more brightly and a light dew begins to fall. As they eat and drink, the talk at the table grows louder and more carefree. Once or twice, Georg notices a face peering out from the lower windows of the house and he decides to drink no more wine, as those around him grow livelier. Sometime in the darkest moment of night, when the stars are at their brightest above them and the chill of evening is kept at bay by the multitude of candles and lanterns, Lord Burlington stands up. More than a little drunk after the meal, he asks all the men to stand and drink a toast.

'I have an announcement to make,' he tells the assembled company, swaying slightly, 'some wonderful news and so please raise your glasses.'

Here it comes, Georg thinks and he grows tense. Who is the new ruler of England to be?

His Lordship raises his voice to a shout.

'To matrimony. I am delighted to be able to say that, after a great deal of wooing and entreaty on my part, Lady Dorothy has agreed to be my wife.'

With that, they all clink their glasses, and, then to Georg's surprise, Burlington leans down and takes hold of Thomas Collins' shirt front to kiss him passionately. As Collins kisses him back, all assembled cheer them and clink glasses again and Georg is aware of watching eyes from the windows of Burlington House. Well, Georg thinks, what does that mean about the other young man, Burlington's companion? After an interval, while everyone else pointedly chat and occupy themselves eating and drinking, his Lordship releases his lover from his embrace and, turning around excitedly, calls to him.

'Georg, some music. To celebrate.'

He points to a harpsichord, a little hidden from view behind the small pavilion. It must have taken at least six men to carry this out here and Georg wonders at the damage they may have done.

'Certainly, my lord,' and he gets up and crosses over to the harpsichord. It is shaded by the tent.

'I need some light,' Georg calls and looks up to see the young man, Thomas Collins's companion, carrying a large lantern towards him. He sets it down in the grass and then goes to fetch some candles to place on the harpsichord. Georg begins to play, the young man standing by his side to listen, and his Lordship's shout of thanks from the far side of the table, urging him to play some more music. When Georg stops playing, the young man thanks him and they stand up and walk back to the table to pour some more wine. In the candlelight, his companion has huge beautiful eyes. He is somewhat taller than Georg, with dark circles under his eyes, a slight fair beard, and in the flickering light, strikingly handsome in some light, sometimes haggard and worn in others.

'Do you like music?'

'Very much. I was trained as a singer but now I work with Mr Collins as a draftsman.'

He makes a wry face of disapproval.

'It is not the work I wished for but it pays well and Mr Collins is very considerate to work with.'

Georg glances over at Mr Collins who is now completely drunk and swaying in the arms of Lord Burlington in a kind of dance under a broad chestnut tree. Something about the quizzical way in which Georg glances at the architect makes his young companion add, 'No, nothing like that. He is not to my taste.'

And his eyes make it clear that his taste lies here.

'You sing, do you? Can I hear some of your songs?'

He nods and when Georg is ordered back to play more music by his

Lordship, the young man follows him and asks him if he knows some of the old English country ballads. They find one that Georg knows and he sings, his clear young voice confident and pleasing in the dark garden, his voice carrying across the still night. Some of the others come to hear him sing. Georg plays on for an hour or so, every so often glancing up at the full chestnut trees, caught in a white light that seems never really to fade at all. The sudden burst of bird song at dawn startles him but he feels no need to sleep, with the excitement of the evening.

He stops playing and still the young man stands beside him while they both listen to Lord Burlington sobbing in the arms of his lover inside the small pavilion.

'Promise you won't leave me, promise me!'

It is nearly fully light as they drink their last wine and watch His Lordship and the architect slip away towards the house, a face appearing at a window unnoticed by the two men. Georg stands up to go, a few men lingering to finish the last of the wine, one or two asleep on their chairs, the candles now all dead, the lanterns black and sooty. The young man, who has been standing by the harpsichord, comes over to shake his hand.

'It was an honour to hear you, Mister Handel. I must leave for my lodgings, by the Strand. I hope we shall meet again.'

'Please. I am Georg. And you are?'

'Peter,' the young man tells him.

The atmosphere is somewhat peculiar in the house over the next few days and his Lordship is nowhere to be seen. Then, unexpectedly, the weather breaks at the end of the next week, and on a rainy day on the Strand, Georg is hurrying to take shelter when he notices Peter walking towards him, intent on getting safely through the busy thoroughfare. Thinking quickly, Georg takes off his hat, to let Peter notice him now, and they stop in the middle of all the bustle to face each other.

'Some wine,' Georg suggests. He nods and they walk off together quickly in the direction of St James's Park to an inn Georg knows there.

Settling in, Peter tells him of the doings in Burlington House. Lowering his voice and looking around, he tells him, 'We have seen little of Mr

Collins at our office this week. It is said, some servant went tattling to Lady Dorothy about the dinner party last week and his Lordship dancing, well, as you remember. She is insisting on his dismissing us all. His Lordship has threatened to move Mr Collins into Burlington House to live with him.'

Peter takes a long drink of his wine and passes a hand over his worried brow,

'Already I have been making inquiries about another position, London is full of building projects at the moment but I cannot leave Mr Collins yet, he has been always fair to me.'

Georg comes to a decision.

'If I had work for you, would you change your profession?'

'What kind of work?'

'Theatre work. I have an opera I wish to see performed here in London and I need an agent to work with the theatre? Would you consider this?'

Peter nods happily and without hesitation answers. 'Yes, I would.'

They pay for their wine and leave, the rain still strong, those around them too intent on getting out of the downpour to notice the two men walking along, staring at each other. Nearer to St James's Palace, in a deserted church porch, they stop and kiss for what seems hours. Georg curses the lack of a place of his own and swears to Peter that, as soon as they can, he will get them lodgings of their own and they can kiss to their hearts content, both of their bodies yearning for more.

They meet now on a daily basis and, one afternoon in the following, a worried-looking Peter tells him that there has been a crisis in Burlington House at dinner the previous night. Her maid regaled Lady Dorothy with a lurid version of the night-time dinner party, telling her of unnatural excesses and of wholesale depravity, of a whole company of men engaging in lewd acts in full sights of the house. On her first formal visit to the house where she will be mistress, in front of the servants, her ladyship demanding the dismissal of Mr Collins and, if he has not immediately departed, threatening to go to the Queen or the Elector or the Stuart, when he arrives, to denounce his Lordship and have him arrested and all the men there thrown into prison. Peter looks worried as he tells this in a low voice, looking around him to avoid being overheard. More than ever, Georg feels the urgency to leave the house. He comes to a decision and tells Peter to take money to secure them both lodgings off the Strand. Over the next few days, Georg arranges to have some of his possessions transported there secretly, all set to fly the perch as soon as the political situation is resolved.

Within a few weeks, more and more rumours abound of Her Majesty's ill health and the atmosphere in the city become feverish. It is announced that she cannot walk to church on Sundays, unheard of for such a pious and punctilious woman. Then it is made public that she has taken an apoplectic fit during a Privy Council meeting late in July and is confined to her chambers and surrounded by her medical attendants. Doctor Arbuthnot invites Georg to dine in his villa on the river near Richmond, as his family are out of the city to escape the dull heavy heat of the summer, and they sit in his garden into the late evening and drink wine. Doctor Arbuthnot confides that her days can now be numbered singly, and to prepare himself in case of the need for flight. Georg duly heeds the warning and the next day withdraws his money from the Bank of England and hides it in a strongbox in his room, along with the Orpheus Statue. He writes to Melusine, suggesting that when the Elector comes into his own, the Doctor should be rewarded. As he seals the letter, he doubts if she will honour this obligation to the Doctor, and wonders if his days in London are numbered, too.

August is a close, sultry month, when London is usually deserted, but all the great and the good have decided that it is in their better interests to stay on and watch the happenings at Court as Her Majesty's life draws to a close. Burlington House is filled with late night visitors and the comings and goings of his Lordship's associates. Georg is making his way out of the house, one afternoon, to call into Peter's lodgings when he hears a church bell begin to toll mournfully. This lone bell is soon followed by another and then another until the whole city reverberates with the sounds of the death knell for the Queen. As he walks on, almost afraid of what he will encounter, the streets are now crowded with people standing quietly in groups, watching each passer-by for some news, some sign of what will happen.

Peter is away from his lodgings when Georg calls and so, oppressed by the watching crowds, Georg makes his way out to Dr Arbuthnot's house in Richmond, to escape from the vaguely threatening atmosphere in the city. He is not surprised to find the Doctor at home, he is now, after all, without employment. Arbuthnot looks tired and a little ashen as he fetches some of his whisky for Georg to try and they go out into the airless garden, an exhausted silence all around them. They say nothing for a while and then Arbuthnot speaks, like a man who has much to say and needs to be listened to, without interruption.

'It was all over at dawn this morning with the suffering woman, not an easy death,' his exhausted eyes reflecting this. 'I wanted to leave as soon as all the necessary formalities were done. At noon, as I was leaving the palace, the heralds came out and trumpets were sounded and Elector Georg,' he smiles, 'I mean His Majesty King George was proclaimed just outside Whitehall. I stood there for a while, too tired to move, and the crowd around me were quiet all during the proclamation. At "God Save the King", a few cheers went up here and there. As I was walking home, the streets around the palace were lined with troops on horseback. I asked one of the officers why and he told me that they had word of a rising in Scotland.'

Arbuthnot laughed.

'When he heard my accent, he looked at me most peculiarly and so I made it my business to hurry onwards.'

He picked up his glass and raised it.

'She was the last of the Stuarts. I suppose, as a Scotsman, I should be sorry to see her go. I do not think her brother in France will ever rule here. Poor woman, it was a hard end. I think sleep was never more welcome to a weary traveller than death was to her.'

And Georg noticed a few tears in his eyes.

For the next week or so, Lord Burlington is constantly receiving visitors and Georg keeps close to his room and his strong box, with no letters from Hanover to keep him informed. And then, one morning, a knock comes at his door and Lord Burlington arrives in person, to show him a letter from the Electoral Court. The date is set. The Elector will be in London before the end of the month and plans a coronation by October.

'I hope he is in a lenient mood with you, Georg.'

His Lordship laughs and Georg remembers the look of contempt in the Elector's face when he first introduced his Lordship to him in Venice and thinks, 'Likewise, my fine Lord.'

This makes it easier for Georg.

'I must thank you, my Lord, for all your kindness to me. Now, that His Highness will be coming to London, he has requested me to take lodgings near the Court and resume my duties as musician to the Elector. I will remove to a temporary lodging in the Strand today, to await his orders.'

His Lordship looks a little surprised but, Georg notices, keeps his annoyance in check, the shift in political power in Georg's favour keeping him controlled.

'Well, shake hands, Georg, and remember me when you are His Majesty's court musician . . . and also remember me to the handsome Peter, who, I hear, is lodging near the Strand also.'

Without a pause, Georg shoots back.

'And my respects to Mr Collins as well, my Lord.'

Lord Burlington laughs and shakes his hand.

'Touché, Georg!'

On a bright October morning, Georg is summoned to wait on Melusine, newly arrived in England, and ensconced in her apartments in Kensington Palace. As he walks up through the garden, he happens upon Nannerl, out with her maids and her little dog. She is pleased to see him.

'Herr Handel, are you coming to see ma tante? Can I walk with you?'

They make their way up into the palace, the young girl now grown into a confident young woman, dressed in elegant silks and with an air of quiet command with her companions. Inside Melusine is waiting for him, surrounded by a host of servants busy unpacking and scurrying all around her, a beaming smile on her face.

He bows low, 'Welcome to England, Madame Von Schulenberg.'

She laughs.

'So formal, Herr Handel, and I see you have met the Countess of Walsingham already.'

He is puzzled and looks around.

'You mean?'

The girl laughs at her mother.

'Oh, ma tante, or should I say, Madame la Duchesse.'

Georg looks puzzled.

'His Majesty announced it at council yesterday. I am to be created Duchess of Kendal, wherever that is, and my darling Nannerl is now Countess of Walsingham.'

Georg congratulates them both, his eyes caught by the immense string of pearls around Melusine's neck. He thinks for a moment and then remembers where he has seen them before. The late Queen Anne. He wonders if they sit comfortably there.

'Come, Georg, there is someone you must pay your respects to.'

She sweeps through her bustling attendants, and ushers him out of the double doors and down the broad stairs, towards an immense pair of double doors, Nannerl following them quickly as their broad silk dresses rustle on the wide steps and over the polished tiles. As they approach the high doors, two footmen stand to attention, and, at Melusine's nod, they bow and throw the doors open wide. Inside a group of men are sitting at a long table, and, as she comes into the room, they all rise and bow to her. In a gilded chair at the head of the table, the Elector stays sitting, looking a little uncomfortable, dressed in a rich blue coat with a high embroidered collar. He smiles at Nannerl and beckons her over to his side. She perches on the gilded arm of his chair of state while he turns towards Georg and smiles a welcome, looking more benign than Georg has ever seen him. After a moment, he even stands up and beckons Georg towards him, and Georg wonders if he has grown taller, somehow, or bigger, or it is just the blue coat.

'Look, gentlemen! It is my errant Kapellmeister, who wrote music to celebrate the undoing of my friends.'

The Elector beams all around him, his face creased with a kind of humorous smile, and the men smile back, a little unsure of his tone.

'Where should I send him, gentlemen? Should I throw him into your Tower of London?'

The men around the Elector laugh gently, and Georg is reassured by a slight nod from Melusine at the Elector's side. He comes forward with confidence and bows low before him.

'Welcome to England, Your Majesty,' and he kneels down and kisses the large ruby ring on his hand.

'It is good to see you, Herr Handel,' the Elector whispers in German, 'you have given good service and now you will be my Kapellmeister again, or what do you call it here? '

He turns impatiently to ask Melusine, and she replies in English.

'He shall be your musician at the Chapel Royal, Your Majesty, and you have kindly decided to increase his pension to 600 pounds a year. All is well again between us old friends from Italy.'

The Elector grunts, satisfied, and Melusine takes Georg by the elbow and draws him towards the open window, leading him back out into the gardens.

'We will leave the gentlemen of the Privy Council to their business with His Majesty, Georg. Have you written a new opera for us?'

She turns and motions towards her daughter.

'Let us go out into the gardens with Nannerl, Georg. The day is very fine, for October and we should make the most of it.'

She takes her daughter by the hand and steps out into the garden, closing her eyes and allowing the sun to shine directly on her face, her pleasure in the feeling of warmth beautiful to see.

'Georg. Our time has come. This is our day in the sun.'

# LONDON
## 1740

He writes it in twenty days, not daring to stop, forcing himself to compose the music for Jennens's passages of scripture and for an overture and a pastoral symphony. He has Peter move the smaller harpsichord into the back bedroom, where unwelcome summer glare can be shut out with black drapes, and he goes at it with a vengeance. His dead arm is newly recovered and so, fearful of a return of the previous year's palsy, he works remorselessly, daring his limbs to fail him again. He sets himself the task of completing three sections a day, and so has Peter wake him every morning at eight. He washes, puts on his dressing gown and then goes straight to work with coffee at his desk, placing himself in prison until each day's work is complete. He works without interruption until late afternoon, Peter blocking all visitors, letters left unopened, all life held at bay. As he writes, he eats nothing substantial, but stuffs dates and grapes into his mouth to keep the sugary sweetness flowing in his blood, and he allows himself no rest until each work is ready to be sent for copying. He has Peter put one of the highly polished tables next to the wall, and here he places the leaves from Jennens's word book in a fearfully intimidating pile on the left of the table and, from the first day, places the completed compositions on the right. He watches as Jennens's sickeningly bulky mountain of pages slowly, painfully dwindles and the other meagre pile of completed music begins to grow and grow.

As a child he had been told again and again of his elderly father's great moment of triumph as a doctor, so many times that he grew sick of hearing it, but it came back to him in those days with a vengeance. A local boy, Ulle, had been playing with his friends one day, when the small knife he threw up in the air came plunging down and, by some kind of wild misfortune, fell into his open mouth and lodged firmly in his gullet. Half-mad with pain and making wild noises, but still alive, the boy stumbled home, his companions all fled in terror, and Ulle's despairing mother brought him to Doctor Handel's house. Instead of accepting the obvious fate for the foolish boy, his father began a slow process of extracting the knife from Ulle's throat, day by agonising day, inch by inch, pouring soothing liquids down his throat to keep him alive and the throat open, and putting him to sleep in a special cage of soft pillows at night. After ten days, his father finally managed to draw the knife out safely and Ulle was saved.

'So, Father,' he told the shade of the long dead old man, 'I am your equal in stubbornness but I am both doctor and foolish patient and the music must be drawn from my throat, inch by inch, like a dangerous knife.'

Some days the music comes easily but, in the main, it does not, and so, often, in despair by mid-afternoon with the clock reproaching him, he ransacks old bundles of music from unwanted operas, seizing any means to complete his day's task, his guts seething with fear and irritation. When this is done, he rings the bell to give Peter the clean sheets of the final draft of music, dressing himself and hurrying out of the house, allowing the housekeeper to clean up the disordered room, and set the manuscripts back in order. Released from his prison, he goes to a Turkish bath nearby to steam away the day's ink and toil and then on to some eating house to read his letters and keep up with his business affairs. When he has eaten, he walks the streets of London and beyond into the fields for hours at a time in the late August evenings. Without fixed destination, but avoiding any house where he might be known, he strides along the summer streets, calculating the number completed, the compositions ahead, ransacking his memory for old tunes, disregarded arias, anything to finish this hellish task. Sometimes, he pauses at street corners and rests, staring at those out strolling on a summer's evening, in awe at their air of leisure and ease, pushing himself to walk further and further each day.

As he walks around London, some evenings it seems to him as if each building, each street corner is a reproach from his lost days in the sun. When he can, he curtails his walks to avoid the theatre in Haymarket, the scene of many of his greatest triumphs and then his later failures and the loss of his carefully accumulated fortune. He remembers a few lines of poetry in circulation in London a few years before. 'Some say compared to Bononcini/That My Herr Handel's but a ninny.' At the same time, all of London was enjoying the very amusing depiction of him as a hog in a rich coat, sitting on a barrel of beer while playing the harpsichord, dubbing him the charming brute. Peter told him that the story had gone all around London that his palsy came on him with his rage at seeing himself depicted as a fat brute in this cartoon. This had not been the case, of course. Georg prides himself on noticing none of the small but distinct snubs and the humiliations of his slow, irreversible slide from fame into unfashionable derision but his hatred of this cartoon can still make his fingers curl with anger.

Thinking back over this time in London during these long walks into the warm August evenings, he tries to puzzle it all out, the first moment of decline, age and obscurity creeping up on him like a vengeful enemy. It had all gone so well at the beginning, when Melusine persuaded the King to set up an Academy of Music to stage Georg's operas at the King's Theatre, as he had in Venice. The nobility, led by Lord Burlington and his new wife, Lady Dorothy, flocked to pay their subscriptions and to be seen at each opening night, waiting for a gracious nod from His Majesty. With money flooding in, Peter was able to leave his work with Mr Collins and took charge of the subscriptions and the copying of the music, his skills at practical matters soon making him invaluable.

For the first season, with almost unlimited resources at his disposal, Georg invites Margherita and her husband to London for a season of engagements and she accepts, singing in his new opera at the King's

Theatre and delighting in Georg's newly acquired home in Brook Street where she and Mr Delaney are his first dinner guests. As he walks Georg remembers the difficulty he had back then in finding himself a house of his own, swearing that he will never be the guest of a great man again. At that time, all the fashionable new houses around London were being bought up by men rich from the trade flooding into London and all the foreign speculations. Hearing of a bargain from his friend Dr Arbuthnot, back at Court due to Georg's pleading, he finally locates a newly built house in Brook Street to lease. The owners did not allow him to buy it, as he is not an English subject and so he takes it at sixty pounds a year. As soon as it is vacant, he asks Peter to move in first, supervising the furnishing and outfitting of the house. In doing so, Georg makes it clear that Peter must, from now onwards, be regarded as his secretary and the manager of his household, and Peter accepts this tacit acknowledgement of his status with a bad grace.

Georg uses most of his Italian gold to furnish the Brook Street house, which is smaller than his father's house in Halle but close to the theatres and to the palace and a short walk down to the church in Hanover Square where he spends his Sundays playing and attending service. When all is painted and his expensive new harpsichord installed and his music room fitted up, he has the workmen build a wooden niche and places the Orpheus statue there. He buys a painting of an idyllic Roman landscape to put beside it, as that reminds him of the place where he and Luca had walked in the country. Margherita exclaims at the beauty of it all, and congratulates Georg on his success when she comes to dinner and is gracious and kind to Peter when she meets him. But when Georg hints that Peter cannot join them for dinner, he leaves the house in a fury. Margherita is too polite to notice.

Margherita comes to London at the time of his greater triumph and when money was flooding into his Bank of England account. He ponders on the slow decline of his popularity and wonders if it all began with the death of Elector Georg. The new King, his son, is well disposed towards him and arranges for the continuation of his pensions. Soon audiences for his operas vanish and the royal family complain about the coldness of the King's Theatre, where they sit loyally in the half-empty opening nights. Watching his money drain away, and desperate for new audiences, Georg proposes that he travel to Italy to engage a new set of singers, the best that money can buy, to entice fashionable London society back to his theatre. He goes to the Bank of England and withdraws the last of his money, now leaving him dependant on his pensions and on this last gamble, to tempt these newest and the most famous of the Italian singers from Rome to London, to revive the flagging fortunes of his company. For a while, Georg contemplates bringing Peter with him to Rome, but he has always kept that part of his history silent in his London life and decides against it.

Georg stops a few nights in Halle, to see his brother-in-law and visit the graves of his mother and his sisters, his young niece now his only relation. Overcome by the emptiness of his mother's house, and the lingering presence of her spirit in her sadly neglected garden, he leaves as quickly as he can.

He arrives in a very different Rome, the wartime city he hurried away from over twenty years now prosperous and peaceful. Like London, there is everywhere the bustle of work on new public buildings and a sense of money pouring into the city. As soon as he is settled, he sends a letter to the Cardinal, asking for the favour of a visit, and sends another to the agent representing the rising star of the theatre Niccolo Broschi, the great Farinelli, whom he had met in London the previous year. In the first few days, he meets with some of the singers he requires for the next London season and arranges satisfactory terms with them all but when he calls on Farinelli, three mornings in a row, each time he is refused entry.

The one reply he welcomes comes from Margherita, who is now widowed and living back in Rome in her father's old apartment. She invites him to visit and he arranges to see her one evening, remembering the route to her house with surprising ease. He is ushered into the familiar drawing room and is shocked when the long dead Madame Durastanti herself stands up to greet him as he enters the drawing room.

'Georg, you look as if you have seen a ghost.'

Margherita's voice issues forth from her mother's mouth. With a start, he realises that this is Margherita herself, grown into a stout middle-aged woman, her mother reincarnated.

'I have,' he tells her before he can stop himself. 'I thought it was your mother back again.'

She looks tearful.

'I wish it was. It is lonely here, with Papa gone too, and my dearest husband also. Only my beloved Anna to keep me company and she has been unwell. Here she is, now.'

Now that he can see her, it is clearly Margherita, her kindly soft expression lacking the sharp glint of her mother's eyes and mouth. Georg has another surprise when her sister Anna enters the room. Like this apartment itself, Anna is almost untouched by the years, still lovely and sweet-faced, except for a single lock of white hair in the dark tresses at her temple, looking as if a child had painted her hair for a play, to mimic old age. Anna comes over and shakes his hand, pleased to see him, and Georg wonders if she is the reason Margherita never had children, the all-absorbing focus for her attention and her love.

As they dine together, they talk of her life here in Rome, and she expresses no longing to return to her singing, clearly contented despite the loss of her husband and the quiet life with her sister. With her usual kindness, she tells Georg that she has arranged for Farinelli's manager to call in that evening after dinner, as he is an old friend of hers and she knows that Georg will needs him for his business success.

When he arrives, the manager Stefano proves to be a man of his own age, prosperous, well-dressed, grey haired and sleek, clearly fond of Margherita and familiar and kind to Anna. He tells Georg that Farinelli may be promised elsewhere for the next season but that he will try and persuade him to travel to London, if the terms are promising enough to tempt him.

Margherita announces that she must attend to Anna and withdraws, leaving the two men to finish their wine in front of the warm fire. As they settle into talking, Stefano asks him suddenly.

'You do not remember me, do you?'

Georg looks at him again, his grey hair sparse on his head, his large dark eyes and wonders.

'I knew you when you were first here in Rome. I was one of Marco's friends, Margherita's cousin. I was there at the palace for your first performance, where you dazzled us all.'

Suddenly it comes to him. This well-preserved middle-aged man was the tall, dark-haired youth Stefanino, the handsomest of them, the object of love for all of the girls, and, according to Luca, a relentless seducer of women, determined to marry for money.

'Stefanino! I should have known you. Forgive me.'

They raise a glass together, Georg embarrassed at his failure to remember him.

'You have prospered, Caro Sassone. Your friends in Rome hear of your great triumphs in London and we are glad that we helped you on your way. Margherita has told us of her wonderful visits to London and of the high regard in which you are held.'

There is something about the relentless tone that makes Georg uncomfortable, as if these compliments are leading somewhere unpleasant. In a moment, he knows who Stefanino will mention and he cannot see how he can stop him.

'Yes, all of your Roman friends follow your success with great pleasure. That is, all who remain on this earth? One has already been taken from us. You remember the Sardinian, our friend Luca?'

Georg nods, not trusting himself to speak, trying to keep a disinterested look on his face.

'We heard last year of his sad loss. Of course, he had been unwell for years. After his accident in Venice, his body healed but his mind....'

The man makes a gesture at his forehead, a twisting of his finger against his temple.

'You know how that can go. He was fortunate. An old friend, who had lost his wife, rescued him and took great care of him. A most noble friend. But last year, a fever took Luca and his friend was inconsolable.

Such constancy. Very admirable and so rare these days.'

The old friend? Maybe the one with the knife? He hopes so. In this, Luca was fortunate.

To Georg's relief, Margherita glides back into the room, sparing him from any need to speak, to respond. With that, Stefanino stands up to leave.

'Thank you so much for this pleasant reunion, my dearest friend,' and he kisses her hand. 'I was just explaining to Signor Giorgio that, sadly, my client will be unavailable to travel to London to take up his most generous office next year.'

Georg bows and wishes him a good night.

During his time in Rome, Georg takes to walking past the palace of the Cardinal at different times of the day, in the hope of a chance encounter, but the large front doors remain firmly shut whenever he passes and his letters remain unanswered. At times, when he walks towards the palace, it is as if the years have fallen away and he is returning to his old room, on the second floor, but then, when he reaches the gates, time intrudes and he halts and then continues on his journey. On one of his last days, one rainy afternoon, walking down the Corso, he sees a familiar figure walking towards him in the crowded street, in a great cloak and wide-brimmed hat. As he gets nearer, it is clearly Lorenzo, his tall figure unmistakable, but he keeps his head down and, just as they walk past each other, Georg slows down and they look at each other briefly but Lorenzo keeps on steadily walking past him, even when Georg does turn back himself to stare at his broad retreating back. He is looking well, Georg thinks, the strong lines of his handsome face mellowing with the years, his figure upright and impressive as ever.

On his final day, his mission over, his money heedlessly spent, Georg climbs slowly up the Caelian Hill to view the new façade on St John Lateran. There, with these stately figures of the saints and the Popes on the façade of the church looking down on him, he thinks about Luca, gone forever, and his younger self, now vanished like Luca, and he shivers and moves on quickly. He had been avoiding it in all his time in Rome but now, on his final day, he makes his way down to Piazza del

Popolo. There he stands under the shelter of a church porch and watches the light die out in the busy square, seeing, dry-eyed, two young men dancing awkwardly on a bright Christmas morning, and, then, the same two young men kissing and sobbing at their first parting. When the square is finally shrouded in darkness, with great reluctance, he leaves, to begin his journey home.

After his return from Rome, Luca, forgotten for many years, now comes back to haunt him. For Georg, in his youth, loving Luca became as natural as breathing and then, suddenly, without noticing it, he was over fifty, corpulent, and few seemed to look at him as before. It was then that Luca's ghost returned. When Georg hurried away from Rome on that Easter Sunday, he never guessed that, with every successive Easter Sunday, Luca would reappear as surely as the new buds appear on the trees. With every year that adds itself unwillingly to his life, he feels more and more keenly the presence of Luca in the cold April winds, the raw days of watery sunshine, the lengthening light of early evening, the first blossoms. Now the young man he ran away from is gone, dying young, but alive as an unshakable ghost in the dim light of an early April evening. On early June mornings, he sees again the unwelcome reproaching vision of his handsome lover rising from his bed and making his way out into his young life. Now a middle-aged man, he looks out of his London window, and watches the evenings grow brighter and the promise of sunshine beckoning, the May days ahead, and thinks, 'Oh Luca, long dead and in your Sardinian grave, now you have your revenge. Every dream that haunts me has the sound of your deep voice in my ear and the touch of your beard on my neck. You followed with me, never to leave, as I walked away from that Roman inn, revelling in my escape, running happily as if you were of no account.'

Does Luca's death blight his life and luck, he often wonders? The house in Brook Street becomes a burden rather than a refuge, the relentless household bills and expenses a series of worrying darts into his peace of mind while all sources of extra income dry up. At night, he has vivid dreams of himself as bankrupt, his possessions thrown out onto the street and the heat of his bed clothes at night, even on a cold night, keep him from the sleep he craves. From time to time, he experiences a kind of dizziness and a buzzing in his head at the harpsichord. One morning, he wakes up after a feverish night and finds that his right hand is cramped and frozen and he is unable to move it. It is as if something he was dreading, something inevitable, has now finally hunted him down and he has been caught in its net. Peter finds him there, stricken with terror, and holds him in his arms, rocking him gently.

His doctors call it a palsy, a word he has never heard before in English and they send him for treatment to the Baths at Aachen, where he is forced to eat little, to forswear his wine and his port and drink the sulphurous waters. One day, lying in one of the hot baths, he manages a little movement in his fingertips. Telling no one, he dresses himself quickly and takes himself off to a local convent, requesting to be allowed to play the fine organ in their chapel. There he forces himself to perform his fingers stiff and ungainly at first, the sounds clumsy and ugly, but he grits his teeth, knowing that his survival depends on his playing again and soon he recognises the playing that the Cardinal remembered, the wings of song he could conjure up, and he persists until he is well again.

Shuddering at this memory, Georg forces himself to walk for miles each evening as he writes *Messiah* and, when he is too tired to walk any further, he limps home to the house, to splash himself with ice-cold water and fall into his bed for the few hours of sleep he needs to keep working. In this self-imposed prison world, with fear tickling his feet like flames, powerful dreams flare up to assail him, fleeting moments of lost desire and half-memories of long-forgotten bodies and faces. He sleeps heavily for a few hours at a time and wakes at random moments to jump up out of his bed and write some tune or other that had come to him in the night from a lifetime's entanglements. In one such hour, he recalls the tune from Rome, on Christmas day in Popolo, and he plays it softly on the keyboard, not wishing to wake Peter, the lively skipping tune now a stately pavane. Another night, he springs up covered in sweat, dreaming that he was back in the Cardinal's palace, out on the loggia, on a moonlight evening, leaning down to listen to Luca whispering something urgent in his ear, his deep voice bathing him like a warm stream of pleasure. He wakes up, wondering how he had remembered all these years later, that Luca was smaller than he and had a deep voice surprising in one so slight and youthful-looking. He could not recall his face or even his body but, for a moment, he could hear his voice again. He longs to bathe in the warm stream of that voice, that deep caressing sound, and wonders yet again why he had hurried away so quickly from him.

During this time, he forces himself to keep all thoughts of money and of business to a minimum, only opening letters before his evening jaunts, walking off the worries, keeping his house free from sleep-troubling anxiety. One day in early September, a letter comes from his brother-in-law in Halle, telling the triumphant news of his youngest niece's betrothal to a worthy local doctor. For hours, he paces the Strand, calculating the cost of the rich gift that would be expected. In the end, he instructs Peter to take the silver statue of Orpheus that the Cardinal had presented him from its plinth in the music room and bargain for a fine gold watch and a diamond brooch at the King's jewellers. His sister's last child, his link with the future. Dorothea was dead now for over twenty years, but he could still recall the feel of her warm hand in his leading him to his first day in school. On her grave they had written – 'I Know That My Redeemer Liveth'. The last gift from Rome, the last memory that he had been young and handsome, and that a kind and powerful man was besotted with him and had laid his heart under his feet. The newspapers all report that the Cardinal is about to be elected Pope in the upcoming conclave and so the loss of the gift is even stronger. Still, he owed his dear sister this much.

Letters too come from Lord Burlington, demands for a visit to Ireland, where his wife, Lady Dorothy, has been sent in disgrace, to arrange the marriage of their daughter Charlotte, and another from the Princess of Orange, hinting at the desirability of a new set of sonatas as a gift.

He is afraid to stop, and wonders at the ferocity of his composing.

The fact was that he had lost his nerve. In all the years since getting away from home, from Italy to Hanover and then London, he had never paused or doubted, as he climbed higher, jumped from stone to higher stone. Grand Duke, Electors, Princess Royal, all thirsty for the music he could conjure up for them, and their money kept pouring in. And then the palsy struck him down and overnight he was over fifty, with his money trickling away. As the money went, so did his courage.

A day comes when the last sheets of Jennens' bundle are gone and the full score ready on the polished table and never did he loathe a work of his more. To be polite, he sends a nicely bound copy of the score to Jennens and writes that, when he was composing, 'I did think I did see all heaven before me and the Great God too', but that was a lie. The truth was that he saw hell beneath, the fall into poverty and failure and oblivion. In the mornings, as he wrote, time and again, the peaceful streets of his home town came to him as in a vision, the neat houses, the pretty trees, the long afternoons of summer, and it filled him with horror. He would die old and unknown and poor in Halle. And so he worked like a fury at music he no longer believed in, day after day forcing himself to his desk and to the keyboard. It was like the knife that his father had extracted from the boy's throat, but piece by piece, cut out of his own heart and his life's blood and it seemed to him that the writing of this music might possibly kill him.

Coming home along Brook Street one warm evening in late August, Georg sees a familiar carriage waiting outside his house. Melusine. His heart sinks. Since the death of Elector Georg nearly fifteen years ago, Melusine had grown increasingly withdrawn, shut away in her immense new villa out in Twickenham. London gossip had it that she had recently adopted a tame raven as companion, believing it to be the Elector, returning to fulfil a deathbed promise to tell her what lay beyond death.

Peter is hovering by the door as he enters.

'The Duchess of Kendal is here. She is in the music room.'

'So I observe,' he snaps.

'I could not stop her. She insisted.'

Georg brushes past him and begins to make his way heavily up the stairs and then slows down as he reaches the landing. He can hear music being softly played through the open door of the rehearsal room. He stands in the threshold, watching his visitor sitting at his large harpsichord, quietly playing one of his arias. 'V'adoro Pupille.' *Giulio Cesare.* One of his most popular operas from over fifteen years ago. On the first night at the King's Theatre, she and Elector Georg had come to honour him. A glittering moment of triumph for Melusine, for all London whispered that the Elector had finally married her, in the wake of his imprisoned wife's recent death. She, Melusine, was now rumoured to be the secret Queen of England and she looked every inch the part in jewels and ermine that night as she applauded Senesino and Cuzzoni and threw a bouquet to Georg and kissed hands to him from the Royal Box. A lifetime ago. She stops playing and sits there in the full glare of the bright evening light, a look of angry bewilderment on her face. As he watches her, he hopes the story of the tame raven is true and that her crazy fancy brings her some solace. Sensing his presence, she smiles at him. He bows ironically, 'Your Grace', and crosses the room to kiss her hands, thinking, as he does so, that any one of the huge diamond rings on her fingers would solve all his financial anxieties.

He goes to pour her wine and, taking it, she stands up and begins to prowl the room, sipping as she goes. She points at an Italian painting by the window.

'Venice?'

'No, a landscape near Rome.

She notices an empty plinth next to the painting.

'Where is that lovely little statue you had here? The one from Rome?'

Grief had not dimmed Melusine's sharp eye.

'Gone to Halle, as a gift to my niece.'

She turns and sits down and takes a drink of the wine he had poured. The humid August evening is becoming a little fresher and a light, welcome breeze begins to stir through the music room.

'Do you remember that supper in Rome?'

He nods.

'Over thirty years ago.'

She smiles.

'You seemed impossibly young and so confident playing your music for us. The Elector was reluctant to go and hear you, you know. I persuaded him. Some pretty young fancy of the Cardinal, he grunted, and when I saw you in your elegant suit, I was inclined to agree. You were very pretty. But your music, well, that changed his mind. He was determined to steal you from the Cardinal.'

'Or His Holiness, as we soon will call him?'

Melusine shakes her head slowly.

'Not to be, I'm afraid. I've just come from Kensington Palace. Her Majesty had the latest dispatches from Rome. It will be in all the papers tomorrow.'

'Another Pope elected?'

'No, not as yet.'

She pauses and sits down to face him. She sips her wine and looks at him.

'The Cardinal is dead, Georg. I'm sorry to tell you. He took some sort of apoplexy yesterday during the conclave and died there. Now another will be chosen as Pope. Such a pity. Just as he was about to take his place in the sun.'

Georg stands up and walks to the open window, his eyes suddenly full of unexpected tears. Dead. He always believed, somehow, that he would see his former patron once again. Below him, Brook Street had become busy with late evening walkers, the cooling breezes tempting out those who had stayed indoors all during the sultry afternoon. Years ago, in the first flush of his London success, he had sent the Cardinal a bound copy of all his operas, in a richly-embossed velvet case. A polite acknowledgement had come back to him, months later, killing off all desire for further correspondence.

'I thought you should know,' Melusine murmurs, breaking a long silence. 'Rather than read it in the morning newspapers.'

He composes himself and turns back to her.

'You are kind, my dearest Duchess.'

She laughs at this.

'Enough with the talk of Duchess. Who would have guessed, at that supper table in Rome, that we had a King, an almost Pope, a Duchess and a celebrated musician, all in embryo?'

'Not so celebrated these days,' he reminds her.

'Nonsense, you will be in fashion again soon and in the meantime I have some good news for you. A letter.'

She takes it from her pocket and hands it to him.

'My friend the Duke of Devonshire wants you to come to Dublin for the winter season, to enliven his Irish exile. He will fund your travel and you may run a series of concerts to refill your coffers.'

He bows his thanks. Dublin. The final blow to his London career. Melusine, like all the very rich, looks pleased and relieved, having found someone else to rescue her old friend from ruin without parting from a penny of her own. Her tasks completed, she looks around her as if preparing to leave.

'You are lucky, Georg, you have your music. I have nothing to fill my days. You know, I begged the King to return to me, from beyond the grave and tell me what lies ahead and he promised.'

She looks at him, her face unusually frank, looking for an answer from him.

'He was usually a man of his word but, so far, nothing.'

Something in his face betrays him, a smile, and she glances over at him sharply.

'Oh. I see. Tattle about my tame raven has reached even the shuttered walls of Brook Street.'

She smiles but looks a little hurt and he murmurs an apology.

'I wish to God there was a tame raven, even if all London laughed at me. There is nothing, is there, Georg?'

He looks at her, shocked.

'He has not returned to me and that man could do almost anything he set his mind to.'

He wishes she would stop talking. To distract her, he walks over to the harpsichord.

'Shall I play some of the new music?'

She nods, her face fallen into her hand, her head bent downwards.

He takes out the score and begins to play to distract her, arias and choruses from the new oratorio for an hour or more. When the light fails and the August night turns a little colder, the room becomes dark and Peter bustles in to light the candles but, glancing at Melusine, Georg waves him away. Long into the dark night, he keeps playing from memory, the music score dark before him, offering the music to placate the shade of those dead men from that Roman supper. Behind him, Melusine sits still, her head bowed, her hand to her forehead, silent, listening with all of her attention.

# DUBLIN
## November 1741

A knock to the door. He stops writing and tears up the pages of the letter to his dead mother.

'Yes?'

With Peter, he speaks the clear English he has learned to master. Only when he needs to distract or confuse does he conjure up the broad accents of his native land, a trick learned from the late king, Elector George.

'What is it?'

'A note, just come, Sir. Mrs Cibber sends her respects and asks you to wait on her today.'

Susannah. Her sweet ways and the twist of desperation underneath. He reaches into his pocket for a printed card. It has a splash of coffee on its fine engraved surface. It reads 'Mrs Honora Power, Hoey's Court, Dublin. Dressmaker and Importer of Fine Fabrics.'

'Tell them I will call at two this afternoon. She must unpack her London stage robes.'

Peter nods, allows himself a comment.

'If Madame's thieving husband has left any behind.'

He ignores this and sweeps on.

'And then bring my card to Lord Mountjoy, at Henrietta Street. Ask if I may call this evening.'

Peter withdraws. He picks up the card again. Good firm paper, professional engraving. Did Peter look at it this morning and wonder? Peter has changed a great deal from the golden youth he had once been but he retained something of that petulance of beauty. He stands up and watches from the window as Peter emerges from the door below into the wet street. The years have worn away much of his interest in Peter but he still likes to watch him, un-observed, as he walks away from whichever house or lodging they find themselves. The hair still retaining some gold, the determined gait, clenched fists, shoulders squared, ready to confront a world that had somehow let him down. The truth was that, despite all his promise, Peter was fortunate to have survived. He could take credit for that survival. Or blame for the narrowing of Peter's life into servanthood.

He looks again at the card of paper. Given to him in a coffee house in Chester. The fourth afternoon, waiting for a favourable wind to allow them to set sail, the urgent desire to get to Ireland. Peter already at their lodgings in Dublin, the scores for the musicians printed and Mountjoy sending polite notes, desiring his immediate presence. A dull afternoon, smoking his pipe in the coffee house, pouring over his music sheets. Someone passing jostles the table and a few drops of coffee scatter on the score in front of him. He looks up in anger. A deep voice, begging pardon, dark eyes and a strong face, a dawning look between them, the language of his eyes urgent and unequivocal. In that swift moment, a calculation made.

'Allow me to fetch a fresh pot.'

Later, names are given in the final moments before parting, his own a pleasant surprise to the younger man.

'This makes you even more interesting to me.'

He says that his name is James Hunter, from Dublin. Travelling for his business. Fabrics and lace. His wife dead these two years in childbed.

'And you?'

'Married to music, as I told His Majesty at Windsor last year.'

Mr James Hunter laughs but it is true. That is what he told the pompous womaniser, young King George, when His Majesty demanded to know why he had never married. Mr Hunter handed over the business card. His sister's address near to Dublin Castle will always find him. Mrs Power, dressmaker.

'I am for Bristol today. When I return to Dublin, come and dine in my house.'

The wind changed that evening and he was soon on the boat for Ireland where he had the leisure to give thanks for this chance encounter, made easier away from Peter's prying, resentful eyes. But, on reflection, he is not so sure. Hunter. Is he the prey? A Jacobite agent, sent to trap and compromise him? He puts the card away and goes up to his room to gather his music.

The hall is clean and prosperous-looking, with a smell of fresh paint. His spirits lift further as he walks towards the stage, pleased to note that the musicians are already in their places. One or two of the men look up at him quizzically but he strides on, and mounts the small wooden steps to the stage and towards the harpsichord. A cloak is strewn across the podium. He stands staring at it until someone hurries up to take it away.

Aware that more and more of the men in the room are watching him, he takes off his cloak, sits down and draws out the sheets of music. When silence has fallen on the room, he turns in his chair towards the musicians. The silence becomes uncomfortable until he nods at the men and gestures towards the keyboard.

'Good morning, gentlemen. As we are all here, we will start with the symphony. Then, if it goes well, we will attempt the pastoral?'

Silence. One or two nod. The rest are immobile and blank-faced. He asks again, a little louder.

'Are you ready?'

A murmur of assent. He glares.

'Good.'

A whisper of paper fills the hall, then a waiting silence and he signals for them to begin. The moment he always dreads. The first sounds of the music in the outside world. They play the slow notes of the opening with a steady pace. And then, with ease, they pick up pace and tackle the lively music with confidence. He begins to feel hopeful. The musicians must be first rate. The soloists are his problem. One soloist in particular. Susannah. These men can play adequately and some of them more than adequately. They finish crisply and he nods his approval curtly and asks them to fetch out the music for the pastoral. In this they excel, playing with discreet elegance, and he allows himself to hope as they play gently through its sweet ripples and dips. It will work, at least this part.

Half way through the piece, a man comes scurrying up the aisle towards him. He frowns at him and the man halts and then moves to sit down meekly. The pastoral meanders on slowly, the tune, the old peasant air he had heard years ago, on Christmas Day in Rome. Played on pipes and flutes by a band of young pilgrims from Abruzzi in the city for the festivities. His first day in Rome and his first sight of Luca. Now, an eternity away, the same music, rendered slow and stately, being played for the glory of the Christ Child in a Dublin music hall. He stands there, long after the musicians have finished playing, seeing nothing but the bright winter light of the Roman square and remembering Luca's hand in his, their stumbling uncertainty, both awkward boys beneath the sleek beards and the fashionable clothes. Someone moves in his chair and the creaking alerts him to the watching men and the uncomfortable silence in the hall. He looks around crossly but recalls his purpose here.

'Excellent, Gentlemen, we shall get on very well together. A short break.'

Muttering breaks the silence of the hall as the men stretch and chat and begin to light up pipes.

Doctor Wynne. He makes his way down the steps, smiling ruefully and holding out his hands. He grasps the man's outstretched hand and folds it into his own, stroking it gently.

'Doctor Wynne, my apologies, we had begun and I was unwilling to risk a break.'

'Not at all, my dear Mr Handel, not at all. Please forgive the interruption. Welcome, welcome indeed. Dublin is very fortunate this season.'

He withdraws his hand to makes an elegant gesture of acceptance. Doctor Wynne is smooth-faced, even boyish, with a kind, wary look. In theatrical matters, it has been his experience that a little wrong footing on the first day always tells him what he needs to know about the men and women he must work with. In this case, he had learned that Doctor Wynne was not easily discommoded and will need watching.

'Tell me, Mr Handel, how may I assist today with your work?'

'You are too kind, Herr Doctor. May I ask, when do the choirs arrive?'

The Doctor assumes a look of regret.

'Just one choir, I am afraid. I have persuaded the Christchurch Choir to attend but Dean Swift is less amenable. He will not allow us the use of the choir of St Patrick's, as is his right, unfortunately.'

One choir. Not enough at all. Too few voices. This work needs a strong chorus; he had written it so, knowing how few singers of note would be desperate enough to forsake London for this backwater. Only poor foolish Susannah, in her hour of disgrace. And it is well known that Dean Swift was in his dotage and beyond all interest in choirs. Perhaps he is being punished for the morning escape? Or held to ransom for more money?

'And do we have a bass?'

'We have, indeed. The excellent Mr Woffington will be available.'

'And one final request and do forgive all these demands. The trumpet?'

Doctor Wynne turns and a tall soldierly man steps forward. Sergeant Wilson.

'May I present Sergeant Wilson to you, Mr Handel?'

They shake hands. A grasp to break all his bones.

'When we resume, we shall rehearse with the trumpet. Now, you shall join me in a coffee. I see my man is here.'

Peter had come clattering in with his heavy tray, incapable of keeping quiet. Doctor Wynne will need to be wooed with cake and coffee.

'Peter, prepare a cup for Dr Wynne.'

He steers the good doctor towards the table where Peter has laid out cups and some cakes. Doctor Wynne takes his with grace and, warmed by the drink, asks in genial tones.

'Will Mrs Cibber sing for us today? I long to hear her. I have seen her on stage and admired her greatly but I never had the chance to hear her sing.'

The good Doctor kept his face bland as he spoke but the question underneath was clear. Few have ever heard Susannah sing.

'No, I'm afraid not. She is still unwell from her travels and ordered by her doctor to rest. I will visit her later and begin work with her.'

'Of course,' nods the good doctor.

He is beginning to be wary of Doctor Wynne's kindly but keen gaze.

'Tell me, how does the opera season progress in London? I had the great pleasure of hearing the divine Senesino perform three years ago and it is no exaggeration to say that I was literally transported by the heavenly sound of his voice. As for the wonderful Faustina…'

As the man droned on, his heart sank. Doctor Wynne was a lover of opera. A misfortune. Then he will be well aware of the sharp decline in popularity for his operas and the failure of his academy and the ruinous descent that has led him to this Dublin season.

'Dr Wynne, may I call on Dean Swift, at some time convenient to him?'

Doctor Wynne made a face of gentle depreciation.

'I'm afraid his health is such that no new visitors can be permitted. I will speak with Dean Swift myself this afternoon.'

Suddenly his patience broke. He stood up abruptly.

'You will excuse me, I must hear this wonderful trumpet before we finish.'

He strode back up to the stage.

'Gentlemen!'

The musicians looked up.

'I thank you for your playing of the pastoral. On reflection, it is not suitable for our purposes and so you will return the music to my man and strike it from our programme.

They nodded, indifferent and a little mystified. The pastoral would not be included. He had plundered everything else, even the Cardinal's silver Orpheus, to survive. This he would not sell. He tapped the lectern with his baton.

'Mr Wilson. "The trumpet shall sound", if you please!'

That first afternoon, Mrs Power was at a loss to place the Englishwoman and she was someone who was rarely at a loss. Clothes whisper to her, telling all the secrets their owners strive to conceal, 'I appear rich but I am near penury, I am desperate, I am gullible, observe my over-elaborate ruffles or my grubby lace cuffs, my stale velvet or my rich, tight-fitting silk and you will see directly into my foolish or impoverished or irredeemably darkened soul.'

But with her, the Englishwoman Susannah, that first afternoon, standing just inside the door of the workshop in the attic and holding her heavy dressing case, something was not quite right. The flowing cloak she wore over her dress looked expensive, made of heavy black wool, smartly trimmed with little buckles down the front and at the wrists, but it refused to give up its secret to Mrs Power. Her arms were too short for the wide sleeves, and there was fresh mud all along the hem yet it would not speak and reveal the soul of this unexpected visitor to her attic in unfashionable Hoey's Court.

The young Englishwoman stayed there in the doorway while Mrs Power waited politely for her to speak. She stood tall, angular, and not beautiful but with an elegant line to her long, thin face, something distinguished about her, despite the strained look around the eyes.

By good fortune, only Jenny was in the workshop that first afternoon, the other two girls out working on fitting Lady Burlington's new silk dress for some dinner that evening in Lord Mountjoy's in Henrietta Street. They would have stared at the Englishwoman but Jenny kept her pock-marked face down and went on with her hemming, discreet, fully aware that no other dressmaking business would have her in the workshop. The room was filled with unexpected bright pale November sunshine slanting through the large windows, and she and Jenny stayed silent for a minute. Some cheap flowery perfume belonging to one of the other girls filled the stale air of the attic room. Then the Englishwoman spoke.

'Mrs Power?'

She sounded like a lady. That was better. More likely to pay.

'Yes, Ma'am. How may I help you today?'

Instead of replying, the Englishwoman dropped her case with a thump, turned and called back down the stairs, her voice surprisingly loud.

'Georg. We are up here.'

A large gentleman came into view behind her, a little red-faced, and so Mrs Power arose from the table, signaling to Jenny to remain where she was. The Englishwoman made to take his arm but instead the large man pushed past her, dabbing under his hat with a handkerchief and lurched forward to throw himself on the sofa.

'Forgive me, Madam, What a climb! Susannah, you walk too fast. I will lie here and expire.'

A foreign gentleman. Dutch? Over fifty and still handsome, despite the falling into flesh. His clothes were much easier to read than hers. Well-cut and expensive, at least five years out of fashion, excellent tailoring on the faded coat. His shirt clean but a little frayed at the cuffs. An abundance of money, but now it had fled. He sat there, taking in the shabby, neat room, the dingy cutting table, the November sun glistening on his bald head, his glances around her place of business a little too measuring for Mrs Power's comfort. Not her father or husband, Mrs Power decided. Too much unguarded affection in her gaze and not enough intensity. They both seemed happy enough to spend all day smiling around them and so Mrs Power felt prompted to ask again, 'And how may I assist today, Madam?'

The Englishwoman smiled apologetically and turned to pick up her dressing case.

'My robes need some renewal and repair, a little like myself, and I was hoping that you could resurrect something from this motley collection.'

She opened the case and began to drag out what seemed an unending bale of green velvet. When it finally emerged, it turned out to be a full length court gown and she held it up against herself. It was a fright to behold.

'As you can see, it is a little out of fashion.'

It was indeed. Even Jenny, glancing up from her stitching, could not help her look of disbelief. An old-fashioned Mantua, dark green velvet, so dark that its folds looked as if they had been painted with black. A skillful copy of a gown from Versailles, some thirty years ago, like a costume from some theatrical entertainment. Theatre. That was it. Something about her

153

clothes had set a niggling doubt in Mrs Power's mind but now she was sure. These were theatre clothes, well-made, good durable materials but over-elaborate and showy in design, meant to please the eyes of an assembled crowd. Theatre. Optimism about money faded.

'A monstrosity, as you can see but I have few options.' The Englishwoman sighed.

'Can it be altered and rescued?'

Mrs Power frowned.

'I can but try, Mistress...?' She paused, waiting for a name.

The foreign gentleman, who had been watching all with half-opened eyes, his hands clasped over his high belly, jumped up and caught hold of the Mantua.

'What a horror, my dear girl! Is that all the despised Theo left?'

He grabbed it from her and bunched it up in front of him to see what it looked like and then shook it out, gesturing to her to take hold of it and spread it out. Mrs Power couldn't resist smiling at his antics, designed to distract.

'Is this at all possible, my good Mrs Power, can we prevail on you to turn this nightmare into a dream in green velvet, fit to appear before the Duke?'

'As I said, Sir, we can try. It may need to be cut down. If Madame would like to go with Jenny, we can have a fitting now?'

'Forgive me, please call me Susannah, and can I call you ...'

'Maria,' Mrs Power told her.

Jenny crossed the room and held open the door to the little side room, standing politely to one side. With a nervous sideways look at her pitted face, the Englishwoman allowed herself to be led into the dressing room.

The gentleman watched them leave and then turned to Mrs Power, his tone noticeably sharper.

'You see what a sorry antique this garment is. Can you make it into a suitable robe for a performance next month, a performance of sacred music? Can we set a figure now?'

She thought quickly. 'I need to see the gown on Madam Susannah first but usually such extensive work would cost around three guineas.'

He nodded. 'The bill for your work will be sent to my house on Abbey Street, to my servant Mr Peter Le Blond.'

She wrote down the address and then waited. He had more to say. She wasn't going to help him say it.

'You were recommended by a business gentleman I encountered on my travels, a relative, I believe, a Mr…'

He fished in his pocket for a card but Mrs Power knew a charade when she saw one. James. So that was the lie of the land. This gentleman was no protector of the Englishwoman, whatever else he was. He takes out the card.

'Mr Hunter. Your brother-in-law, I believe?'

She tormented him slightly, taking some time to recall.

Her face cleared, 'James, yes indeed, my dear sister's husband.'

He looked puzzled.

'My departed sister, I should say, bless her soul. Dead now these three years and her baby dead of smallpox the following spring.'

'Mr Hunter said you are a business woman of great discretion.'

She nodded, wondering exactly what she would be asked to stay quiet about. If he was prepared to pay properly, she wouldn't object. Her business was no longer fashionable, mouldering away in the attics of Hoey's Court.

'And our dear Susannah has been unwell as a result . . . of so much public odium.'

'Indeed?'

'Yes, I've known her since she was a young girl and she is as honest and as true as you or I.'

They both smile at this.

'But that devil of a husband of hers. Ach, a terrible devil, Theo. Theo Cibber.'

He finally drops the name. Cibber? The story began to come back to her. That Drury Lane actress, caught up in some court case with the husband suing the lover for money or her earnings or some such grubby transactions. Now here she was, in her changing room. She coloured. Had her stock fallen so low that she must sew the hem of the sweepings of the London stage? It seemed that it had.

'Shall we say four guineas for the dressmaking, Mrs Power?'

'I'm not sure if I have the time . . .'

'Then five. I'm sure I can rely on you.'

He turns as Susannah sweeps back into the room in her trailing gown, Jenny catching up the clumsy train, like her attendant lady in waiting.

'You look majestic, my dear.'

'I look like a frump, you mean. Rescue me, Mrs Power.'

If anything, the gown now looked infinitely worse on her. It had been made for someone smaller and even slighter, and the outmoded train dragged from her tall, thin body like the wet bedraggled greenery from a pond, while the dress itself clung to her thin body with embarrassing clarity. For a slender creature, her belly looked a little swollen. Recent childbirth was Mrs Power's guess, her small breasts looking unnaturally full.

'We will do our best, Madame.'

A touch of frost, which the Englishwoman is quick to notice and she colours slightly. The accursed name has been spoken and her polluted past revealed.

The foreign gentleman makes an impatient bow to them.

'I must go, ladies. Susannah, I will be in the music hall in Fishamble Street so walk around and join me when you are finished. We must begin rehearsal this afternoon.'

As if it is an afterthought, he takes out a card and an envelope and hands it to Mrs Power.

'I leave you a note for Mr Hunter. My address, to be forwarded. I promised him some tickets for our new musical work.'

She takes it but cannot resist a little torture, putting it down carelessly on the work table among the shards of silk, and then picking it up again.

'My silly head. Now I will leave it here on my mantelpiece or it will be forgotten. Forgive an empty-headed woman.'

He charges out the door and she turns again to the dress and walks around the Englishwoman, gesturing to her to hold out the skirts, pulling the nasty old train back to its fullest extent.

'Jenny, get my large shears, we can take velvet from the train and use it to let out the bust and waist.' She looks pointedly at the distended stomach, and taking hold of the dress, spreads out the skirts as wide as she can. When she takes out the shears from Jenny, the Englishwoman flinches.

'Hold still, Madame. These blades are sharp.'

She begins hacking at the voluminous train, relieved to find the cloth solid and not too worn, throwing large swards of stuffy green velvet in Jenny's direction, finding some fresher materials hidden under the skirts, while the Englishwoman stands there, accepting the silence for the punishment it was.

'So Ma'am, when will you need the robe?'

'We will be performing next month.'

Another pause as she rips at the ends of the train, hunting for spare velvet.

'May I ask you, Mrs Power, can you recommend a nearby parish church? I promised my dear mother that I would attend mass regularly while I was here and I cannot find one.'

Another mistake. Mrs Power draws herself up. Trying to make common ground with mealy-mouthed talk about churches. Not just a Drury Lane strumpet, but a popish one at that.

'I'm afraid I cannot be of assistance, Madame, St Werburg's church around the corner is my own parish church.'

Jenny, to Mrs Power's surprise, mumbles something in her soft voice about her own church, Adam and Eve on the Quay, a blush spreading unpleasantly over the pits on her face. Momentarily sorry for her discomfort, Mrs Power orders her into the storeroom to fetch some linen strips to pin under the skirts.

As soon as she is gone, the Englishwoman whispers.

'Is smallpox prevalent in Dublin at the moment, Mrs Power? The girl…her face?'

She keeps her eye on the door and her voice low, not to offend the girl and Mrs Power likes her a little better for it. But not enough to wish to reassure her.

'I'm afraid it is, Mistress Cibber. Last spring my poor sister and her baby were taken from us within three days and poor James was desolate, as we all were. But time moves on and we have hopes of a new marriage for him soon with a nice young lady from Celbridge.'

The young woman looks frightened. And takes the civil answer as permission to start talking.

'I have a small child, a baby…,' she goes on.

Mrs Power stares at her grimly, without a word.

'And I am concerned to protect her from illness. She is all I have, my other two angels were taken from me. She is called Maria, like you. I took it as a good omen. She is here with her father. I never knew there were such good men like him in the world.'

Mrs Power wishes she would stop talking, drawing her in, making her complicit. Was she simple-minded or merely without shame? She stares at her but the Englishwoman seems unconcerned.

Luckily Jenny returns with the linen and they continue pinning up the dress, but, as if the conversation had never stopped, she asks, 'And you, Mrs Power, do you have children?'

Before she can stop herself, she tells the truth.

'A son. He died, at four weeks. So many years ago now.'

Mrs Power looks around, wondering what made her say that which had never been said in that room. Her life, her girlhood, so many years ago, or so it seemed.

Jenny looks startled but then resumes her pinning.

Having said it out loud, she hears the words hang on the stale air of the attic workroom, words she has never spoken here before. Mrs Power waits. Something more must be said. The Englishwoman sighs.

'Such a sad, sad time.'

It is not clear whose time is sad but Mrs Power has had enough of her disturbing talk.

'That will do, Jenny, we have sufficient velvet to rescue the gown. If you would like to change again, Madam, we will detain you no further.'

The Englishwoman smiles, as if this confidential talk has made them friends, and drags herself and her despoiled gown back into the other room, Jenny trailing behind her like a faithful puppy. The door is closed but Mrs Power wanders over and pushes it half open again, making her way back to her work table.

At the same time, she can hear Abigail and Lucy chattering and bustling as they run up the stairs, full of the excitement of their excursion to Lady Burlington and her daughter. They burst into the room, and immediately Mrs Power puts up her hand to quell them. They tear off their hats and cloaks in silence and Abigail, the senior, scurries over to Mrs Power to deliver her account book.

She opens it.

'Hm, three pounds for the silk and another pound for Lady Charlotte's fur cloak? For once, her ladyship is prompt with her payments.'

She puts out her hand and Abigail hands over the notes.

'And did she give you two anything?'

'Yes,' babbles Lucy, the younger, less cautious, her own secret favourite. 'A shilling each and a cup of chocolate and all the latest London gossip. It seems Lady Charlotte is to be married to some duke or other, the Duke of Hartington, wherever that is?'

'No, she is to be married to Lord Hartington, the heir of the Duke of Devonshire, you goose,' interrupted Abigail, who took a keen interest in the peerage.

'Wait, wasn't that Lord Euston, her ladyship's own beau, the young man she was . . .'

'Such nonsense,' Mrs Power cuts her off, filling out some numbers into her ledger, but listens nevertheless, unwilling to stem the brook of Lucy's unguarded babblings.

'And that Mrs Cibber is hidden here in town. Lady Burlington told us. You know, the famous actress, the one that was in all the newspapers last year.'

'It is pronounced Kibber, like Kipper', interjects Abigail, 'and Lady Burlington says that she is to sing some holy music, even though she is a known strumpet and is hiding in Dublin to get away from her husband, who sold her to a man for 100 pounds. And he forced her into the man's bed at gunpoint. She has a bastard child with her and her husband is on the hunt for her.'

'I love going to visit Lady Burlington,' Lucy said, dreamily, 'the chocolate and all the London news, it is like heaven there.'

Mrs Power considers hushing her, but she keeps quiet. The inner door opens wide and Jenny comes out, frowning at the other two girls, who are startled into silence at her unusual impertinence. The Englishwoman follows after a short pause.

'Here it is, Mrs Power. I've given Jenny my address. She will deliver it next Sunday when she calls to bring us to mass in Adam and Eve's.'

Jenny bobs a curtsy.

'Yes Ma'am, I'll be there at noon on Sunday.'

Which is the most the other girls have ever heard her say and they look on open-mouthed.

As she leaves, the Englishwoman pauses, turns to Abigail.

'In fact, my dear, the sum involved was 500 pounds, more than I've ever earned on the London stage, and the bargain was mine. I do wish such fortune comes your way, too...someday.'

At eight o'clock precisely, he alights from the carriage and watches Peter knock at the door of Mountjoy's house in Henrietta Street. Although it is a few streets away from his lodgings, and a mild evening, he decided not to risk mud on his boots by walking. Settling his hat, he hears barking from a window above him and glances up. A woman laughs at his surprised face and he sees her face bobbing out and barking at him again. He bows. It is Lady Dorothy. He waves cheerily, his heart sinking. He sends Peter away and bustles into the opening door of the warm house, welcome after the damp air of the street, and up the wide stairs, a footman leading the way. Lady Dorothy. He had heard that she was visiting Dublin but it never occurred to him that she would be present. The Mountjoys were hardly of her set.

At the turn of the stairs, he sees her standing with her back to him on the landing above, looking into a long mirror and he stops. When she turns and notices him hesitating, he hurries up the last few steps to kiss her hand.

'Georg, what a pleasure. Charlotte and I have been staying here for the last few days and we have a feast planned to welcome you to Ireland. We know how you love your food.'

Her voice, low and pleasing, and her eyes ringed with dark shadow, she is dressed in soft red silk, with deep red rubies gripped by thin silver clasps worn at her throat and in her hair.

She offers her arm and he walks her through into the dining room where Mountjoy stands just inside the door.

'Welcome to you, Georg. Our table is now nearly complete.'

They shake hands and, glancing quickly over his host's shoulder, he casts an eye around the large room. Varieties of red everywhere, the rich crimson carpet, the patterned velvet curtains, even some of the hothouse roses at the centre of the long table. Lady Dorothy laughs as she glances down at her dress.

'My lord, I am dressed to melt into the floor. Should I change?'

Mountjoy is determined not to be wrong-footed and tells her she completes the room, and then moves quickly past her to welcome another guest.

Looking pleased to see someone he knows, Doctor Wynne nods at him as he enters the room but Lady Dorothy puts her hand on his arm.

'You must sit with me during dinner, Georg, I want to hear all about this new work and your friend Mr Jennens just sent me all the gossip from London.'

It is news to him and unwelcome news that Jennens is a friend and has written to her from London but, before he can respond, she calls out, 'Charlotte'. He turns and sees Dorothy's young daughter standing at the other side of the room, hiding behind Lady Mountjoy. Charlotte is wearing a red silk evening gown, a replica of her mother's and looks over nervously at him. Lady Mountjoy also catches his eye, smiles at him but turns back to her companions, a young gentleman and a boy, listening while the young boy, bright-eyed and confident, talks and the man smiles on approvingly. At this summons from her mother, Charlotte moves unwillingly from her hiding place and stands behind her. He looks at her, her face, broad and handsome like her father's but somehow too big for her thin body, her eyes already marked with the same dark shadowing as her mother. He remembered the day that Charlotte was born and her father Burlington's delight. At last a healthy child, he told everyone, after all the stillbirths and one sickly elder girl. Surely sons would now follow to inherit his riches. They never did.

Charlotte is too shy to speak when he asks how she likes Dublin, but she is relieved to see a familiar face. This is Charlotte's first time to be allowed to sit at dinner in the evening, her first time to wear a silk gown like her mother, her first time in Ireland and all of these novelties keep her silent. When dinner is announced, her mother gestures her towards the table. She curtseys to Lady Mountjoy as she was taught and crosses the room to sit, enraptured by the beauty of the gown, its softness against her arms, and the whispering sound of the full skirts when she moves. Charlotte wishes the girl Lucy, the dressmaker, could see her now. She wonders where Lucy lives and if she might meet her one day on the street. Then Charlotte would invite her to come back and have more chocolate and tell her all about the man, the Duke's son, the one she is to marry in six years' time when she will be of age. Lucy's French scent, she told Charlotte, was called 'Fleurette' and it was the most delicious she had ever known. But her mother comes over with the German man, Papa's conductor, and insists that he sit between them at dinner. When Mamma takes her seat, then the others begin to move to the table, the young boy escorting Lady Mountjoy to table with a confidence that she envies.

When everyone else is seated, Lord Mountjoy takes the head of the table and booms out the names, and each person has to smile and nod and Charlotte tries to remember each name as Mamma ordered her to. The polite-looking Irish gentleman is called Doctor Wynne, and he bows to the table, then Lord Mountjoy calls the German conductor, 'Our Celebrated Maestro, Signor Giorgio', and everyone titters with cheerful agreement and then, with a flourish, he calls her and Mamma, the two goddesses of the red room, Goddess Dorothy and Goddess Charlotte, which she likes, but she can see that Mamma is annoyed. The father and son are called Mr Wellesley senior and junior, and the pretty lady in the white silk gown is Mrs Wellesley, wife to one and proud mother to the boy and he finishes by saying, 'you all know my good lady and myself and now I must eat,' and everyone laughs politely as he sits down with a thump.

It has been Georg's observation that, at every table, where a person of great influence is present, the attention of all the others is always fixed on the conversation or the behaviour of that person, covertly watching even as they eat or chat to one another or sit silently pondering their own affairs. He has sometimes been that person, particularly in the days of his fame, when singers and musicians courted him for a place in his theatre and, of course, royalty has always taken that role, Elector George, a plain and shrewd man, as much as any, the Cardinal of course, but tonight it is Lady Dorothy that all at table observe.

Charlotte notices that Lord Mountjoy turns quickly to Mrs Wellesley at his side, and so instead Mamma begins talking to the conductor and asking him about the music that Papa has commissioned from him. When the food arrives, Mamma laughs every time the conductor takes another slice of meat, or helps himself to some other dish, and tells him, 'Georg, you have had enough, you are too greedy', which the man dislikes but must smile at. Mamma has warned her, she will play the flute after dinner. The Duke of Devonshire will be calling in and the young boy across at the table will play the violin and so she must be prepared to perform. She knows that her flute playing is poor, much poorer than her singing, which she loves. Papa has asked her to surprise Mamma tonight by singing one of the German conductor's songs. She wishes Lucy could hear her sing, Lucy, who told her that she adores the theatre and wishes she could see the famous Mrs Cibber, who is the toast of the London stage. Charlotte has been lost in admiration for the sheen of the crimson silk on her forearms but when Mamma mentions Mrs Cibber, she begins to pay attention to the talk around her.

'Now Georg, tell me, you know the family, her own name was …?'

'Arne,' says the conductor, sharply, his mouth full of roast goose.

'Arne? Is she related to Thomas Arne, the composer?'

'Her brother. Susannah has been my pupil for over ten years now and the best I have ever had.'

'Good,' she nods, putting down her fork, her food untouched.

'I wanted to ask you about these terrible rumours, and you are the best person to ask, I find.'

She raises her voice again and, as she does so, the whole table begins to listen. Someone once told him that Lady Dorothy was in some way a descendant of Anne Boleyn. He often wondered if her predecessor's ghastly fate ever gave her pause for thought or checked her tongue. Evidently not, he sighed, as she continued with her story.

'Is it true that her abomination of a husband sent her at gunpoint into her lover's bed?'

Doctor Wynne stops eating, listening closely from the other side of the table. He is flattered to be so near a countess and cannot believe his good fortune to be so close to London gossip as dramatic as this but he glances at the children and wonders if this was a suitable topic for the table. Why was he here? Georg wonders, and that nice Wellesley family. Not Lady Dorothy's usual hunting ground? Curiosity winning out, Doctor Wynne overcomes his scruples to venture a question.

'My lady, was this the court case we were all reading about last year?'

So he knew all about Susannah this morning, Georg thought.

Lady Dorothy looks sweetly at Doctor Wynne and the man visibly purrs.

Purr not, Georg thought, you may be next for discomfort.

'Yes, but Georg knows the real story, don't you?'

As she continues to look at him for further elucidation, he puts down his fork and faces her.

'Theo Cibber is a dangerous man, and Susannah is fortunate to have escaped him.'

Lady Dorothy now has the attention of the table and is intent on the pursuit of her story.

'They say that La Belle Susannah was playing Desdemona one night in Drury Lane and a wealthy man saw her and fell in love there and then. He went to her husband with a great sum of money, and the bargain was sealed. Of course, it all went wrong when she ran away with the wealthy lover, and then her husband had to try and steal her back!'

She laughs and looks around the table.

'As good as one of your operas, Georg? And now Susannah has her lover and her by-child hidden away in Dublin.'

He marvels at her uncanny ability to know so much unpleasantness. Does she bribe her servants or pay men to spy for her? As she talks on, he watches her, the table now silent before her tale. Lady Dorothy was a woman who always seemed to be on the brink of nervous exhaustion, her blue eyes underscored with dark shadow and yet he felt sure she would live to be a nervous octogenarian, long after he had been buried from the travails of fending her off. He takes some more wine and thinks, Lord Burlington, the Apollo of the Arts, as he is called, and a generous man to his musicians and painters. Lord Burlington had been kind to him when he first came to London and long may he enjoy vast wealth and build beautiful houses to his heart's content but the hell of family suppers can only be imagined. Sometimes, listening to her voice, which rarely moved above a gentle whisper, he imagines that a spurt of her blood would hiss and sink through the fine mahogany in front of them.

In an attempt to distract her, Lady Mountjoy asks some question about her silk dress, and while they chat about such fripperies, he looks around the room, admiring the strong crimson drapes, the dull glow of the silver in the candle light, the faces of the others made gentle and soft by the candlelight, the children's clear eyes watching their elders with curiosity. He finds himself thinking, 'Luca could paint such a room with pleasure, the backdrop of darkened walls, the soft blood red velvet curtains, the handsome faces.' Why does he thinks of Luca and about his life long ago in Rome these days? Perhaps because the newspapers are full of speculation about the recent papal elections. The Cardinal was almost elected Pope, his moment arrived at last. He wondered at the twists and turns of a world where, in a time now unimaginable, a time when he was young, the Cardinal, a powerful and good man once loved him. He drinks some more wine, and begins to listen again. Dorothy, having exhausted the neutral ground of fashion with Lady Mountjoy, turns her attention back to Doctor Wynne.

'Are you the doctor who takes care of the famous Dean Swift?'

Doctor Wynne smiles and nods.

'Have you met the Dean, my lady?'

She shakes her head curtly but Georg knows that she has. It is one of her husband's favourite stories. Once Burlington invited Swift to his London house but omitted to enlighten his wife, Lady Dorothy, as to the identity of this voluble cleric in the rusty black cassock and so when Swift, with his accustomed confidence, commanded her to sing for him, she glared at him and stalked out of the room, not knowing whom she had snubbed. To her credit, when enlightened, she returned and gave her apologies and sang but Georg always felt that the story reflected least well on Burlington, who always relished the telling of it as a great joke. He watched as she toyed with her food and then put her knife down.

'Yes, someone told me, I forget who,' Dorothy continues, 'that the same Dean Swift just last Sunday attacked one of his curates. Or I may be mistaken, did the curate attack the Dean in a drunken fit and beat him with his wig?'

She laughs, as if it was a merry tale.

'Now, tell me, was it you? Did you topple our Gulliver?'

Doctor Wynne is shocked into blurting out.

'But it was Dr Wilson...' and then he stops as he notices Mr Wellesley listening with great interest.

Mountjoy, scenting danger, makes to speak but before he does, young Mrs Wellesley cuts across him, gently but firmly.

'I have not seen the Dean since he has fallen into bad health but he was a great friend of my late father's, and very kind to my dear Mamma and to us all.'

Lady Dorothy turns a look of surprise in her direction but smiles and nods, as if they were both gossiping in the same malicious vein.

'I can believe that. He had two wives, or so I am told, and one was his secret sister, a Mrs Johnston.'

Mrs Wellesley also nods as if agreeing, but continues in her gentle way.

'Yes, Mrs Johnston was also a dear friend to us, his Stella, as he always called her, and she was kind and true, as I was fortunate to know for myself. When his Stella died, the Dean put a lock of her hair into an envelope, wrote something on it, and has kept it always by him at his desk.'

The room falls silent. She is a quietly-spoken woman, her fair hair in girlish curls, her white dress equally youthful but she has a quiet authority, determined to maintain her tone.

'My father once saw that envelope on the Dean's desk, and summoned up the courage to ask what was written on it. It said, "Only a woman's hair."'

She pauses and picks up a piece of marzipan from a pewter dish, and then puts it down on her plate, knowing the whole room was waiting.

'When I was younger, I thought, what a harsh thing to write, as if the lock of hair from our dear Mrs Johnston was as nothing. Now that I am a wise old married woman and I have lost my own little girl, I know what he meant.'

She paused and reaches over to stroke her son's dark curls.

'It was only a woman's hair, and it is a marvel that so slight a thing could carry a world of longing in its few precious strands.'

There is a silence, and before Lady Dorothy speaks again, Georg finds himself saying, somewhat to his surprise,

'Once in Rome, a million years ago when I was young and had a full head of hair, someone told me that the first sight of my golden hair was like a glimmer of sun in the dawn of heaven.'

He rubs his shaven head under his wig and they all laugh, Charlotte finding it impossible to imagine the German conductor with any hair, let alone golden.

'And who was that, Signor Giorgio?' asked Mountjoy, hoping for some ribald talk, 'some beauteous diva from Rome, the divine Vittoria perhaps?'

Georg winks at him but remains silent. It was actually said to him by a man who was nearly made Pope, he thought to himself, but not for worlds would he tell anyone here.

Lady Mountjoy chooses this moment to rise and signal to her husband and all the guests prepare to leave table. With an unpleasant sensation of dizziness beginning just over his eyes, he sits down again abruptly and pretends to fuss with his boots. He has a curious sensation. It is as if suddenly the vast foundations beneath Mountjoy's grand house have revealed themselves under the crimson carpet and he is sitting precariously on the brink of a great yawning pit, about to topple in. A tingle along his arm warns him to close his eyes. Fortunately, the fragrance of coffee comes drifting in from the next room and the room quickly empties. As he braces himself to stand, the others are already proceeding out the door and so he remains sitting, his eyes firmly closed in the emptying room.

To cool his head, he tears off his wig and splashes some water from a jug on his face. It is tepid, warmed by the many candles but already the dizziness had slowed down and he gets up slowly and moves towards the curtained window, trailing his wig in his hand. He pushes open the heavy velvet to press his head against the cold glass of the windowpane, and as he does, his face looms up before him, the candle light transforming him into a twisted old gargoyle, his face dark and deeply furrowed in the distorted pane. Is that how he truly looks? He notices that the hasp on the window is unfastened and pulls the window open, stooping down to breathe in the damp night air. Below, three floors down, the kitchen garden is shrouded in mist, like a fetid graveyard. He imagines Lady Dorothy falling through the air and landing with a thump on the rotten cabbage stalks below.

Behind him, some of the servants have returned to clear the table and so he stands up and makes his way slowly into the other room. A harpsichord has been set up and, as he enters, the young boy is preparing to play while Mountjoy beams at him. Mrs Wellesley is doing duty by the coffee. He walks over to her.

'Your boy, he will play?' Georg asks as she pours him a cup and she smiles and nods.

'Oh yes, our hosts are kind enough to allow him to play tonight. Please do not feel you must praise the child, we know his limitations.'

He smiles, 'I promise that I will not.'

She glances at him with amusement, and tells him that she believes him and he drains his cup.

'Tell me, Mrs Wellesley, do you think I may visit Dean Swift?'

She frowned.

'I'm afraid I cannot help you, I have not spoken with the Dean since my father's death last year. When I saw him in St Patrick's last Easter, he looked very ill and I dared not approach him.'

Lady Dorothy, who had left the room, now re-enters holding some music while Charlotte follows carrying a flute.

'Has the Duke arrived? Will our little concert begin?'

They all look at Mountjoy, who looks sheepish.

'Yes, indeed, the Duke has promised to call in after dinner for an hour, on his way back from Dublin Castle.'

So that's why he was here. Lady Dorothy was intent on enforcing the engagement between the Duke's son and Charlotte and this evening was to make her look better as a musician, to help in the transaction. To cover, Mountjoy claps his hands and announces:

'Our two latest discoveries, first Master Garrett Wellesley and then Goddess Charlotte will play the music of Maestro Giorgio.'

The boy moves forward, throws a look at his mother and she hurries to sit at the harpsichord while all the adults turn their chairs towards them. Georg sits and watches as the boy opens with the andante from his own violin sonata. His playing is slow, confident, his face a little flushed but already making his presence felt with a few quick flourishes, taking the music as quickly as he dared. He pauses before the allegro, meeting all eyes but Georg's and now he knows that the boy is playing this for him. His mother accompanies him, watching him a little anxiously as he unfolds the next movement with an increasing vigour. When it comes to the final allegro, the boy is now in his stride, and it is with regret that Georg realises that he is finishing. As they all applaud politely, Georg catches his mother's eye and nods once, and she smiles back at him, a smile like the sun appearing on a December afternoon.

Lady Dorothy, seated in front, turns back towards him and gives him a curt nod towards the harpsichord and he makes his way over to the instrument. It is one of his own compositions again, the sonata for flute and, he fears, somewhat beyond Charlotte's capabilities. She comes dutifully forward with her flute and her dress appears even odder as she stands in front of the harpsichord, her pale face overwhelmed by the red of the dress, her short hair boyish and unflattering. She begins and is as competent as a good teacher can make her, but, as they play on and reach the livelier section, he struggles to moderate his tempo to make Charlotte seem less plodding and to contain her wayward playing, her uneven pauses and her uncertain runs as they labour through the piece. Those listening, he realises, will know the playing for what it is, and he hopes the child will be able to reach the end of this second section, when he will stand up, thank her, kiss her hand and end this as quickly as he can.

Before he can do so, behind him, he hears a door open and although he cannot see him, it is clear that the Duke has entered, as all eyes shift away from the performers and towards this new arrival. As the music ends, Charlotte bows as she has been taught and Georg stands up to begin the applause. To his great satisfaction, the Duke comes straight over to him and shakes his hand.

'My dear Maestro, welcome to Ireland. Thank you so much for honouring us with your presence this season.'

While they talk, Charlotte remains by the music stand, the sheets for the song in her hand and wonders if the concert is over and what should she do about the song. Papa was very insistent that she sing tonight and he will expect a letter from her all about it. The German musician has left the harpsichord and is now all smiles and bowing with the Duke and Mamma is attempting to intervene but the two men keep talking over her and everyone else in the room is hanging on every word the Duke says.

Remembering Papa's strict instructions, Charlotte makes her way to Mrs Wellesley and asks her if she will accompany her. Immediately she agrees and hurries to take her place at the harpsichord, her face a little odd as she realises which song Charlotte plans to sing. Someone told Charlotte that one of the maids is Lucy's cousin and she hopes this girl will hear how well she sang and how everyone applauded and Lucy will wish that she had been there to hear. This made Charlotte determined to proceed.

'So Georg, when will we hear this new work of yours that Jennens tells us about, the new marvel of biblical proportions?'

Georg smiles and prepares to answer when, from behind him, he hears the opening chords of a new piece of music. Someone is about to sing 'Lascia Ch'io Pianga.' He turns and sees that it is Charlotte, her flute dropped carelessly onto the floor, standing in readiness to sing in her red dress. His heart sinks. He has never heard the child sing but if her flute playing is any indication, her musical ability is not strong and this aria needs the full voice of an adult, not the voice of a child.

There is a pause, and then she begins to sing. As if from nowhere, a fully developed voice begins to issue from the child, and a shocked silence falls on the room and they all look at her. Georg moves nearer as the others sink back into their chairs and he listens. This song, heard so many times that he no longer even knows it, now seems new and troubling and presses on his attention. 'Let me weep, my cruel fate and sigh for liberty,' the child pleads and there is something almost unseemly in the fullness of her voice as it issues forth. With all eyes fixed on her, Charlotte feels with satisfaction the rich reverberations of the sounds that she is making and wishes Lucy could hear her as she moves into the second section. She takes a few breaths and allows her voice to open up and get slowly louder as Papa's tutor had taught her.

As the song fills the room, Mrs Wellesley glances up in surprise and pleasure and almost misses her place in the accompaniment. From where he is standing, Georg can see Lady Dorothy's face, and, as the song progresses, she moves forward in her chair, a pained look on her face as she watches Charlotte's performance, oblivious to all around her.

He cannot decide what that look is, it is not quite shock, but Dorothy seems trapped and in some kind of distress as she listens to the voice of an adult, sorrowing woman coming from her own child, decked out in her first silk gown.

Suddenly Georg realises where he has seen this look before. It was nearly fifty years ago. It was the look on his father's face when he was caught in the attic room playing the little spinet that his mother had smuggled into the house. While his mother and his younger sisters cowered behind the door, afraid of the impending violence and braced to throw themselves between them, his father stood there, watching him play, seemingly unable to move. Certain that he would be beaten, Georg remembers playing on defiantly, his fingers running over the keyboard with increasing energy. He finished the piece and turned to see that same strange look come over his father's face. His father was afraid, just as Dorothy is now afraid, afraid of the music issuing from this changeling child. Georg watches Dorothy as Charlotte finishes her song to startled, sincere applause and cheering starting up in the music room and feels more than ever the painful lack of a child to stand between him and death, even at such a cost.

# DUBLIN
## April 1742

At the beginning of April, spring suddenly descends on Dublin, and the grim city Georg had come to hate all during that long raw winter vanishes overnight. Oppressive frowning skies and unrelenting rain now give way to lengthening days of warm spring sunshine, revealing a new city to his unbelieving eyes. This gentle light fills the vast spring sky, drawing out tender new buds and early blossoms on unnoticed trees in the city gardens around his house. At the corner of Abbey Street, a gaunt tree stood like a gallows all winter, jabbing its thin black branches at him as he passed, or so it seemed. Now gradually, the old tree, dead to all intents and purposes, awakens with tiny green shoots, then a great mass of white blossom appears in such profusion that to glance up amongst the boughs is to glimpse a bower of heaven. By mid-April, Dublin has become a wildly beautiful place and he delays his walks home along by the river to delight in this newly remade world. Once or twice, he ventures up to the gates of the Duke's great deer park beyond the river late into the evenings, to watch the sun move slowly down between the tall oaks. On his way home along the banks of the Liffey, gulls scream at him as they swoop down on gusts of warm salty wind in from the Irish Sea, bringing the promise of escape back to London.

All during his Dublin exile, he wondered if the unrelenting drizzle of the Irish winter might kill him. The bright evenings of November soon gave way to the dark gloom of December, each day growing dimmer and shorter as he rehearsed his concerts and prepared his first performance for the Duke. He soon came to dread the walk home from Neal's Music Hall through the dismal narrow streets, where light disappeared much too early and the heavy skies above him seemed to press down low like a vast shroud of wet, begrimed linen. By Christmas the biting frost was nipping at his feet in the mornings as he walked up to Fishamble Street, the sharp breath of the grave. Raining or not, he forced himself to walk for an hour or so in the streets around Dublin Castle in the evenings, petty showers of rain sniping at him and getting under his hat. Then, sitting in his chair before the fire in his lodgings in Abbey Street, his legs and arms ache from the cold that seeps right into his bones. Once Peter showed him a coat left in a cupboard for a few days, grey mould already blossoming on the insides. On some nights, a full moon shining down on the Liffey made the dark waters dance in the icy light, as the lumbering old barges pass him, the shifting and swirling black currents under their bows looking like molten tar to his tired eyes. At night, he found it difficult to sleep with the unending cold in his feet, despite the fire he insisted Peter keep in his room and the warming pan to take the worst of the damp from the sheets. Worse followed when, after Christmas, a sharp chill wind pounced on the city in early January, blowing in from the North, freezing the Liffey and coating the streets with treacherous ice. Strange arctic birds flew in from the North Sea to stare at him from their perch on Elector Georg's statue, patiently waiting for him to slip and fall and then swoop in and peck out his eyes, or so it seemed to him. One day he caught himself shaking a fist at them and muttering that he was not dead yet, much to the amusement of some passers-by on the bridge. 'I am turning into an old mad man,' he decided.

At his concerts, his hands and feet seem never again to thaw out as he plays the harpsichord. The failure of the previous year's harvest in Ireland drives many of the destitute of the countryside into the city and Georg instructs Peter to distribute food to those sleeping in small makeshift huts around Abbey Street and to keep him supplied with small coins for the many families begging on the streets around Dublin Castle. One bleak morning in February, he arrives early at the steps of Neal's Music Hall to find a poor beggar woman lying on the doorstep, frozen to death, her hands cradling her head in a final gesture of despair, and he stands looking down at her, helpless and guilty. As the days crawl by and, one by one, his concerts are performed to full houses, the money he desperately needs begins to flow in and he dreams of his release from his Irish exile. He yearns for the dry air of a London winter and his bed in the warm house on Brook Street, remembering with longing the crisp snowy air of his childhood home in Germany, and he counts the days towards the spring and the ending of his Dublin stay. At all costs, he cannot permit himself any thought of the January sun in Rome, a dream likely to make him howl with grief at this unexpected twist in his life, this downward lurch leaving him stranded here in this sodden, mildewed place. One night in his chilly bed, he dreams of the balcony in his old room in the Cardinal's palace, and it is as if he is standing there again in the early morning with the sun on his face, feeling a warmth right down through his body, penetrating to his chest and filling him with a feeling of bliss. Slowly but with deadly menace, the Roman balcony begins to tilt downwards, and he finds himself sliding down into the murky tar-like chill of what now looks like the Liffey. He wakes with a start, and sits up in the darkness of his Dublin bedroom, cursing everything in this city, afraid of tears of rage welling up behind his curses.

From their first day in Dublin, Peter insists on taking all the London newspapers. Every morning at breakfast he would read out accounts of the season's theatrical triumph until, finally goaded, Georg orders him to stop and banishes the papers from the table. Peter sulks and takes to leaving the papers open here and there about the apartment. Georg can't resist the temptation to read about the resounding successes of his musical rivals. It was the first time in nearly thirty years that Georg had been absent from the London winter season, all his successes now melted away from popular memory like sleet. In all these papers, they chattered endlessly about English opera, his own Roman operas languished neglected, now apparently in the dung heap, each word of praise for his rivals was a further nail in his Dublin coffin.

To add to his problems, Dean Swift was proving increasingly difficult, or so Doctor Wynne reported, calling Neal's Music Hall a 'club for fiddlers' and forbidding his choristers from singing in the first performance of the new oratorio. There has been another rehearsal with the choir of Christchurch and the musicians and, although they were fine singers, the scanty number, less than twenty boys and men, had made the whole oratorio sound feeble and the singing was overwhelmed throughout by the music. Georg called twice to the Deanery in January, each time leaving friendly notes, and presents of snuff, reminding Dr Swift of their one encounter in London years before with Dr Arbuthnot. No response. In late January Georg accepts an invitation from Doctor Wynne to play the beautiful new organ at St Patrick's Cathedral in the hope that the Dean might attend but, the service, although well attended, fails to tempt Dr Swift out of seclusion.

In London, Georg had engaged a young German soprano, Christina Avoglio, to sing at these Dublin subscription concerts. This had cost him a substantial fee, demanded in full in London by Christina's shrewd manager husband, a capable young musician from Naples. Christina herself is a pleasant young woman from Munich, who leaves all the financial decisions to her husband, and her sweet, pleasing voice is well suited to the many roles he assigns her in Dublin that winter. She pleases the Dublin audiences very much and is enjoying all the money from recitals at Lord Mountjoy's musical evenings but she and Susannah have not met so far.

One afternoon in early February, Georg summons them both to a rehearsal in Abbey Street. From the first moments of conversation, it is clear that Christina has never heard of any of the scandals surrounding Susannah, as she is gracious to her and takes her hand without hesitation. To prepare, Georg first asks Christina to sing 'I know that my Redeemer liveth', and it impresses him, her gentle voice filling the small room on Abbey Street and bringing Peter in to listen. Turning to

Susannah, Georg notices a frightened look on her face, and begins to think he has made a mistake. Susannah has been in better spirits since her dangerous husband had been bought off by her lover. That danger averted, Susannah decides to risk the wrath of Dublin public opinion by taking to the stage in January and performs in a comedy for the Duke and the assembled Dublin Castle people. Much to her relief, her performance is received with great acclaim, leaving her in better health and Georg now risks teaching her the new duet. Today, watching her listen to Christina's beautiful voice, he is not so sure about Susannah's return to health, despite her lively smiles and her graciousness to the other woman. It is singularly unfortunate that Christina's voice ripples with youthful strength and an unending reserve of powerful sweetness. There is a grey colour in Susannah's face that unsettles Georg. When Christina finishes 'Rejoice greatly', her energy throughout undaunted, Georg asks the two women to rehearse their duet, 'He shall feed His flock'. They stand side by side, as he begins to play. He has taught Susannah this note by note, to prepare for this rehearsal and is relying on her dramatic skills to carry off the aria. After a brave start, her voice begins to go flat on the lower notes and he realises that he has come to this too soon. As her voice makes a kind of harsh rasping noise on a lower note, Susannah stops and then bursts into tears, tells him between sobs that she has failed him and that he should seek another singer for the performance of *Messiah*. Christina, a good-natured girl, puts her arms around the sobbing Susannah while Georg wonders 'What other singers?' As he also attempts to console Susannah, he tells Peter to bring her down to the dining room for some chocolate and to rest. Later, when he and Christina have completed their work, he calls in to find Susannah being fussed over by Peter, who shoots him a look of reproach for upsetting her. Susannah always did have the knack of drawing the devotion of servants to her.

During the winter, Georg had got into the habit of inviting the young Wellesleys to dine, enjoying their gentle good humour and encouraging their young son to play more of his own music. The following evening, as Peter is clearing away supper, he produces the sheets from his new oratorio and asks Elizabeth Wellesley to sing the first part of 'He shall feed his flock' for him, as he has heard her fine contralto voice. He desperately needs to hear it again, this time from a voice untroubled by ill health and fright.

Elizabeth reads the music, her large grey eyes sparkling.

'May I make a suggestion?'

'You don't want to sing it,' he asks, surprised and disappointed.

'Not at all. Signor Giorgio, I like it very much. But we have a singer here who can sing the second part.'

She turns to her son.

'Garrett?'

She nods to the boy who springs up from his supper plate. She hands him the music and he reads it intently for a few moments, then stands by the harpsichord. Elizabeth begins to sing, her voice deep and strong for such a thin willowy woman. Then, as the key changes, the boy takes over the aria, taking his place without a moment's hesitation, his reading of the music true and clear, like his playing of the violin. His young voice, repeating the slow, stately melody that his mother had sung, resembles hers in tone, opening out the full beauty of the melody. This is a voice he could use. By the end of the first section, he knows that one of his most pressing anxieties has been solved. This music, if properly sung, will succeed, but not with Susannah. Christina shall sing it alone.

'My dear Garrett, will you sing for me tomorrow at rehearsal, I have a shorter piece in mind for you?'

The boy nods happily and his father thanks Georg for his kind indulgence.

'I have no time for kind indulgence when people are paying to hear my music. Now, that is one problem solved. Now for another. Dr Swift? How can I change his mind about his cathedral singers?'

Richard Wellesley frowns.

'But I hear that the doctors examined him last week. It is rumoured that he may be confined to an asylum.'

'The poor man.'

His wife looks shocked.

'Perhaps I could…' the couple glance at each other and the husband nods to the wife.

'Yes?' Georg asks.

Richard speaks with conviction.

'We could call there tomorrow afternoon, after rehearsal and ask after his health. Lizzie, you will come too?'

She nods.

'There is always a welcome for my wife at the Deanery. You will accompany us, Signor Giorgio. I can introduce you to the Dean? '

He nods and thanks them, hoping that his kindness to their child was not seen too directly as an appeal to their aid with the Dean.

Garrett is brought to Fishamble Street the following morning and acquits himself well at the rehearsal, singing his short solo with clear precision and with the same confidence as he had shown in the parlour on the previous night. His solo finished, he sits quietly for the next while listening to the choir and watching the musicians closely with his large serious eyes, grey like his mother's, as they play the overture and then accompany the choir. Promptly at noon, his parents arrive to collect the boy and also to bring Georg to the Deanery. It is, for once, a bright crisp day and Georg proposes that they all walk the short distance down the hill to St Patrick's. As they pass Christchurch Cathedral, Richard advises him.

'We can leave all the questions to Lizzie. She is a long-time favourite of the Dean and of all in the house.'

The boy, released from his long morning's rehearsal, is skittish and full of energy, badgering his mother with a thousand questions and pestering her for food, which she produces from a small basket. His mouth full, he spots a small wagon trotting its way down the hill towards St Patrick's Cathedral and shouts at his mother to watch as he races the horses. In the clear noontime sun, Garrett runs to outstrip the trotting wagon and when he passes the horses on the small bridge, he punches the air in triumph. Walking swiftly down the narrow hill past the small cottages near the

Cathedral, his parents watch him carefully, signalling for him to wait for them. Georg remarks to his companions that he has never seen them in daylight. They are a well-matched couple, walking on either side of their chattering boy, placid and elegant in the weak February light. Turning towards the Deanery, they pass high walls with the tips of the tall trees swaying in the sunshine. Elizabeth tells him that this is Dr Swift's own walled garden, where his renowned pears and plums are grown.

'Naboth's Vineyard. The Dean's own nickname for it, though no evil King Ahab has managed to steal it from him. When I was a child, Mrs Johnston, our beloved Stella would bring me to pick plums and then over to the Deanery to toast oranges by the fire.'

Turning into an open gateway, they walk up to the door of the Deanery, and Elizabeth moves forward to knock, signalling her boy to stay quiet. The two men fall in behind her. There is the sound of a door being flung open inside. Silence. Elizabeth knocks again. After a long delay, the door opens and a woman peers out, her face creased with a frown. The frown soon disappears when she recognises the young woman.

'Miss Elizabeth. And Mr Wellesley. Is that my fine boy, all grown up, my Garrett? I held you on the day you were born?'

'How are you, Mrs Ridgeway?'

Elizabeth beams at her. A look of caution dampens down the smile on the woman's face.

'Passably well, my dear Miss Elizabeth. It is such a pleasure to see you.'

The older woman moves out from the door to embrace the younger woman warmly but Georg notices that she takes care to shut the door firmly behind her. Elizabeth emerges from the embrace and smiles in his direction.

'Mrs Ridgeway, this is Signor Giorgio, the famous musician. All the way from London to play his music for us.'

The older woman bows courteously and Georg takes off his hat.

'You are welcome, sir. We have all heard of you. I hope Dublin is honouring you as you deserve.'

Georg bows again, waiting silently as Elizabeth makes her request.

'Can we trespass on the Dean's time for a moment? I would like them to meet again. Signor Handel is a great admirer of his writings and I believe they met once in London, some years ago.'

Mrs Ridgeway looks worried and takes a moment before she answers, looking back towards the house and not meeting the younger woman's eyes.

'Can you wait one minute, and let me go and see, Miss Elizabeth? Forgive me not bringing you in. Bridget has been washing the floors, the great oaf, and they are so wet, you could break your neck.'

Mrs Ridgeway pauses to caress Garrett under the chin and then withdraws, closing the door firmly behind her. As the door closes, Georg catches the clear sounds of someone else running in the hall, with heavy, thumping feet.

Elizabeth stands there, looking at the closed door, a little tearful, as she apologises.

'This is the first time the door of the Deanery has ever been closed to me, in all my years coming here. How things have changed?'

'My dear, many doors have been shut in my face, believe me, and I have survived to tell the tale.'

Georg jests but regrets it, his jest simply paining her further. Her husband presses her arm gently and Garrett amuses himself by leaning over the low wall and then trying to peer in through the large front window. He turns and whispers back to his mother.

'An old gentleman has just gone by, Mamma, stalking into the library. He looked very angry. I think it was the Dean. He has a very sore eye and he threw some books against the wall.'

Garrett turns in again to look and his mother orders him to come back to her side. He ignores her while the adults all stand there in the February sunshine, not looking at each other. There are muffled noises inside and then a loud banging of a door somewhere within again. Elizabeth calls Garrett away from the window, more sharply. This time, he comes obediently to stand at her side. They are all too intent on listening to the sounds inside to speak.

After a few moments, the door slowly opens and Mrs Ridgeway

reappears, her face grim, more than a little upset. She looks at Elizabeth with a hint of resentment behind the kind smile.

'Wouldn't you know, now he has decided to go back to his study, and won't be disturbed? Strict orders.'

She shakes her head in anger and they all feel that it is somehow directed at them.

'Such a contrary man, as you well remember. What a day it has been.'

Elizabeth makes to ask again but she is interrupted.

'He will be so sorry to have missed you, Miss Elizabeth.'

Her tone is clearly one of firm dismissal. The older woman looks sheepish as she says this but Elizabeth Wellesley smiles at her.

'Never mind. We will come another day. It is so good to see you. I am sorry I've left it so long this time.'

'Wait. This is for my Master Garrett.'

She brings out a covered dish wrapped in a cloth and hands it to the boy.

'Your favourite pie. Plums from the orchard. Be sure and heat it for your supper and eat it with my love.'

With the sounds of another door banging somewhere inside, she starts and then quickly returns inside, closing the door as fast as she can, without another word of farewell.

Elizabeth looks forlorn and stands there, unwilling to leave.

'I'm so sorry that we could do so little, Signor Giorgio.'

Richard Wellesley takes his wife's arm and looks over to Georg.

'Are you at leisure for a few more minutes?'

Georg nods.

'Then come with me. I have an idea.'

The couple set off in the direction of St Patrick's Cathedral, with Georg following and Garrett running ahead again after some dispute with his mother about the immediate eating of the pie. They make their way down the steps and into the gloom of the Cathedral. A verger nods at the Wellesleys and putting his finger to lips, tells them, in a whisper, 'The choir is in rehearsal, Mr Wellesley, Madam.'

'Is Doctor Wynne with the choir?'

'He is indeed, sir. If you'd like to make your way up to the side chapel, he should be at liberty within the half hour.'

'Good,' Richard whispers, 'we will go to him.'

They make their way quietly up the darkened cathedral towards the choir stalls by the main altar. The sounds of the young voices singing fill the empty old cathedral and give Georg a feeling of savage determination. It is not an especially large choir but they sing well, voices fresh and strong. Combined with his present singers, they would make a very competent task of his oratorio. He listens to them enviously, thinking that nothing must prevent his acquisition of these voices, but something warns him that he must leave all of the talking to Richard Wellesley. Georg has been in Dublin only a few weeks but he knows already that the well-tempered inhabitants of this island are full of good manners and kindness to foreigners but speak honestly only to each other on important matters like money or position.

Doctor Wynne is sitting listening to the choir. When he sees the visitors, he waves a friendly greeting and rises to join them in the side nave.

'You are all welcome indeed,' he whispers, 'the rehearsal will soon be over.'

They sit down, waiting for the choir to finish. When they do, Doctor Wynne stands to thank the singers and dismisses them, turning to ask, 'What brings you to St Patrick's, Herr Handel?'

'You,' Richard cuts across, determined to lead the conversation. 'We need your help with the choir from St Patrick's. Signor Giorgio requires them for his oratorio.'

Doctor Wynne spreads his hands out, a gesture of his own powerlessness.

'I wish I could be of assistance, but the Dean is unhappy with the idea of his cathedral choir performing in a music hall.'

'This is different. Sacred music for the benefit of a charitable hospital. My own boy will sing. If it is suitable for him, then it is suitable for the choir.'

Wynne glances at the boy as if unwilling to speak in front of him. His mother calls the boy.

'Garrett, can you go back outside and play in the garden? We will be only a few more moments.'

The boy stands up and races away down the church, glad to be free of adult talk, taking the pie with him.

'I didn't wish to bring this up but there is disquiet about Mrs Cibber appearing in this oratorio. I myself have no objections but Lady Dorothy . . .'

Before Georg has an opportunity to roar his anger at him, Elizabeth interrupts.

'I can understand her ladyship's unease, indeed; I once shared it. Now I understand that all has been made regular with her husband.'

Doctor Wynne looks interested and Elizabeth hurries on.

'It is not ideal but, given the charitable nature of the event, I am permitting Garrett to sing. Mrs Cibber will be an invaluable asset to the performance, as will the Dean's choir.'

Wynne looks dubious.

'An actress, from the London stage, the subject of a scandalous court case. Really Elizabeth.'

'We have seen her perform on the stage ourselves, John, just last week and she was splendid and very amusing. I would be happy to meet her myself. Should the performance be cancelled and the hospital lose funds because of the lack of a full choir?'

Wynne frowns.

'She is a dear friend to the good Signor Handel.'

Wynne bows to him. Georg cannot stop himself and breaks in.

'And Madame Avoglio is happy to sing in her company.'

One look on Doctor Wynne's face tells him what he thinks of the approval of another performer, even one as respectably married as Christina Avoglio. As the three of them stand there, circling him, Wynne looks uneasy and unwilling to agree.

'But if only it were up to me. Dr Swift has been most explicit...'

Richard laughs, a determined look coming to his face.

'But it is up to you, Wynne, and we all know that. Our poor gentleman is hardly in control of his own senses. They say that he will require a guardian soon'...Richard pauses...

'Come, Wynne, do not force us to go to the Duke with this. You know the Duchess herself saw Madame Cibber on the stage with us last week.'

By the look on his face, Wynne clearly did not.

'You can make the order yourself. Let's call it a sacred oratorio in the posters and the newspapers and all will look well.'

Wynne looks unhappy but promises that he will reconsider. They all shake hands and Wynne tells Elizabeth that his wife will call next week, as arranged.

Georg is uneasy as they walk back down towards the Cathedral and back out into the fresh air at the porch, bright and sunny after the gloom of the old church.

'I am still worried…' he begins, but Richard cuts him off.

'You will have your extra singers, Signor Giorgio. I promise you that. Just be sure to call it a sacred oratorio as I have suggested.'

Georg turns to face him.

'How can you be so sure?'

'Because the Duke is your patron and the Duke, as Lord Lieutenant, must authorise the appointment of a guardian for the Dean.'

'And that guardian will be…?

'Doctor Wynne, our own dear friend. He will become, in reality, the new Dean. And, as Doctor Wynne needs the Duke at this point, we are fortunate that the Duke thinks so highly of you.'

Georg feels an immense relief. He thanks Richard and, turning to Elizabeth, adds: 'And thank you for speaking so warmly of Susannah. May I invite her to come and meet you both at my house next week for supper, my dear Mrs Wellesley?'

Elizabeth Wellesley turns to look at him, a little startled. Just then her boy runs up to her and she begins to scold him.

'What is that on your face?'

The boy blushes, traces of pastry around his mouth.

'You have eaten the pie, I knew you would. I warned you to wait until supper time. You greedy child, what will I do with you?'

She takes out a handkerchief, spits on it and begins cleaning his face, much to the boy's embarrassment.

Georg stands in the sunlight, smiling at her ministrations, wondering if he could simply slip away and leave them all there but Richard takes his arm and they walk back together to Dublin Castle. Georg knows that there will be no dinner invitation for Susannah, that she spoke only to support him and to rout Doctor Wynne.

Now, with all his preparations in place for the performance of the oratorio, and his time in Dublin drawing to a close, unexpectedly, with this change of season, he finds that he is a little unwilling to leave. April reveals the beauty of the city to him, the cry of excited seagulls swooping in the swirling updraughts of the spring breezes, the warm gusts of air carrying stray blossoms past him. One morning on his way to rehearsal, he is amused to see a scattering of tiny white blossoms on the Elector's statue, flecking his granite coat.

Memories of his young self fill him with a kind of tender loss, beautiful, unaware, afraid to linger, and he dreams of Rome that night and of the taste of cabbage soup on the Corso.

Then as the Dublin evenings began to lengthen, unexpectedly tender and with light that goes on forever, he takes to rambling further and further out of the city. The sky landscapes beguile him in his long walks along the river, leading him up to the gates of the great deer park. There was a painting in the Cardinal's study that Georg had admired, a pastoral scene in the Rome countryside by Claude of Lorraine. A large dream-like painting with the soft light of late evening, the gentle gloss of the budding green trees, a lazy bird circling slowly homewards, high above a tall oak. On those April evenings, these immense Irish skies recall this painted landscape to him, the gentle quality of the soft air and he finds himself drawn to the deer park again and again to lose himself in that sky.

As if in response to the warm spring air, the elusive Mr Hunter suddenly bursts into voice and shows a renewed interest in meeting. In November, Georg's two letters to him had elicited no reply and then a scribbled card came in the New Year, with no address, pleading an unexpected and prolonged absence in London on business but with no mention of a meeting. Mrs Power parried all of his attempts to get information from her. Then, in mid-April, when Georg had given up all hope of seeing him again, a card was left in person last night to a suspicious Peter in Abbey Street. The few scribbled words were warm, begging forgiveness for the delay. Mr Hunter hopes for tickets for the sold out performance of the new oratorio, and mentions he is staying in Hoey's Court with his sister-in-law, Mrs Power. Mr Hunter invites Georg to dinner that night, after the performance of *Messiah*, or so a sulky Peter tells him. Georg keeps his face bland at the mention of this invitation but his heart lifts. In addition, on the same day, a surprise parcel comes from London.

*2nd April*
*Georg, I saw this statue languishing in a shop window near the Strand and thought to return it to its rightful owner, with my sincerest regards. May it be an omen of good fortune for your new oratorio? It cost me a great deal of money and excuses me from remembering you in my will. Your friend,*
*Melusine*

He tears open the parcel to find a plush red lacquered box. He opens it. The Orpheus statue. He takes it out to hold it in his hand again, believing he had seen the last of it. How slight it feels, this thin sliver of carved metal, the singer with his lyre looking heavenward. A scrap of silver with all of his life bound up in it. He thinks of the beloved hands of the dead man who had held it. He knows how tight-fisted Melusine has become in old age, despite being swollen with bribes from English politicians during the Elector's lifetime. How it must have hurt her to hand over a hefty purse of gold to the London jewellers. He kisses the statue in gratitude to her and to the dead man who had first given it to him and places it on the table beside his bed in Abbey Street.

Finally, all preparations complete and tickets sold, the day of the performance of the new oratorio arrives. Georg, sleeping little, haunted by the memory of that rasping note in Susannah's voice, rises early, dressing himself in a new black coat and a fresh shirt. Unable to sit still after his hasty breakfast, he sets out for a walk around the busy city streets, paying his morning homage to the statue of the Elector on Essex Bridge and pausing to ask for his help. The stone face of the Elector looks back at him, as sour looking in granite as he was in life, but Georg imagines the merest of nods and takes that for a benign omen.

He strolls along the river before presenting himself at Hoey's Court. The morning is fresh and surprisingly warm, and he walks up the hill towards Mrs Power's house where he plans to leave some tickets. He crosses into the side street just as the bells from Christchurch Cathedral are ringing ten. Hoey's Court is, for once, deserted at this time of the morning, a lone carriage rattling past him as he walks towards the dressmaker's house. As he approaches Mrs Power's door he notices something bulky lying on the ground right outside her door. He slows down as he gets nearer, the black form now revealing itself as the inert outline of a man lying face down. When he reaches Mrs Power's door, Georg stops. The man's body is blocking his way in. Unsure, he steps out onto the narrow road to get a better view and stares down at the immobile figure stretched out at his feet. It is an emaciated old man, dressed in black, his head pressed into the muddy ground, a trace of blood on the puddle by his side.

His eyes are closed and there is no audible sound of breathing. Georg looks around the empty street, spotting a servant girl much further up the street, sweeping in front of a shop. He waves to catch her attention, but she turns away and goes back into the shop, slamming the door. He grows uneasy, wondering if he could just leave the body where it is, but he thinks of the dinner with Mr Hunter. He scans the ground around the body, looking at the bag and hat lying about in the mud. Probably some old man escaped from a nearby house, slipping away from his family unnoticed as they eat breakfast. Or maybe an old drunk from the Bull's Head Tavern. Georg notices a small shiny metal snuff box on the road, next to the hat, its contents spilled everywhere. He stoops to push it with his stick. Then, with some difficulty, he picks it up and examines it. It is tawny in colour, not quite gold, made of beaten metal and with an inscription inside. Georg places it carefully on Mrs Power's windowsill, and then turns to look again at the prone figure at his feet. A wagon comes clattering down the street, with a young man holding the reins. Georg holds up his hand to get his assistance but the driver, seeing the body lying on the ground, flicks expertly on his reins to hurry up instead and swerves to avoid the fallen man, splashing the inert form with more mud.

'This is impossible,' Georg thinks, and shouts a curse at the retreating back of the wagoner. After the wagon has disappeared from sight, he decides to give the body a gentle prod with his stick. Much to his relief, the corpse stirs a little at this, shudders and then mutters something incomprehensible. 'Alive, at least,' Georg thinks and then, no other help in sight, he comes to a decision. He steps carefully over the old man and raps loudly on Mrs Power's door. At this noise, the old man turns over towards him, slowly opening his eyes and then struggles to get up. He fails in his attempt, his arm entangled in his great black coat, and he curses roundly. The old man turns his head to glare upwards at Georg, one eye swollen, a look of anger creasing his blood-flecked face. He begins to growl at Georg, who stares back down at him wordlessly.

'Help me up, sir. This is my uncle's house. I was born in that house and I wish to die there today.'

The old man barks out his orders at him. Georg is startled at the strength and volume of his voice but raps at the door again even more urgently. This side of Hoey's Court is in shadow, away from the bright April sunlight and the lingering chill of winter creeps up from the ground and into his feet as he stands there, hammering at the door.

Despite his grubby clothes and his emaciated appearance, the old man is well-spoken and dressed in sober good clothes. Georg wonders again if he should help him up but is unwilling to get his own new clothes fouled. The man shouts up at him again.

'Help me up, sir, and cease gaping down at me with that foolish look.'

The old man attempts to wipe the blood from his face with his muddy fingers, brown snuff all over his clothes.

'Are you deaf, sir, or a fool? Do you hear me? I wish to get up.'

To Georg's great relief, the door opens and Mrs Power looks out.

'Mr Handel,' she says, in surprise, pleased to see him, not noticing the old man on the ground behind him.

'Handel. I know of him. A German and a genius. Where is he?' the old man exclaims. Mrs Power, a little puzzled, peers down to see who is speaking. Georg shrugs at her, unwilling to be associated with the fallen man and makes a face of deprecation. Mrs Power looks annoyed when she sees the figure on the ground, his face now buried in his coat as he struggles to free himself.

'Get up and away from my door. Are you drunk? Go or I'll fetch you away with my broom.'

Catching sight of the blood on the ground and on his face, she suddenly turns pale and puts her hand out to steady herself on the wall. She closes her eyes and then turns back to the house.

'Jenny, Lucy,' she shouts, 'come down here at once. It is the blood, it make me ill.' she explains. She looks to Georg as if she will faint. He hurries to her side and takes her by the elbow firmly, holding her with all his strength.

'Close your eyes. I have you in my grasp.' He tells her, 'Breathe as deeply as you can.'

On the stairs above them, much to his relief, he can hear the thumping sound of footsteps descending. Mrs Power's girls all appear and Georg thrusts Mrs Power firmly into the arms of the pock-marked girl.

'Bring her up and find some brandy or some salts. She has seen blood.'

Jenny nods, takes a firm grip on her mistress's arm and, with Abigail's half-hearted assistance, begins to walk her slowly up the stairs, Mrs Power's head swaying a little. The old man roars again at Georg, annoyed at being ignored.

'You. Sir. Help me up. I am entangled.'

The other girl, Lucy, comes down the stairs and, hearing the shouts, pushes past to look out of the door. Seeing the old man lying on his back in the gutter, she puts her hand to her mouth.

'We must help him up, Mr Handel. He is cut.'

Georg puts out an arm to stop her but she moves past him and goes to kneel down on the ground beside the old man.

'Be careful, girl, he may be dangerous.'

The old man, hearing him, says, 'I am of no danger, my girl. I am already dead.' He laughs.

'Hush. Let me help you,' she tells him. 'You have cut your forehead.'

Before Georg can stop her, she stoops down over the old man and takes his arm in hers.

'He may be intoxicated?' Georg tells her.

Lucy sniffs at him.

'No, sir. Not a whiff of brandy. Just a fall. We must get him up. Let me call for help.'

She straightens up and goes back into the hallway, and starts calling loudly.

'Mr Hunter. Mr Hunter. Can you come down here, please, sir?'

She turns to Georg and explains,

'We need to get him upstairs and Mr Hunter can help. You will only get all your clothes dirty, Mr Handel, so stay there.'

Before he can stop her, the girl kneels back down and, pulling out a clean handkerchief from her sleeve, begins to wipe off the blood from the old man's face and forehead. The old man gazes up at the girl.

'Thou art a soul in bliss while I am bound upon a wheel of fire that mine own tears do scald like molten lead.'

She tut tuts lightly.

'Now, sir, there is no need for tears. We will get you fixed up soon, and you'll be in bliss again yourself and as right as can be.'

Georg is about to follow Mrs Power and the girls upstairs when this halts him. Whoever he is, this old man can quote Shakespeare. Mr Hunter comes down the stairs and smiles at Georg. Finally. Standing tall and as handsome as Georg remembers from the bedroom over the inn in Chester, his fine dark eyes gleaming, he takes George's hand and grasps it warmly.

'Good to see you again, sir, and my apologies for the long delay. I have been away on business for months now and not at liberty to show you my city.'

Georg smiles back, determined to be gracious.

'No need to apologise, Mr Hunter. I have some tickets for our performance and I was hoping you and Mrs Power will be free to hear the music today?'

'Indeed we will, and will you dine with me tonight as my guest, to celebrate the new oratorio?'

Before Georg can answer, Mr Hunter looks over his shoulder at the old man, now cleaned of blood and mud. Hunter gives a low whistle.

'The Dean!'

Hunter moves quickly past Georg and goes to the old man, now struggling to rise with Lucy's help.

'Dr Swift. May I assist you?'

Hunter leans down to take his other arm. Between them, with some effort, they get the old man to his feet while Georg stands there watching, his face reddening.

'Please allow me to assist you upstairs to my sister's rooms, Dean. We have a fire to take away the chill and a drink to warm you.'

The old man looks gratefully at Hunter.

'Thank you, sir, this fool over here was of no use at all. But first my hat. And my snuff box! I've dropped it. My snuff box. Find it. A great man presented it to me.'

Georg, full of contrition and embarrassment, looks around and sees the snuff box in the window sill and runs over to retrieve it. It is still besmirched by some kind of slime. All its contents have fallen on the ground. He picks it up with his handkerchief and cleans it off.

'Dean. Allow me. My apologies.'

He hands the old man his snuff box.

'I did not recognise you,' Georg tells him, by way of excuse, 'it is many years since we have last spoken, at Dr Arbuthnot's I think? I am Georg Handel.'

'Why would you recognise me, Mr Handel?' the old man glares at him. 'I would not recognise myself. I am no longer the Dean. I am now the shadow of the shadow of Dean Swift. Now help me upstairs. I am wet through and through.'

Georg takes over from Lucy in assisting him to his feet and motions her up ahead.

'We can get him warm by the fire and I'll send a message to the Deanery to have his servants come and fetch him,' Lucy suggests and she runs up the stairs.

Swift hears this but shakes his head vigorously.

'No, no. No one from the Deanery. I will hear this music today, in the hall, but first I want to see my uncle's house. Up!'

Georg and Mr Hunter link arms to bring the Doctor slowly up the many steps to the second floor, Mr Hunter's warm hand taking his to support the old man as they walk him up. For a brief moment, he thinks of Luca's hand in the dance on Piazza del Popolo in the slight caress of Mr Hunter's large fingers along the back of his hand.

At the top of the stairs, all too soon, Mrs Power is waiting impatiently to take the Dean on her arm, her face contrite with concern.

'Here, let me.' She takes his arm under hers and leads him into the large work room.

'You must forgive us, Dean. I didn't see you down there and your poor face is cut. First you must allow me to dress the wound.'

As she is talking, Mrs Power runs her hand over his coat and frowns. She is dressed in a fine dark silk gown and stands away from the wet and dirtied old man.

'Now, this won't do. The coat is soaking wet.'

She signals to her brother.

'Here, James, help me get it off. He is wet through.'

Swift thanks her and stands there obediently, allowing himself to be divested of his mud-stained coat. Mrs Power bustles around, giving orders.

'James, bring Dean Swift into the back room and fetch one of your shirts and a coat, it will keep him warm until he returns home. Jenny, boil up some water and fetch that bottle of wine. Abigail, my medicine basket.'

The girls, all in their finest clothes, run to obey her while Mr Hunter leads the old man into a small inner room where Georg glimpses a bed through the open door. As the door closes, Mrs Power turns to her girls.

'Abigail, get your cloak on and run around to the Deanery. Doctor Wynne must be told immediately. They will be looking for him everywhere and Mrs Ridgeway will be worried sick. He must have slipped out this morning.'

Mrs Power talks on, as she sits by the fire and searches her medicine basket, while Georg stands there, wondering if he should go. Finally she looks up at him, cotton and medicine bottle in her hands.

'Forgive me, Mr Handel, I was forgetting you.'

'I've brought the tickets for the music at noon, if you and the girls are still at liberty to attend.'

Mrs Power beams.

'We would be delighted. You see us in our best frocks to honour you. Madame Susannah mentioned it yesterday, and it was kind of you to deliver them.'

She permits herself a quick glance at the door where Mr Hunter is helping the Dean, as if to tell her true opinion of his calling in person to her premises.

'We would so like to see her gown. It looked like new when we fitted it yesterday. And of course we long to hear your new music,' she hurries to add. 'We will close for an hour or so at noon, our customers can wait.'

Georg glances at the clock. It is past ten-thirty and he needs to be in Fishamble Street by eleven at the latest.

'It will be little longer than an hour, I fear. We begin at noon and will be playing until at least three o'clock. Here are the tickets. I must leave shortly.'

Georg places the envelope of tickets on the table next to her, just as Swift is walked back into the room by Mr Hunter, delighted to be wearing a clean shirt. The old man beams as he looks around himself at the large room and begins to question Mrs Power.

'Madame, this is now your house?'

'I rent it for my business, Dean, and sometimes I sleep here when I have work to finish.'

'Your business?'

'I am a dressmaker, sir.'

Swift looks around, in disbelief, at the bales of silk, the cuttings all over the floor, the boxes of buttons and the flimsy trails of ribbon and lace on the broad work tables. The girls all stand attentively in their Sunday best, smiling at him. The old man shakes his head in a kind of wonder.

'But this was once my uncle's home. Never mind. I see you have a bed in the smaller room. Perhaps I will remain here tonight. There was trouble in my house again last night . . .'

He stops, a frown passing over his face. At a covert signal from Mrs Power, Jenny pours wine for him, adding in some hot water, and brings it forward and offers it to him. He takes it and drinks with pleasure.

'Thank you, child.'

He looks closely at her ruined face.

'Your face. Well, your eyes are kind and that is beauty enough.'

Georg looks over at Jenny but she seems unconcerned at the old man's insensitive chatter and, handing him Mr Hunter's great dark coat, begins to help him put it on. The sleeves are too long and flap over his hands and Jenny hurries to tuck them in. Swift watches her as she turns the cuffs with gentle care.

'You know, she had kind hands and dark eyes, just like you, my child. When she died, I stayed in my room in the Deanery and when it was time to bury her, I moved into another room away from the road. I could not bear to see the lights pass my house, bringing her to her grave.'

Jenny listens without comment, assuming he is rambling.

'Did you ever meet her, child?'

'No, sir,' Jenny murmurs, her task finished and anxious to get her cloak and leave for the music hall, standing patiently, listening to him.

'Of course not, you are but a girl and my Stella is dead many years now and soon I will be dead too, and here in my uncle's house where I was born.'

He takes the glass and raises it in salute . . . . 'But not today, perhaps' and drinks.

His coat fitted, Mrs Power guides him over to the large comfortable chair by the fire and settles him down, the better to dab at the clean wound on his forehead with her cotton and her bottle of spirits.

As he drinks his wine, Mrs Power cleans his forehead and the old man grows more expansive.

'I am obliged to you for this coat,' he tells Mr Hunter, who bows.

The old man points to Lucy, now in her cloak and gloves, dressed up for her excursion.

'This girl was my saviour, my Cordelia,'

As he chatters, now Georg can see a faint resemblance to the man he met in London years before, but it is only a ghostly resemblance and it rattles him. With a slightly frosty look, the old Dean turns towards Georg.

'Tell me again, who you are, sir? I seem to know your face.'

'Georg Handel, Dean. We met many years ago.'

Mr Hunter draws up another chair for Georg and motions him to sit, pouring him some wine. Georg shakes his head, inclining his head towards the clock, and Mr Hunter sips it himself, toasting him silently first.

'Why are you in Dublin?' the old man asks him but, Georg, watching Mr Hunter, fails to answer and the Dean rambles on, uninterested in his answer.

'You should leave. They told me I would return as a bishop to England but here I am, like an oak, dying from the head downwards.'

Conscious of Mr Hunter's eyes on him, Georg tells him.

'I leave for London in a week, Dean. My time in Dublin is nearly over.'

'They told me that. They promised me so much in London I had the ear of the great and so many promises and now, look at me, here I rot.'

Georg shakes his head.

'My passage home is booked and now that my time is nearly done, I find I am sorry to go.'

He says this to the Dean and smiles at Mrs Power but thinks – are you listening, my elusive Mr Hunter?

Mrs Power offers Georg some food but he shakes his head, unwilling to delay, but the Dean accepts like a greedy child, pushing a pastry into his mouth as if it is the first food he has seen in months.

'And so, Madam, I wish to stay here tonight.'

Mrs Power shakes her head.

'I'm afraid, sir, we must leave soon to hear Mr Handel's music. There is a dress we must see, a green mantua.'

Swift looks downcast but brightens as an idea occurs to him.

'Then I will join you. I don't care for music but it will be an excursion and I have so few these days.'

Georg and Mrs Power exchange glances but Mr Hunter intervenes.

'It will be my honour to accompany you to Neal's Music Hall, Dean,' and he looks at the others, as if to reassure them. Georg shrugs his shoulders.

'I must leave now. If you are all ready, you can come with me and take your seats before the doors open for the public at eleven-thirty.'

Much fuss is made by the women to get the Dean ready. At first Swift is unwilling to leave the warm fire but when it is made clear to him that he will be abandoned, he rises quickly. Again Mr Hunter and Georg walk the old man slowly back down the stairs, but without linking hands, the sharp eyes of Mrs Power right behind them.

In a short hour, Hoey's Court has been brightened up considerably by the April sunlight, the sky softly blue overhead, a few blossoms drifting past on the warm breeze. As they make their way slowly up the street with the Dean, the three girls skip ahead, despite Mrs Power barking at them to slow down, all giggles in their best clothes. Their young voices ring out in the April air as they crest the hill, and laugh when the ribbons on their good hats dance in the warm breeze. The Dean is surprisingly sprightly as they walk, taking his arm and asking Georg all about friends in London, many of them now dead. It seems incongruous that this lively old man was lying inert on the ground only an hour before but, when Swift pauses at the top of Fishamble Street, he takes Georg by the arm, pulling him away from the others.

'Promise me,' he says in a low whisper. 'Promise you will leave this city as soon as you can. Let nothing detain you,' and he glances at Mr Hunter.

Georg assures him that he is returning to London, uneasy at the surprisingly sharp glance.

This fails to satisfy the old man, his eyes glassy as he stares at some inner fear, all around him forgotten.

'Leave this living graveyard. Heed my words.'

On the steps of Neal's Music Hall, a crowd has already gathered to await the opening of the doors and carriages are starting to rattle down the street from Christchurch. Georg leads his group into the large rehearsal room right at the back of the hall where the musicians and the singers are already assembled and they all stand up on his entrance. In the far corner, by a small fire, Susannah is sitting, her hands tightly clasped. She begins smiling when she sees Georg enter and, releasing her hands from the tight, painful-looking knot she has made of them, waves at him. The girls rush over to her to admire the dress, and Susannah stands up to show them the new elegant lines of the resurrected green velvet, the smart black trim on the collar, the simple cross at her neck.

Mrs Power looks at the dress, pleased with her handiwork.

'Excellent, even if I say so myself.'

Susannah holds out the small cross for Jenny to look at.

'My mother sent it from London. Blessed by His Holiness himself in Rome, Jenny.'

Jenny puts her finger out to touch it very tentatively. Susannah nods, to encourage her.

'Blessed by His Holiness in Rome,' she repeats as her finger delicately strokes the thin silver cross. 'I feel holy myself now, Madame Susannah.'

Georg signals Peter to bring the case of his papers, and taking out the new running order, walks over to Susannah and takes gentle hold of her elbow. Something in his face making the girls slip away respectfully, to return to the Dean's side.

'How are you, my dear?'

She looks up, a little frightened by the intent behind the kindness in his voice but smiles wordlessly to reassure him.

'Susannah, remember, if your voice fails you, just stop. The musicians have been alerted.'

'I feel much better,' she tells him, her face looking more and more grey.

'I know, but for today, Mr Woffington will take over "But who may abide" and Christina will sing all of "He shall feed his flock". This will leave you strength to concentrate on your own arias.'

Susannah looks up at him, her eyes full of pain and surprise, and he continues, afraid she might say something to try and stop him.

'I have transposed "If God be for us" for your voice, as we rehearsed. And the musicians have all been told.'

Still silent, she sits there, refusing to speak, but he is determined.

'It will be better, my dear. You must trust me.'

'As you do not trust me,' she whispers.

He looks intently at her, too worried about that rasping sound in her voice to change his mind, and finally she nods her agreement.

Doctor Wynne comes into the rehearsal room, looks around and then rushes over to the Dean with relief.

'Dr Swift! Mrs Ridgeway charged me specifically to bring you home directly, to eat.'

The Dean waves his hand in Wynne's face and turns to bow to Mrs Power.

'Nonsense, I have eaten. This kind woman has taken good care of me and her blessed girl rescued me from the street . . . .'

He looks briefly at Georg, who colours.

'And now Mr Handel has invited us all to hear his new oratorio.'

Doctor Wynne looks at Georg, as if to say, 'Is this wise?'

The Wellesleys arrive with their son and Elizabeth comes forward to take the Dean's hand and kiss it.

'Dr Swift!'

'My little Lizzy. Come, let us go in and you can sit by me. This German seems a little slow to me but they tell me his music is sublime.'

Wynne looks unhappy but helps the Dean out into the main hall. However, at the door, Swift stands still and looks around.

'The dear girl. My Cordelia. Where is she? Ah, there you are. You will sit with me today and hear this music.'

Lucy comes up hesitatingly to his side. He takes her hand, signaling to the other girls and to Mrs Power to accompany him, the Wellesleys following with Doctor Wynne, shutting the door behind them. Chattering among the boys slowly dies out as the minutes move towards noon, Georg taking his seat quietly beside Susannah and Christina. Susannah is not looking at him, or at anyone, but stares ahead, a look of increasing resolve on her face and in the line of her shoulders. Christina, who seems to Georg to be completely without nerves, sits calmly at her needlework and the men and boys of the choir stand around patiently, scores in hand. A silence falls on the rehearsal room and soon the only sound to be heard is the distant hum of chatter from the main hall as the audience take their seats. In the silenced room, a sudden burst of laughter from the hall draws an involuntary shudder from Susannah. At one point, Christina takes Susannah's hand in hers and Susannah presses it but then returns it.

Finally, Neal sweeps in, in full plumage, trailing a cologne scent, the open door unleashing the terrifying roar of excited chatter from the crowded hall.

'His Grace is arriving, his coach is just now drawing up, with Lady Dorothy in his party. When you are ready, Georg....'

Georg stands up, motioning to the choir and the musicians to walk out. The boys file out quickly, followed by the men and the musicians while Susannah stands up and waits next to Christina and Georg. When it is her turn, she sways a little but composes herself and processes into the hall, a bright, professional smile appearing on her face to meet the many watching eyes.

With Neal, Georg makes his way out of the side door of the rehearsal room and into the bright April sunshine on Fishamble Street towards the front entrance. Here the Duke is already alighting from his carriage, all smiles to the waiting crowd in the sunlight, and he waves happily when he sees Georg approach. Georg bows low to him and to Lady Dorothy and Lady Charlotte at his side.

The Duke takes Georg's arm and nods graciously at Neal.

'A full attendance, I believe. The hospitals will be happy with that.'

Lady Dorothy laughs and puts her arm on Georg's sleeve.

'Sacred music, Georg. Who would have believed it of you? All your popish friends in Rome would be proud of you today.'

Georg grits his teeth and offers his arm to Lady Charlotte, while the Duke takes Lady Dorothy. Together they proceed up the steps and into the packed hall. Their approach hushes the audience and all assembled rise for the Duke. Georg conducts the party down the aisle to the front row where Neal has placed six seats. The tallest is for the Duke, with a gold footstool, but the Dean has appropriated the ducal chair, with Lucy on one side and Mrs Power on the other. The Duke graciously bows to the Dean and insists on his remaining there, leading Lady Dorothy and Lady Charlotte to their seats and choosing to sit on the end of the row himself. It amuses Georg to see the look on Lady Dorothy's face when she realises that she is sitting next to her dressmaker.

The hall falls silent as the Duke is seated and all resume their places. Georg crosses to the harpsichord. He looks directly into the body of the hall for the first time. Every place is taken, rows of well-dressed men standing at the back and all around the sides, a light breeze from the high open windows at the sides of the hall, the faint unhappy cry of a gull heard far away above the roof. The singers wait, the choirs of St Patrick's and Christchurch all standing, Susannah and Christina seated right at the front, next to the small group of musicians. There is a calm on Susannah's face that is costing her dear, while Christina settles the folds of her dark crimson velvet skirts, as if sitting at home in her own parlour waiting to drink her tea. Dublin sunshine, pure clear April light, and Georg meets the faces in the hall, hundreds of eyes watching him. He waits until the silence has stretched out over their heads, making them slightly uncomfortable, the light breeze stirring a feather on a hat in the front row, and then Georg sits and the music begins at his curt nod.

Mrs Power sits, hardly daring to look at Lady Dorothy, who has glared at her several times, and she wonders how long they will be trapped there as the music begins. She listens as the violins play the opening chords slowly and a little dreary, so far, she thinks. Then the pace quickens, with the music becoming more dramatic, like something from an opera, and she stops thinking about Lady Dorothy next to her and begins to listen, wondering if she might enjoy some of this tedious sacred music after all. Next to her, Mr Hunter looks with interest at the white shirt stretching over Georg's chest, and thinks of the older man's body. The overture comes to an end and the tenor stands up, a thin-faced man from St Patrick's Choir, and he begins to sing. Doctor Wynne glances over at the Dean, with the little seamstress next to him where they all seem to be enjoying the music. The Dean is showing none of his restlessness, no sign of the constant shaking of his head to clear away the noises that are always the prelude to an outburst or an attack. Wynne sits backs and allows himself to concentrate on the civilised singing of the tenor. Nothing too exciting, he thinks to himself, but when the choir stands up to sing of the Glory of the Lord, Wynne sits up again, something unusually lively in the singing. It seems to Wynne that the voices of these boys and men, here in this crowded new music hall, with the elegantly dressed crowd in front of them, are fresher and more exciting than he has ever heard them sound before.

Sitting in front of him, Mrs Power, a little bored by the tenor, is pleasantly surprised by the exciting sounds of this chorus. When the bass stands up, his long, dramatic dueling with the orchestra is like something from a dull play and she finds herself wishing for the chorus to sing again. Nearby, Charlotte watches Mrs Cibber, the infamous Susannah, right here in the hall before her. Mamma would not let her attend the play last month, even though the Duke and the Duchess, her new Mamma and Papa, had invited her. Charlotte thinks that Mrs Cibber is a sorry disappointment for a scarlet woman as she sits there demurely in the dark green dress, almost holy-looking. Madame Susannah is not exactly beautiful, certainly not as beautiful as Lucy, sitting a few seats away from her in a lovely grey dress with pretty lace at the sleeves, next to that mad old clergyman. Charlotte glances over at the German musician, a severe expression on his face today as he plays, none of the kindness and playfulness that Charlotte knows. The musicians and the singers are clearly anxious to please him, their eyes on him, except for Mrs Cibber who seems to be smiling to an invisible audience, miles away from here. Oh good, Charlotte thinks. Now she is standing up to sing. Now I can hear what a scarlet woman sings like. She is taller than Charlotte noticed, her dress elegant, stately, if a little old-fashioned, but it is sacred music, she supposes, and she begins, a light pleasing air, almost a parlour song, 'Oh thou that tellest good tidings to Zion'. Susannah's voice surprisingly deep for a slight young woman, Charlotte thinks, low and quiet and her voice somewhat hoarse at first but gaining in confidence as she progresses. As the choir comes in to echo her, joy and energy in the voices, especially as they command the audience to 'Behold', Charlotte thinks this excursion well worth the trip.

The Duke has not seen Mrs Cibber sing yet but has heard whispers that troubled him about her uncertain voice and her clear, somewhat mournful singing and modest demeanour reassures him. Lady Dorothy had given him trouble about the scandalous Susannah and it gives His Grace some satisfaction to hear the lady-like sounds she makes, telling the Dublin audience of good tidings to Zion. The chorus then all rise and the violins announce a lively tune. Mrs Power almost sings along as they move toward a great shout of 'Wonderful, Counsellor, the Mighty God, the ever-lasting King, and the Prince of Peace.' The violins build up to add to the excitement, and Mrs Power finds the back of her neck tingling with the lovely unexpected rise of the voices, almost shouting with joy herself as they sing. She thinks of her child, wonderful to her, despite the terror of exposure, for such a brief few days. Mrs Power is not sure that she can keep her composure in this public place, with the Duke nearby and Lady Dorothy throwing her filthy looks and so she forces herself to think of her account books and of the dresses to be made later that day, to stop herself from falling on the ground and sobbing.

The young boy, Garrett, at a nod from the German composer, comes forwards and Charlotte wonders if he can sing as well as he plays the violin. He can, she thinks, with some annoyance, as he tells of shepherds abiding in the fields, his face grave, his voice clear and light, the audience straining to catch the perfect notes. Behind Charlotte, Elizabeth Wellesley watches her boy sing, his air of concentration the most beautiful of the many beautiful expressions she has even seen on his face, afraid to look at her husband sitting next to her, knowing that he is thinking as she is thinking, or pleading rather. Please. Please. He is now our only child. Please. Spare him.

The Dean sits there happily and watches the German play and his singers working hard at their task, this endless music meaning less than nothing to him. For once, his head is clear of the noises that come and torment him day and night and he is content to be on this comfortable seat, in the warm hall. Next to his a young woman sits, her eyes full of tears as she listens to this singing and he wants to ask her why it moves her so much but he knows not to disturb those around him. He is learning, slowly, painfully, that to say as little as possible these days is to be left alone, not to be rebuked or forced to eat or sleep when he would rather not. He looks down at the small hand on the seat next to him, and he takes it gently in his. She smiles back and presses his hand. Who is this girl? Not Stella, he knows that. Now these singers, they are singing about a child. Stella would have wanted one. It was said around Dublin that they had a son but, of course, that was all rumour and nonsense. What kind of blighted child might they have produced, despite her pleadings and her reassurances? Later she took in a poor boy, some charity case and paid for his education, and the rumours began again. This music seems to go on forever. She loved such singing, and he never cared for it and nothing she could ever do would persuade him.

When Christina Avoglio takes her place to sing her first aria, 'Rejoice greatly', a murmur of satisfaction can be heard throughout the crowded hall, the Duke impressed with her youthful good looks and buxom figure. She begins by giving a lively shake of her head and she plunges into the ringing scales of the aria, and startles all there with her sweet-voiced singing, her modest demeanor adding greatly to the confident energy of her voice. Although soft, Christina's voice gives the impression of muscular rippling sweetness, of vast reserves of power behind the pleasing tones. At one moment, her powerful voice fills the hall, seeming to strike the roof. She stays standing, to sing the duet meant for Susannah and herself, and Susannah, one of her solos now over without a breakdown, looks kindly at her and smiles in congratulation as she passes her on the way back to her seat. Lucy decides that she will be a singer, if only to look as beautiful and the Duke has resolved to hold a dinner in the young German woman's honour, now that the Duchess had returned to England and wonders if he can dispense with inviting her husband.

At the interval, they all stand briefly for applause and then the singers and the musicians make their way back into the rehearsal room, away from the suddenly noisy hall. Unwilling to face Susannah yet, Georg crosses over to the Duke, who is standing attentively over Swift. Neal is babbling to the Duke of the great honour that His Grace has conferred on the occasion and, as Georg arrives by his side, tells the Duke that Mr Handel has promised to return to Dublin next year for another season. 'Not for a million pieces of gold,' Georg thinks and the old Dean catches Georg's eye when he hears Neal's boasting of a return, a look of warning on his face. But, before he can contradict Neal, the Duke waves Georg away, telling him to go and rest, that his great labours demand it. In the rehearsal room Susannah still looks more than a little grey but determined, knowing what lies ahead, refusing all offers of wine, sipping a little water and then throwing some on her brow. The boys chatter as they drink some fruit juice and grab at the food, jostling each other, the decorum of the stage abandoned. Georg stands alone, drinking a little water, and tries not to watch Susannah, who looks as if she is about to be sick as the time draws near. He knows that he should have allowed her to sing with Christina, to give her voice more exercise but it is too late now.

All too soon, Neal, his face beaming, comes to recall them and they return into the main hall, and, as far as Georg can tell, most of the audience has stayed to hear the rest. While the chorus sing 'Behold the Lamb of God', Susannah sits waiting, watching Georg for her cue, her full skirts rustling as she stands, dignified and resigned, as if on her way to her own execution. Mrs Power watches the gown with admiration, remembering the sorry sack she had been given and now the elegant green falls into admirable lines around Madame Susannah's tall elegant figure as she faces the packed hall. The slow mournful sounds of the violins introduce the aria and then, as if casually, Susannah begins to sing, her deep sonorous voice hushed in the opening moments, forcing the audience to listen intently. As her aria unfolds its tragic message about the man of sorrows, she seems to be keening, telling the audience of loss, while the violins accompany her tactfully, and adding their own sorrow, their own lament. Mrs Power wonders how such a sweet, pleasant creature as Madame Susannah could know so much about the loneliness of her own soul as she sings her way towards the gentle conclusion, her voice true to the last, revealing to this crowded hall private grief. How can she sit down again, as if it were nothing, simply a singing engagement?

Later, it is said all round Dublin that Doctor Wynne stood up, interrupting the music and proclaiming to Susannah, in a voice of biblical certainty 'Woman, for this, be all thy sins forgiven'. In fact Doctor Wynne said nothing, just sat and listened and it was Georg who wanted to get up from behind the harpsichord and beg Susannah forgiveness for ever doubting her. Her smile as she took her seat again was enough, pale, exhausted but triumphant and she looks over at Jenny and touches the cross at her neck and Jenny smiles back.

After that, something possesses the choir during the 'Hallelujah Chorus', a kind of energy that fills the large space of the hall and lifts all around them, the musicians, the soloists, Georg himself, the fashionable audience, Charlotte in her new dress, the discontented Dorothy, the complaisant Duke, the weary unloved Mrs Power and the ruined old man, his life finished, all of them are changed while Georg, too busy with the music to notice, keeps all the singers and the musicians under control. Christina stands again, to sing, 'I know that my Redeemer liveth', and the mood of triumph continues, as her youthful, almost brash strength, in direct contrast to Susannah's, the aria building in waves of blinding lyrical sweetness pouring effortless from her towards the final moments of affirmation and belief.

At the front of the hall, as the music draws to a close, an afternoon shaft of light slowly moves in to brighten up the empty space between Georg and the audience. A few stray blossoms drift down in the warm air and land on the ground before him. When Sergeant Wilson stands up to play, Mr Woffington answers the trumpet with his strong, confident singing, announcing 'and we shall be changed'. As the bass sings, Georg watches as, one by one, his beloved dead appear and begin to make their way, unseen, through the body of the crowded, enraptured hall, summoned by the sweet clear sound of the trumpet. The hall has seven hundred people crammed in, but still, the shades of his lost ones find a place with ease. There they stand, looking at him, their eyes full of love or amusement or shrewd appreciation. Mother, Elector George, Madame Durastanti and her lovely daughter, the Cardinal, a recent addition to the ranks of his dead.

Finally, to his great relief, Luca walks up to stand amongst them, beautiful and untouched by the remorseless years. His precious shades, slipping in unnoticed amongst the living to listen, invisible to all eyes but his. His mother takes Luca's arm, her face as beautiful as he remembered, her sight restored, flattered by the attendance of the young nobleman next to her, her nods of approval at the singing and at his playing. His sister, young and strong again, stands behind her mother, nodding her head in time to the music, pleased at the sight of her brother grown up an important public man. Elector Georg, looking as he had known him first in Rome, stands next to the Cardinal, a look of grudging approval on his face. 'Melusine,' Georg wants to tell her, 'you were right. Your lost love is no raven, but stands here, dead, woken for a few precious moments by music.'

By the Elector's side stands Margherita's mother, Madame, as plump as ever, her shrewd face watching the audience. Her lovely daughter Anna holds her mother's hand, showing her pleasure in the music by the strange noises she makes. Ah Margherita, you have lost your Anna, you will be lonely for her in your Roman apartment. The Cardinal comes to stand in full view, caught in the April sun, and Georg can barely look at him but the Cardinal smiles. And Luca. In the final moments of the trumpet's call, the caressing notes of triumph and confidence, Luca comes into his direct sight. Standing straight and undamaged, his dark face as beautiful as when he had first seen him. No shadow of another parting on his beloved face. They, the living and the dead, listen with pleasure as Sergeant Wilson's strong clear notes scatter all before him, and Mr Woffington's voice answers the trumpet in its ringing certainty.

When Susannah and Christina stand to sing ' Death is swallowed up in victory', the dead bring others of their kind with them, Vanessa and Stella, standing unnoticed at each side of the ruined old Dean, Susannah's lost infants now grown into solemn children sitting at her feet, watching with intent eyes, Mrs Power's unacknowledged son, Elizabeth and Richard's dead children. Susannah's voice, released from her fears, weaves with Christina's to fence with death, gladdening the invisible shades in their midst as his music had promised, incorruptible.

At the end of the performance, there is a silence and then the Duke stands. Behind him, the audience begin to clap and the singers and musicians stand, looking well pleased, and they call for Georg. He rises and walks over to stand in the shaft of warm sunlight to join his lost ones, and he bows his head in thanks. It had never occurred to him, in his frantic haste to write this music, that such a thing could happen, that his lost ones would return, made flesh again by the call of the trumpet. They were waiting for him, they promise, as they stand by his side on that April day. Soon, soon, they would be there when his enemy the palsy finally wins. Tears come as he turns to smile at Luca, already fading away. In that moment, he is young again, standing there in the beautiful Dublin sunshine.

*Eibhear Walshe*